SEEDS of FIRE

Karin Kallmaker
writing as

LAURA ADAMS

Bella
BOOKS

Ferndale, Michigan
2002

Bella Books, Inc.
P.O. Box 201007
Ferndale, MI 48220

Printed in the United States of America on acid-free paper
First Edition

Editor: Greg Herren
Cover designer: Bonnie Liss (Phoenix Graphics)

ISBN 1-931513-19-8

For Maria, to love and be with you

Acknowledgements

This tale could not be told without the inspiration of Hildegard of Bingen's music. Many beautiful recordings exist, but my personal favorite remains "11,000 Virgins" by Anonymous Four. Not only is the 4-woman harmony sublimely rich with emotion and purity, the translations by Susan Hellauer are equally moving. Hildegard's music was meant to be sung by women with voices like these.

Kelly Smith at Bella Books has been a continuous source of encouragement, especially her frequent refrain, "Write a good book, would you?" Therese Szymanski provided wisdom in judging fine lines of behavior and how to shade the dark so that some light remains.

Equally as important as the kindness and support of other publishing professionals, is the unquestioning caring of my partner, Maria. She slaves in the corporate world so I can be the rare exception: a writer without a mandatory day job. When writing overwhelms me to where I need a break from being a mom, she's there for that, too, as well as "the aunties," Joan and Paula. Other friends have been especially important this past year — a tumultuous one for so many. (epearce, Frog, mcyoda, Martian, Wahinemoa, you know who you are.) Truly, I don't know what I've done to be so blessed in family and friends, but the reality of it comes out in my writing; my success is theirs as well.

BOOKS BY LAURA ADAMS:

Sleight of Hand (Tunnel of Light, Book 1)
Christabel
Night Vision (Daughters of Pallas 1)
The Dawning (Daughters of Pallas 2)

Writing as Karin Kallmaker:

Substitute for Love
Frosting on the Cake
Unforgettable
Watermark
Making Up for Lost Time
Embrace in Motion
Wild Things
Painted Moon
Car Pool
Paperback Romance
Touchwood
In Every Port

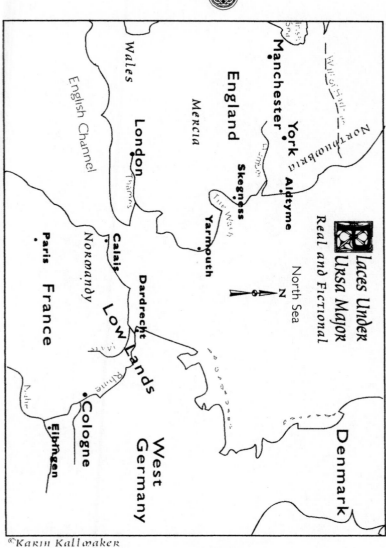

Laces Under
Ursa Major
Real and Fictional

©Karin Kallmaker

Embers

The night danced over her. The axe was in her hand.

The bonfire cast orange light on the sacrifice. She knew him immediately, though it mattered nothing to her purpose this night. Small and white-haired, from the far north, they would miss his laughing way. He had been chosen and she let herself feel his joy at the journey he began.

A flash of light — the axe fell. The acolytes took his body so it would ripen their harvest, ease the coming cold and continue the turning of the seasons. Now waited the last sacrifice, her gown white and tread steady.

The virgin was stretched out on the altar, willing, honored.

The Axe of the Goddess raised the once-blooded weapon as the hood was removed.

This time, recognition took her breath away.

* * * * *

Her memory was veiled with shadow. Ursula knew she had not always been like this and did not remember what had happened to change her.

Soil broke in her hands, and she led bees to the nectar of the young orange tree Autumn had brought her. The flowers she did not know, nor the plants that prickled with spines, but she planted all that Autumn brought her because it was all she knew how to do. She called birds to their rightful feast on the tiny bugs that nibbled at the blooms. She stroked the new plants and the leaves reached for the sun.

This was peace. She understood that. But she knew it wasn't a lasting peace. Something would change. Perhaps it would be her. There were moments when she felt as if she could almost touch her past, but she had grown wary of the biting headaches.

She was aware that Autumn loved her. She worked in the garden and knew that Autumn was not asleep, that Autumn's oceans-deep eyes followed her movements. She did not know if she had loved Autumn in return. She wished it were so, and prayed that when her memory returned she would find herself loving Autumn in the same, unwavering way that she was loved. But the future and past had been disconnected.

There were voices behind the shadows of memory. Three called to her, wanting her to come back to them. A chorus of women sang of their longing. A lone, weary voice wept in despair, while another muted despair with crashing anger.

She worked in the garden and felt Autumn's gaze on her shoulders. She heard the voices, but memory was veiled by shadow. This peace was healing, and she was caught between wanting to remember and wanting to stay in this place, loved and guarded. She could not stay. The budding leaves and ripening fruit told her, as was the way of things, that life was change.

* * * * *

When sleep abandoned her yet again, Taylor St. Claire wanted to abandon the bed, the house, and her life. Liz stirred and, for a moment, Taylor thought that she, too, had woken before dawn once again. When Liz settled back into slumber, Taylor used the dim light from clock face to study the curve of her lover's cheek. Liz needed sleep more than she did.

She had not seen Liz smile since the first of August, since the disastrous outcome of their Lammas Night working. Taylor blamed herself for those failures and for Liz's ongoing turmoil.

She had underestimated the forces at work. Ursula was lost. Kelly would not speak of Lammas Night nor the distant past they had all shared. She and Liz, of course, had studied every nuance of their dreams, when a long-ago Ursula, surrounded by her companions of an ancient time, had been ambushed in an abbey near Cologne.

Taylor believed it was a memory of a past they had all shared, which explained why the memories were only from their own perspectives. Taylor's contribution to the past had begun the moment she, then known as Abbess Claire, had left the abbey's cloister and tried to draw on her powers in the Old Ways to defend the women who had arrived in the foregate.

There had been one moment of clarity: three women — herself, Ursula and the murderous Uda of Jutland — had all worn the complicated Norn braid of the Goddess, the great she-bear who guarded and nurtured the realms under her constellation of Ursa Major. She interjected herself between Uda and her first victim. Later she knew that woman was Elspeth, who was also the Liz who now slept by her side. At the time

3

she had only known one thing: the woman's voice, her eyes, her touch had all evoked an astonished recognition within her. Her distraction had been fatal. Her senses stunned, her heart leaping gladly, she had forgotten, for a moment, that they were in mortal danger.

Uda of Jutland had not forgotten why she was there. In an instant Claire's braid lay in the foregate dirt, and the shock from its cutting had left her nearly unconscious in Elspeth's arms. Light flashed on the broadsword raised by Uda's cruel lieutenant, then her blood mingled with Elspeth's in the dust, finding and losing each other in less than a minute.

Liz frowned in her sleep and Taylor was tempted to try a spell to relax both of them, but she knew it would not work. Nothing worked. She didn't even have the resources to put herself in a light trance where she might be able to pursue these thoughts more fruitfully. Liz's pain came from Taylor's wildly swinging emotions: frustration, rage, helplessness, anguish. They spilled out of her and Liz bore the onslaught, day in and day out, because she refused to use her shields to shut Taylor out. Their rapport was continuous and that intimacy was the only thing they had left. Taylor could not imagine trying to survive the destruction of her circle — battered and broken on Lammas Night — without Liz in her mind.

Liz's pain was mounting with each passing day, and Taylor knew she would eventually have to urge Liz to raise her shields between them. They were the shields Taylor had taught Liz to use, the only thing that had ever shut off the emotional noise that bombarded Liz every moment of her life. Even more dire, Taylor could tell Liz's shields were weakening as time passed, as if they could not be sustained without Taylor's help.

With conscious effort, for both their sakes, Taylor turned her mind to happier memories. The day she had met Liz — yes, that would certainly do. She had been officiating at a wedding. Liz had arrived while the ceremony was in progress. Taylor had sensed her the moment she entered at the back of the church. Envisioning the day did bring another pang of pain, for she had given up her parish, her vestments, her Christian calling, to prepare her circle for the deep Lammas working. Church and circle had been pressing her to choose between them, neither accepting that she could work equally for both without a conflict of loyalty or a paradox of dogma. Meeting Ursula had seemed like a sign. She had chosen circle, only to watch it shatter beyond repair.

Vexed that her thoughts had so easily gone back to that bitter night, Taylor envisioned again the moment that she had seen the ethereal Liz for the first time. Taylor had thought of an eggshell — fragile, but capable of holding the very essence of life within it.

Then she had looked at Liz with her other senses and seen the unrelenting suffering of Liz's spirit. She had been like a lightning strike in the peaceful clarity of the chapel. As the ceremony progressed, she felt the rising joy of the bride and groom, of the congregation, and gave of herself for the blessing she wove into the couple's life and the day. It had been the Vernal Equinox and there was hidden but equally joyous magic in her choice of her chant for her solitary blessing.

In a garden of fruits, in a splendor of flowers, we are joined. We gather as one, in this garden of blessings, in this splendor of love . . .

Her exultation in the day and the ceremony only increased, and so did Liz's pallor.

She had not allowed that to detract from her duties as she followed the happily married pair down the aisle. But at the moment she came abreast of the last pew, she had looked directly at Liz, curious about the woman's distress. Liz had met her gaze with stunned, relieved recognition that had mystified Taylor.

Liz had stayed in the church while Taylor had given her

5

further blessings to the couple and accepted the thanks of the extended family. Some time later, having not seen Liz emerge, she went inside again, not knowing that with her mind clear of her duties she would be utterly changed by her next look into Liz's tortured eyes.

"I knew I would find you," Liz had murmured, almost as if against her will.

For a fleeting moment Taylor had thought, "The woman is mad," but then she knew that this madness was hers to embrace. She had sought completion all her life, and found measures of it in the twining magics of religion and spirituality. Church and circle were her callings. But when she looked into Liz's eyes she had been flooded with an ache of incompleteness. She only had to believe, to find her perfect trust, her perfect love, and the ache would be healed.

She believed, she trusted, she loved. The forces of life she had been studying since she was a child had brought Liz to her. Scarcely a minute later, in a tiny room surrounded by linens and altar vessels, she found the missing piece of her soul in Liz's kiss.

Liz stirred again, drawing Taylor out of her contemplation of their past. She had taught Liz how to shut out the chaos of a world full of emotion, and shown her how strong she really was to have survived without going insane. They had found each other, and had been almost inseparable for these past eighteen months.

Her mind turned inexorably to when the daily joy of their lives had changed, on the Fourth of July. Liz had brought cousin Kelly and her lover Ursula back to their house after family festivities. One look at Ursula and Taylor had felt her life veer from its course. She had no way of knowing if it shifted away or toward her fate.

What she knew was that Ursula was exhausted. It showed in her eyes, her shoulders, in the way she carried herself. They shook hands and Taylor had felt then the hungering darkness that hunted for Ursula and, even from beyond the gate, drained Ursula's spirit. Another touch and Taylor had easily pushed the darkness away. Why couldn't Ursula do that?

And then the music had caught them both. *We long ever after you in tearful exile . . . semper suspiramus post te in lacrimabili exilio. Chants for the Feast of St. Ursula* — how could Ursula not even know its name?

It's what ministers do, Taylor told herself. Confronted with a suffering spirit, who carried power but did not know how to use it, she had naturally wanted to help in any way that she could. More intriguing, this fragile woman was hunted from beyond the gate and seemed the embodiment of a legend most thought was pure myth. The mystery and the challenge had captivated Taylor. Arrogant fool, she cursed herself. She had been so busy looking for a sign for her own destiny that she disregarded everyone else's.

They had only unbraided Ursula's hair, planning to rebraid it in a ritual designed to unlock knowledge that Ursula ought to already have. But each uncoiling lock had been an agony for Ursula. Her pain had shaken the circle to its foundation. The rapacious darkness had done the rest. At the utter end, fighting oblivion for herself and those who had given their trust and fate to her to raise the circle, Taylor had not seen Ursula taken. The darkness had screamed, then it was all gone, leaving Taylor and her companions unconscious until Kelly had roused them.

She could not help her groan of defeat when she realized her mind was back where it had started when she had awakened from a vague, disquieting dream.

Liz reached for her then. "I know, my love. Let me help."

For a while there was only Liz in her mind, but solace ended when Liz finally rose from their bed. Liz left for work and another empty day loomed ahead of her. The well of failure was there for her to dive into, yet again. She could not stop herself from falling into its depths.

* * * * *

7

If she did not strike the acolytes would tear them both apart and they would be forever lost to each other.

She would profane the love the goddess gave them if she struck, and profane her vows, blight her people if she did not.

"I will find you again," the virgin whispered.

As she hesitated the acolytes took up a ululating cry as sharp as the knives of bone they carried.

The axe fell . . . and fell . . . and fell . . .

* * * * *

Kelly Dove stirred as the shimmer of daybreak touched her face. There was no instant between sleep and waking that she did not remember that she had lost Ursula.

Another day to go through the motions of living: bathing, breakfast, checking the progress of the late summer shallots or onions that were scheduled to be picked, sorted, seeded and readied for winter. Fall was unmistakably in the mid-September air. It had seemed to come the day Ursula was taken, as if even the fields knew she was gone.

She had cried only twice in her life. Self-pity was a stranger, and regrets just as foreign, until the night Ursula left her. But now she woke every morning weeping, not believing she deserved to lose Ursula's love. She wept and wished she had never let Liz's girlfriend anywhere near Ursula no matter how much Ursula had said she needed Taylor's help. She let herself grieve, trying to reap the bitter harvest and move onto the frigid winter. Winter always brought the promise of spring. Spring would never come for her, not again, and so she was caught, ever falling into tears.

She rubbed her shoulder where Ursula had kicked her in her struggle to leave. Were it not for the bruise that ought to have long since healed, Kelly might have been able to lie to herself and pretend that Ursula had simply returned to her home in England. But the bruise was a constant reminder of

8

the night when Taylor and her circle had unbraided Ursula's hair, though Kelly had had to help at the last. She had only helped because Ursula told her it would prove her love.

In her mind, Kelly had heard Ursula's fear. *:I won't go there again. I won't.:*

The darkness had seized Ursula then, her body shimmering with an eerie blue-green glow. There had been screeching — almost musical but for the volume — and Ursula had begun to rise toward the swirl of roiling light above them.

Ursula had gone to it willingly, pulled into the air, into the spiral of darkness, lifted by a woman's hands that had gleamed with purpose and power.

She had gone willingly to that other woman and was forever lost to Kelly. Kelly would have never let go, but Ursula had kicked her, wanting to be free, and said once again that Kelly had to prove her love.

She slammed her hands into her pillows. Her love had never been in doubt. Ursula knew that. What Ursula had meant was that Kelly had to atone for hurting her, to atone for the bruises she had left in the night of passion that had been their last.

Her tears didn't mask the chilling echo of a distant time when she had hurt Ursula. Killera had been her name in that dream, and she had known she was losing her goddess, her Ursula, to the daughter of the captain who sailed them to Ursula's arraigned marriage. Killera had taken revenge in an act of intimate violence that Ursula had neither resisted nor reproached afterward. Kelly's soul was burdened by guilt, by the pain she had caused in the past and in the present.

She would never have let go otherwise. She should not have let go no matter what Ursula asked.

Fall came early, mired in tears and regret. With regret came a curse. She did not curse Taylor, whose useless mysticism and nonsensical magic circle had delivered Ursula into danger.

9

She did not curse Uda, the demon of past dreams. Not even Ursula, though she had not trusted Kelly's love or strength.

The only curse in her was for the captain's daughter, the thief who had stolen Ursula's heart, for Kelly was certain that the hands that had taken Ursula on Lammas Night had been Autumn's. Were it not for Autumn, she would have never hurt Ursula, and Ursula — her Ursula, in this life — would have never doubted their love.

Ursula was with Autumn, a gift Autumn did not deserve.

So she cursed Autumn, wherever she was now, in whatever life, in all her pasts and all her futures. She willed evil into whatever peace Autumn might find.

Part One:
Splendor of Colors

Memory is a liar.
Lies are what sustain me.
— Lea Battle "The Sybil's Feather"

One

She would not have done it, except for the money.

When it came to dealing with people, Autumn knew patience was a virtue she neither possessed nor wanted. But she stayed where she was, did as she was told, smiled and smiled and smiled, all for the money.

The House of Cards was gone. The decrepit club where she'd performed nightly had been sold and demolished. Autumn knew she could make a living at poker or blackjack. Cards held no secrets from her. It was only a little magic to change the cards so she was the winner of a large pot. But it was technically cheating and any form of a lie made her nauseous. It also upset Ursula, though even Ursula didn't know why. Of course, Ursula didn't know much of anything, her past still as blank after nearly seven weeks of living with Autumn as it had been the first day.

Their dreams were empty, if they dreamed at all. There were no mutual dreams of a past they might have at one time shared — at least Ursula said she was no longer having the dreams either. There were no nuances of other women they might have known, now or then. There was only the darkness lurking beyond sleep, beyond the gates they both maintained to keep it out.

The darkness wanted Ursula back. Autumn wasn't going to let that happen. If sparing Ursula the ravage of the darkness was not reason enough, she had her own painful history, fifty generations of herself dying in attempts to bring Ursula back to her side of the *Spiralig Tor*, the spiral gate. She had finally succeeded, at no small cost in pain to either of them, and she was not going to lose Ursula again.

None of it seemed real under the hot lights and brash assault of ringing slot machines. She sat calmly in the dealer's chair of a blackjack table. Assured that only her hands would be caught on camera, it had seemed an easy five grand to make. After three hours, and with dawn approaching, it didn't seem that easy after all. The movie stars were being made up again. The scene ended with a drink tossed at the male lead. All traces had to be removed before the scene could be redone. The makeup on her hands, which masked the livid scar she still bore from the night she had found Ursula, likewise had to be reapplied often. The puncture wound in her knee, also from that night, had ached for the past half-hour.

It was tedious, all the waiting. She could wait centuries for a second of Ursula's love, but waiting minutes on other people's whims made her testy in the extreme.

Why am I doing this? Because you need the money, was the answer.

Two takes later the female lead announced that she was done for the night, shrilly advising everyone that she'd never done more than three takes for Scorcese and wasn't about to do a dozen for a movie-of-the-week.

Autumn didn't understand what most of that meant, but the bottom line was that she could go. As she gathered her coat from under the table, one of the production assistants plucked at her sleeve. He let go when she fixed him with a long, steady gaze. "Can I help you?"

He couldn't have been more than seventeen. "Yeah, sure. See, the producers cut their costs by renting out the sets to other productions when they're done for the day. There's these infomercial people who are going to shoot here now and they want you to deal for them."

"I'm going home," Autumn said.

"It'll only take about a half-hour. Believe me, they have no standards. Pay is two-fifty. Cash." He was older than she had initially thought, but years never equaled maturity. She was all too familiar with the fluidity of age, memory and wisdom.

"I'm not in the union." There had been some sort of waiver arranged for her with the actor's union because of the special skill she had that no union member provided.

"As if these people care. It's easy money, honey." She didn't answer, and he finally gulped. "It's Bradley, right? I'll tell them you're in."

She glanced at her watch. "If we're done by six a.m. I've been up all night."

"Yeah, you got it." He mimed a pistol shot at her and she returned the favor. He looked down at his chest with a start, but Autumn was already turning away to hide her smile. It was just a little trick, and they came so easily to her these days. Knowledge came out of nowhere, and Autumn often felt as if she'd stepped into a new skin when the burns she'd suffered in Ursula's rescue had healed. She reminded herself, then, that she had to be more cautious about using these new gifts.

Ursula — she clung to the name like a prayer, though it

caused her distress as well these days. She'd been driven so long to find Ursula. She'd died so many times. And still she died, every day when Ursula smiled at her and did not know who she was. They spoke only of today because they had no past that Ursula could recall. Ursula accepted that something extraordinary had happened to her. She seemed aware she had a power and knew how to use some of it. The orange tree, already half-grown and bearing late fruit though Autumn had planted it six weeks ago, was proof of Ursula's power. A lush garden sprang from desert-packed earth and uncertain water. It seemed to Autumn that the blossoms turned toward Ursula when she was near, instinctively wanting her nurturing.

Autumn knew how they felt. She tried to hide her feelings from Ursula — she had promised she would take nothing of her that Ursula did not freely give. She didn't want obligation to manipulate Ursula's emotions. They shared the same bed from necessity, but were rarely in it at the same time. At night, Autumn prowled the casinos and clubs for roulette winnings no one noticed, and she slept by day. Ursula was awake with the sun. Autumn wished it were otherwise, gods how she wished it. A touch, a smile of recognition, a kiss, anything, anything, anything at all.

"Places!" The sharp call brought Autumn out of the familiar ache. She went back to the table. The draping had been changed, but otherwise nothing was altered.

The production assistant came back to introduce her to the director of the infomercial, who drawled, "Can you set the deck so player two always wins with twenty or twenty-one? And players one and three bust?"

She nodded. He didn't have to know that she didn't need to pre-deal the deck. The cards would be what she willed them. It was the easiest trick of all. Since no money was involved it wasn't cheating and thankfully, her inner sense of fairness wouldn't balk. She heaved a sigh of relief as her stomach settled. She made it look as if she was setting up the deck while they did light checks.

They ran over on time, but Autumn was disposed to give them fifteen more minutes. She was paid in cash, which improved her mood even more.

It was always evening inside a casino, and though she knew it was early morning the sunlight was still a surprise. Mid-September was warm in Vegas. The temperature was already over eighty degrees, she judged, and she was just too tired to walk home. But cabs cost money. Pay from the movie company would be slow coming. The cash she had just made needed to be stretched.

Midnight had always held fewer secrets than noon for Autumn. Perhaps that was why she felt naked in sunlight. She could not be a creature of shadow in the harsh heat of Las Vegas, and she found it a trial to move in the unaccustomed glare. Her knee throbbed suddenly. The walk home would be endless. In the daylight she would have to go all the way around the train yard — no cutting through under cover of darkness.

Until a month ago she had still been a creature of the night, in spite of all that had happened this past summer — in all her newly remembered pasts. Ten years of not knowing who she was, ten years of struggling to make ends meet on the meager income from the House of Cards — ten years gone with the stroke of a pen and a swing of a wrecking ball.

She still did not know where she had come from the day she'd been found in a casino bathroom more than ten years ago. She still didn't know what had happened to put her there. But she trusted the past of her dreams because they had brought Ursula back to her.

She paused in the shade of a palm tree, ignoring the exhaust and rising heat. It took two heartbeats to calm her nerves. The merest thought of Ursula still unsettled her. She knew even now Ursula was quietly working behind Ed's workshop in the garden that bloomed from nothing. She might speak with Ed for a while, or to a neighbor who dropped in just to admire the rapidly growing plants as well as the beauty that worked among them. From the rear window of the loft they shared over Ed's workshop, Autumn had listened to the *Chants for the Feast of St. Ursula* and watched the steady pilgrimage of new and old acquaintances to the garden. She watched but could not join in.

Every visitor unconsciously deferred to Ursula, sought her advice, and shared their sorrows and joys. Autumn could not go to Ursula that way, in need of her innocence and unconscious healing. She could not play supplicant or acolyte, not when she had survived death itself on the power of *beloved*. As far as she knew, they shared only one distant past, which came to utter ruin, and this stagnant present.

In between was Autumn's struggle to survive and find her beloved again, overflowing with lifetime after lifetime of failure and madness. She did not know where she had pulled Ursula from and Ursula did not remember. Autumn tried to keep to the rhythm of the life that had helped her survive the waiting. It was all she knew. Ursula drifted, too, knowing only the garden and that she felt safe. They both waited for something to happen.

Her nights weren't what they had been. She won at roulette to keep them financially afloat. It wasn't exactly cheating. She wasn't changing where the ball landed. She just knew where it would come to a rest. She had offers to take her magic act to new clubs, but her future was not as an entertainer. Her instinct for self-preservation constantly cautioned her to keep her profile low, her head down.

Her future was to be what Ursula needed. That was everything. Autumn understood why she had survived to this day: to love and be with her, offering the small magic she possessed should Ursula need it.

Those women who had journeyed with Ursula to the abbey had been part of Ursula's circle of the great She-Bear, but

Autumn had watched them die at the hands of Uda of Jutland. At the last it was Ursula who had saved her, trying desperately to fight off Uda's attack while protecting the remaining lives in her care. Ursula had used Uda's own power source to fling Autumn and Hilea, their bard, from the abbey's confines. Life had meant nothing to Autumn after Uda had taken Ursula. She had taken her life, and never known what had happened to Hilea.

She shoved herself out of the shade of a sculpted dolphin, and for a moment the sweltering heat from the pavement hid the searing of fire down the scar between her breasts. When she realized part of the heat was coming from her, she knew without looking that the scar was angrily red. The itching pain was a reminder that in this lifetime, as in all the others, she had made a grave mistake, one that would some day have a reckoning. She hoped it was her only mistake. Now that she had Ursula there was no room for more.

The scar was her door prize from the night she had died, the Fourth of July, not even three months ago. She had not yet begun having the dreams of her past, and so she had not recognized the striking, seductive woman who called herself Rueda. She would dream in the weeks of her recovery, and learn that the chestnut-haired woman was Uda, who walked a dark and violent path. She would dream as well of Ursula, who had given her back to life.

The leather-clad Rueda had been headily seductive. Having no memory of anything before the age of seventeen, Autumn's ingrained habits of safety had been overwhelmed as she remembered being in a woman's arms before. She had not known it was Ursula she remembered and hungered for. Until that night, all the failure and madness had left her empty.

Breathless confusion had made her forget her dog, Scylla, waiting for her in the train yard to walk her safely home. Autumn had no doubt Scylla would have recognized Uda. She had taken Rueda hungrily, dizzily into her bed. She hadn't yet learned that she had shields that could have protected her.

She had not expected Rueda to drug her, manacle her to the bed, draw a dagger. She had not been prepared to die.

She dodged in and out of tourists photographing faux Roman statues and fountains spraying precious moisture in the desert sky. It was hard not to rub at the scar.

In the hospital and recovering at home she had dreamed of undertaking a journey with Ursula, of falling in love, of being wrapped in Ursula's innocent power. They were sailing to their death, she knew that now, but then a compulsion to intervene in the past had helped her realize for the first time that true magic flowed inside her.

Driven by flashes of memories from centuries of failure and raving madness, Autumn had stretched through forces that tore at mind and body and used magic she hardly understood. Her lifetimes of yearning were ended. She had found Ursula again, and pulled her to safety. Death had been almost a friend, but finally, in this disjointed life, she had a reason to live.

The pain between her breasts increased. It felt like the scar was on fire. She wanted to touch it, but would not show weakness in a public place. She stumbled toward the nearest casino in search of the privacy of a restroom.

"Where do you think you're going?"

The laconic voice stopped her, made her focus. She was in danger. "That's none of your business."

Detective Staghorn, LVPD, eyed her with a potent combination of dislike and avarice. He had seen her dexterity and knew she would make an excellent pickpocket and a cunning thief. He'd hoped to turn her to his service. If she worked for him he'd protect her from arrest. She hadn't known her revulsion at the idea stemmed from centuries of adherence to a moral code, refining herself constantly, striving to be worthy, to be strong enough, to find the warrior she had once been.

That warrior was more here than she had been when Staghorn had begun his harassment. She now frightened him. She kept her gaze cold and deadly. That he frightened her was also true, but he could not know she had seen his face in the final dream of Ursula, in the abbey, when he had wielded the heavy broadsword that cut Elspeth and Claire nearly in two. He didn't know she had killed him then with decisive vengeance. It was possible he would goad her into doing so again.

It was hard, though, not to show some sort of reaction to the increasing heat from her scar. She had borne pain, borne fire and madness, though ultimately they had taken pieces of her memory until she'd nothing left.

Everything she had learned to be was still inside her, if only she could remember it. So far, memory had only been recalled by pain and fire.

The voice she carried within her spoke. She'd only recognized recently that it was her own voice in many languages over the centuries of her endurance. *He will have nothing of you. He never has.*

"I'd forgotten about you." Staghorn tried to seem casual, but Autumn knew he was lying. She'd humiliated him too thoroughly to be forgotten. He glanced at the black on black bodywear and leather jacket that were her public persona. "You don't look so good in the bright light."

"You don't look good in any light," she snapped. She turned her back on him. Touch me, she thought. Just go ahead and try.

"I thought vampire wannabes couldn't stand the sun. Is that how you got stabbed? Trying to bring that babe in leather over to the dark side?"

She started walking. The skin around the scar was sweating profusely. Was it Staghorn's proximity? He had been Uda's tool in the past. Was he in this life as well?

The idea that he'd somehow been Uda's cohort the night that ended with Uda's dagger in her chest made Autumn lose her focus on him. Her reaction was slow when his hand grasped her upper arm.

Slow, but still fast enough.

Pain and fire brought memory, and memory brought skill.

It was a simple thing for her, now, to mentally move something from one place to another, even things that weren't solid, even things that are ideas or energies. She took the thing she had the most of at the moment — the burning pain between her breasts. She channeled it to his hand.

His howl made people turn their head. He drew his weapon quickly with his other hand. Autumn spread out her jacket to show she was unarmed. Witnesses she needed paused in their daily life.

"You're under arrest, you vicious bitch!" Staghorn's hand was blistered. Autumn didn't care. She could think only of timid Elspeth and brave Claire dying in the dirt with Staghorn grinning over them.

"For what?"

"It doesn't matter," he snarled.

Her luck had changed for the worse. A passing patrol car stopped and the officers leapt out. Staghorn identified himself.

"This worthless piece of crap attacked me!"

Autumn was still standing there with her jacket open. "I'm completely unarmed. He grabbed me and then he started screaming." She couldn't say she didn't know why. Lying made her ill. She draped herself in her most innocent air. She whispered a suggestion to the officers' minds, simple truth. :*She's not armed. She's no danger.*:

"Take off the jacket," one officer ordered.

Autumn complied. The sun on her bare shoulders was unfamiliar and only added to the heat that was turning her heart into an inferno. If she broke into a head sweat they'd think she was on something. She didn't want to go to the nearest precinct. Staghorn would know where she was and for how long. If he was working with Uda, then Uda would know, too.

Ursula would be unprotected.

:*Staghorn's an idiot. She's no threat. Staghorn's crooked. She's no threat.*:

The taller of the two cops, who'd finished searching her jacket and found only her wallet, turned to Staghorn. "Exactly how did she attack you?"

"I don't know. Look at my hand!"

Autumn shrugged. "Ask one of the witnesses. He grabbed me and started screaming. That's the honest truth." But not the whole truth, and she had to clamp down hard on the part of her that never wanted truth to go unspoken.

With a little mental encouragement from Autumn, witnesses eagerly and truthfully told what they'd seen, which was exactly what Autumn said. Staghorn was hollering for a paramedic, the wimp. He'd felt only a portion of what Autumn was enduring. She needed to get away, fast, because she was reaching her own limits of endurance. She let herself be patted down.

:She's unarmed. Staghorn's a user. This is a waste of time.:

"Let's get you to a hospital," the shorter cop suggested. They had to forcibly drag Staghorn away.

"She did it, I'm telling you. I don't fucking believe this! You can't let her go."

She watched the patrol car speed off. Staghorn would not forget this. It was the second time she'd humiliated him in front of brother officers.

She signaled for a cab, desperate to get away from the scene and close to Ursula. The searing pain was not dissipating with Staghorn's absence, prompting a new fear. Maybe the pain was a warning that the woman who had cut her open — woman, demon, dark face of an ancient goddess — was back.

She threw a ten at the cab driver and scrambled out of the car. "Ursula!"

The garden was deserted. Though the plants were all

flourishing at astonishing rates, there weren't so many of them that an adult could hide. Ursula was not there. *She's always there in the morning.*

Upstairs to the loft they shared over Ed's workshop. The door was locked — unusual. She opened it with her mind, even though she sensed Ursula was not inside. Scylla wasn't there either, and she was both comforted and dismayed.

Down the stairs to Ed's workshop, where he was bent over his welding. He didn't hear her until the second time she called his name. "Where's Ursula?"

He doused the torch and turned. His safety helmet blurred, becoming a puzzling vision of a protective helm emblazoned with a crusader's cross. When he raised it to gaze at her he was just Ed again, not a Moorish survivor of an ancient conflict. He had survived a conflict in this life, though, and walked with a permanent limp, courtesy of mortar shell. "Isn't she in the garden?"

"No." Autumn couldn't hide her panic. Ed knew nothing of the dreams, but understood that Autumn was a magician, and her magic was not confined to a stage. He asked no questions, and never had in any of those lives Autumn was slowly remembering. He had always been there for what she needed of him: father, brother, servant, bearer of burdens, source of comfort. He did not understand where Ursula had come from but he swelled with the same desire to protect and shelter Ursula from darkness. It was an ancient debt. Someday she would tell him why he felt its burden.

"She's not there. I don't think —" she pressed her hand to the burning heat between her breasts.

Ed's dark, lined face further creased with worry. "What's wrong?"

"My scar — I have to find her."

She dashed outside again, finding the presence of mind to whistle for Scylla. Scylla had been the one to rouse the neighborhood while Autumn had lain dying from Rueda's dagger strike.

There was no answering bark.

"No, no," Autumn groaned. She took a deeper breath and whistled again, adding mental energy to the volume.

Had that been a distant reply? She didn't remember running to the street. Peering into the shimmering distance she saw two figures, one human, one canine, walking together as if they had no cares in the world.

She went to one knee to catch her breath and because the pain was easing, finally. The fire was still almost beyond bearing, but as Ursula grew closer Autumn felt the cool, soothing balm of her presence. She knew she could stand it as long as necessary. Ursula was her endless strength. Nothing could break her.

"I'm sorry," Ursula said when she was in earshot. Autumn could only think that skin so fair was not meant for the harsh desert sun. Ursula didn't seem to feel the heat, however, and her luxurious red hair floated behind her as she walked, the ends brushing the backs of her knees. In Autumn's dreams it had always been braided, but the woman she had pulled from the *Spiralig Tor* had been naked, unbraided, gaunt and in agony. "Did you need me?"

How not to scream Yes? "I was worried," she said baldly, hiding a shiver at the dream memory of Ursula's braid coiling around her body. Ursula had regained her glow of health since that night, and Autumn could not stop reliving how her skin had felt in that distant past. "You've never been out."

"Today seemed like a day for it. Scylla wanted to go for a walk and Ed was busy. So I took her. I knew she wouldn't let me get lost."

Scylla licked Autumn's hands with doggy bliss. Ed went back to work while Autumn gazed into the luminous black eyes that had haunted her for centuries. She'd panicked for nothing. Well, not quite nothing. Staghorn had almost had her arrested and her chest was on fire.

Ursula lofted a plastic grocery bag into view. "I hope you don't mind — I took some money from the drawer. I thought you'd be hungry."

"I don't mind at all." She *was* hungry, and tired, and in pain. Her mouth didn't know when to stop. "Everything I have is yours, without asking."

Damn it, she had said too much. She could see the pity in Ursula's eyes. What else could Ursula feel? She knew Autumn was deeply in love with her. How could Ursula return an emotion so intense that it was beyond her grasp? She could only pity Autumn's distress, in the same way she would pity any stranger in pain.

She turned toward the garden to avoid the question in Ursula's eyes. Ursula remembered only the dreams she'd had after coming to the safety of Autumn's loft, beginning a few days before she reached the abbey and the terrible events within its walls. She knew Autumn had shared those dreams, but they hadn't discussed what it could mean. Autumn had not brought up her earlier dreams, either. That would require speaking of Autumn's feelings and losing the last of what passed for normal in their current situation.

Normal. Who was she fooling? Autumn plucked an orange from the tree she'd planted a short time ago. Now she had a beautifully ripe fruit in her hand. Normal? Hardly. The fragrance alone was healing. Staghorn and her fears faded to the back of her mind.

"What did you bring me?" Autumn asked in hopes of diverting the conversation from any chance at unwanted revelations. She offered the orange to Ursula, who dropped it into the bag.

"Potatoes. I thought I'd make you eggs 'n chips. We only eat it in the evening, but after being up all night, it's your suppertime."

Autumn carefully asked, "We?"

26

"We Brits," Ursula said easily. "Back in —" She choked to silence and was utterly still, one forearm across her forehead. She stared at some distant point for perhaps a minute, shaded by the spreading leaves of the orange tree. Her gaze slowly returned to Autumn. She shook her head slightly. "It's gone," she whispered. "Damn."

"Don't push it," Autumn said. She knew only too well what straining to remember could cost. She, too, had an intimate experience of migraines after ten years and more of not knowing for certain what her name was, nor where she had come from before the age of seventeen. With the migraines came a disconnected life, never feeling more than a faint conempt for everything. Even after all that had happened, the only thing she knew for sure was that her name had been Autumn in her past and her soul was irrevocably bound to Ursula.

The questions were back in Ursula's eyes. She still wondered why Autumn loved her, helped her, and what Autumn had saved her from. Added to that was renewed anguish. *Who am I? Why am I here? What happened to me?*

"Eggs 'n chips sounds great if you're up to it." Autumn didn't know exactly what was going to end up on her plate, but Ursula had proven a more than able cook. She led the way to their stairs and opened the door for Ursula. Scylla stretched out under the cool shade of the orange tree with an audible sigh of pleasure.

Ursula set the bag down, and slowly turned. "You weren't just wondering where I was. You were upset. Worried." Not questions, not yet.

"Yes." Autumn said nothing more as she hung her jacket in the tiny wardrobe. She wanted to rush to the bathroom for a cold washcloth to press to her scar, which began to burn again the moment she left the shelter of the garden. She had managed to hide the scar from Ursula, and still did not want to explain how she had gotten it, or from whom.

"Why?"

"Why what?" It was a childish evasion.

Ursula's sigh had a good measure of vexation in it. "Why were you — no. That's not the right question. Why do you care what happens to me?"

A tougher question. "You know why."

"Tell me."

"Because . . ." She couldn't say it. "You know why."

"Because you love me."

Autumn nodded, her face as like stone as she could manage.

Ursula's eyes did not fill with the expected pity. Before Autumn could discern the emotion that *did* flicker in the black depths, Ursula's gaze focused on her chest. "You're hurt!"

She glanced down. The area around her scar was puffed and red. No surprise, but she hadn't realized the swelling had become visible above the top of her thin black sleeveless shell. "It's just a scar. I need to put some burn ointment on it."

She felt Ursula's gaze on her back as she went into the tiny bathroom. But she forgot Ursula was there for a moment after she yanked the top over her head and pushed her black sport bra down. She hadn't looked long and hard at this scar. The scars on her hands and knee, similar to bullet wounds, were newer but almost old friends. She'd gained them in honest battle for Ursula, those and the burns in the explosion that followed. Autumn did not mind wearing those reminders. Ursula knew all about them.

But this scar between her breasts was different. The blade had been sharp, but thick, and the sutures done in great haste to save her life. The burning heat emanating from it had left the surrounding skin purpled with blisters. She closed her eyes, trying not to relive that night, not the passion, not the surrender, not her choking helplessness and terror as the blade descended.

"What happened to you?"

Autumn opened her eyes to see Ursula in the doorway, too

close. She'd longed to have Ursula look at her, really see her, but not like this. She busied herself with opening the burn ointment. She thought of a hundred different evasions, but the truth won as always. "I was stabbed."

"My God."

Autumn got the tub of goo open, remembering in time that it stained clothing. She pulled the sport bra over her head, intensely aware of how close Ursula was. She was about to dip her fingers into the ointment when Ursula spoke.

"Wait."

Surprised, Autumn glanced at her in the mirror. She was unprepared for the look on Ursula's face: uncertainty mingled with hope. "What is it?"

"I can heal you."

"I know," Autumn whispered. "You already have, more than you know."

"I'm serious."

"So am I," though you don't seem to get that, Autumn wanted to add.

"I can feel —" Ursula put her arm across her forehead again, straining to remember. Finally, she shook her head. "I have done this."

With an aching, pounding heart, Autumn watched Ursula's fingertips approach her chest. An intimate touch was so longed for, but not like this. Her body was melting, straining, yearning toward Ursula's touch. She clamped down on a moan. Ursula seemed to waver in light tinged with the red of her hair.

At the moment of fingertips on skin, Autumn felt an agonizing flash of sensation, as fierce as that of the dagger breaking through her sternum and piercing her heart. The pain stopped in an instant and she saw that the scar had disappeared.

Then everything went black.

Two

The air was heavy with the scent of harvest. Kelly stacked another empty sorting bin in the growing pile that wouldn't be touched again until spring. One small task accomplished, she sat down heavily on the workbench, glad of the dim coolness of the barn.

Though Kelly had long since scuffed out the circle Taylor and her cohorts had made in the barn's dirt floor, she could still see it in her mind's eye. She could feel the tingle of power on the back of her neck and in the one bruise that had yet to heal.

If you don't help me now, I will not forgive you. If you don't help me now, it will mean you never loved me. The last words Ursula had said to her, shuddering with pain, her voice hoarse from screaming: *This is the last time I will ask you to prove you love me.*

To prove her love she had let Ursula go, let her be drawn impossibly upward, out of Taylor's circle and into a spiral of violent light. She would never have let go on her own. Even unconscious she would have clung to Ursula. There was nothing she would not have done to keep Ursula safe.

She shook off the memory, though it was harder today than yesterday, and would be harder still tomorrow. She told herself she did not believe in past lives, nor in Taylor's circle. All that had mattered to her was that Ursula believed. She'd tried to be what Ursula needed and failed her in this life, the only one that mattered.

The dreams weren't real. They were just Ursula's dreams. Ursula had taught her a way to talk with their minds. That had opened the door to experiencing Ursula's sleeping life. Everything else was bullshit. Everything else was a lie. Everything else meant nothing. All that mattered was that Ursula was gone. It didn't matter how.

Had she been sitting there an hour? A day? She felt dizzy, overwhelmed by the dusty blend of drying herbs and grasses. She was so tired. The exhaustion of that night, not quite seven weeks ago, had never been vanquished. Taylor said she was feeling the darkness that had destroyed the circle and taken Ursula. Taylor, Kelly told herself for the millionth time, was full of shit. She was tired because she was grieving the loss of a love that had wrapped her in joy, lifted her into rapture again and again.

"Miss Dove?"

She wasn't surprised that she hadn't heard the arrival of a visitor. She was so deep in her own pain she sometimes could only hear the pounding of her heart. She recognized the voice and rose. "What can I do for you, Rachel?"

The Amish woman didn't seem to mind the dim interior of the barn. "I need some herbs. I've got a wheel of our first cheese in the buggy. Your favorite."

31

Kelly ought to have been overjoyed. Among the many wonderful things produced on Amish farms in the fall was a rich farmer's cheese that she adored. But she didn't have any capacity left for pleasure over something as pointless as food. She made an effort. "I could use a treat. Thank you. Take what you'd like." She knew Rachel well enough to trust she would be fair to both of them.

Rachel gazed at her for a long moment. Kelly abruptly remembered that she'd sometimes entertained less innocent thoughts about Rachel, before finding Ursula in that little herb shop in Aldtyme, England.

She was dizzy and tried to hide it by sitting down. Rachel moved past her toward the dried parsley and marjoram on the nearest shelves. Kelly could think of nothing more to say.

"Are you alright?" Rachel's voice was tinged with concern.

"Just tired."

"Is that all it is? I noticed . . ."

After the silence grew too long to bear, Kelly prompted, "You noticed?"

"She's gone. Your lover."

Kelly glanced up at Rachel, surprised by her frankness. The Amish didn't tend to ask about the lives of those outside their clan. Doubtless they disapproved of her sexuality, but the sins of outsiders were of no consequence to them. She had other qualities that did have value in their eyes. She was an able farmer and the area's best source for a variety of specialty herbs and the only source for some varieties of tomatoes and onions, all organic. She bartered fairly and did much of her labor without benefit of machines. A second pair of hands, Ursula's gifted hands, had made it all seem so easy.

In response to Rachel's observation, she could only say, "Yes."

"I'm sorry," Rachel murmured. And she put her hand on Kelly's shoulder.

She hadn't realized Rachel's eyes were blue-now-green. A healing wash of warmth seemed to cascade from Rachel's

32

hand, down through Kelly's arms and her stomach. She realized she was hungry. She felt awake and energized suddenly. She remembered Ursula's fragile softness in her arms, her cooing voice, then the sharp pleasure of Ursula's nails on her back the last time they had been truly abandoned together.

"Think of her." Rachel seemed hardly to be breathing.

Kelly could think of nothing but Ursula, the way she smelled, the way she moved, the way her hips curved.

Rachel's hand left her shoulder and gently cupped her jaw. Kelly looked up and found it too dark to see Rachel clearly. When had the sun set?

She pulled Rachel on to her lap and kissed her then, breathing in Rachel's excitement. Her head was spinning. It almost seemed as if the sun was breaking through clouds, but then it was the still dark again, broken only by Rachel's hungry, rapid gasps against Kelly's mouth.

Rachel seemed to be no bigger than Ursula. Kelly could almost put her hands completely around Rachel's waist. She lifted Rachel off her lap, then rose to push her onto the nearest sorting table. Rachel was pulling up her skirts with eager whispers of desire.

Ursula, she thought. *:Ursula.:*

:Ursula.: Rachel seemed to echo Kelly's prayer as she bared her breasts. She pulled Kelly's head down. *:Make me yours.:*

Passion unfurled in her, anger and regret mingling into a potent mixture that seared through Kelly's body. She could see herself as if from above, her body hard against Rachel's, feasting roughly as Rachel encouraged her.

:Make me yours. The way you made her yours.:

No, Kelly thought, but the denial did not stop her hands. Her last time with Ursula was rising from the blackest hole of her memory, from the depths where she had pushed it, trying to forget that she had hurt Ursula. From deeper still came an uglier memory, when they had rocked through the sky in a crow's nest far above the deck of an ancient sailing ship. Ursula had told her she loved another and Kelly — Killera — had hurt her for the first time. Ursula had let Killera hurt her, just as Rachel was letting it happen now.

Not just allowing, but encouraging. Kelly wanted to draw back. This wasn't her. Rachel was inside her head, but Kelly didn't know how that could be.

:The way you were with her. Be that to me. Show me.:

No, Kelly thought, but she could not escape the pleasure of touching. She did not care what bruises she might leave. She heard the rending of fabric and Rachel laughed, throaty and triumphant.

Kelly had heard that laugh before, in her dreams.

She'd heard it just before Killera had died, in the past. She didn't believe in the dream. It wasn't her dying on the rough-hewn steps of an ancient abbey. The laughter filled her ears.

:What are you to her? What do you give her? This? Just this?:

Never this, Kelly wanted to answer. She felt Rachel's determined search of her memories, her mind flicking through images of Ursula, sullying all of them.

:What are you to her? Show me her magic. Show me her face in the circle.:

:No.: Kelly tried to shout it but her mouth was covered by Rachel's. She pulled back, struggling to free herself from Rachel's kiss. It wasn't Rachel's face in front of her, but Ursula's. Her Ursula, her goddess, her life.

:Show me everything and I can be her for you.:

The promise was so seductive that Kelly yielded to it. Since Midsummer's Night she'd not slept restfully, she'd not stopped longing for even a moment. She'd sunk further and further into depression and memory, and now Ursula was back, not just tolerating her forceful touch, but begging for it.

Rachel's mind pressed into the dream memories. Kelly could no longer deny that part of her knew she had also been Killera. Ursula had walked as the goddess, and Killera had been there when the goddess had possessed her. The ritual was in Killera's memories for Rachel to take.

:She liked what you did to her. Take me that way.:
Ursula . . . Rachel . . . hips arched against her and her fingers found familiar sweetness. She wanted it to be hers. She wanted Ursula to be hers.

Belatedly, her mind a fog, and aware that she could not be watching all this happen from above, Kelly knew this woman could not be Rachel. She was not Ursula, either. She had to be Uda, from the abbey, the woman who had killed Killera and incited the killing of Claire and Elspeth.

She panicked because she was wrapped by strong legs, clasped by a body that seemed to pull her inside. The walls of the barn wavered — the sun was coming out. She shook her head.

:No!:

She rejected it, all of it, the passion, the anger, even the regrets. She had to let it all go or Uda would use it.

Letting go of the past, she found a core of strength to push herself from Uda's grasp. The walls of the barn melted to gold.

She woke up on her back on the floor next to the bench where she had dozed off. It had just been a dream. It was still morning. There was light and air. She could breathe.

Just a dream, she told herself. Only a dream. No scent of passion lingered on her hands, though it was still strong in her mind.

The laughter that echoed from sleep was drowned out by the approach of a car. She rose and dusted herself off. It was all she could will herself to do.

When she saw who it was she turned her back, twisting her hands into fists. She didn't curse Taylor the way she did Autumn, but she wasn't far from it.

She heard Taylor's shoes on the driveway gravel, but was

equally aware that the breeze had developed an edge of chill to it. Rain would settle in by evening. Good for her fields, which were mostly harvested or going fallow next season, but not so good for many of her neighbors.

"I can't stand it anymore," Taylor said.

"What do you have to stand?"

"I lost everything —"

"You lost nothing but your friends." Kelly wouldn't look at her, even though Taylor had moved to within a few feet. "You still have love."

"No, no." Taylor's voice was thick with tears. "You don't understand. You don't really know who she was."

Kelly whirled around at that. "Don't start! Don't start that crap with me again."

"I didn't know who she was, I still don't. She didn't know who she was — how could you know?"

"I had her in my arms. She loved me. Don't tell me I didn't know her. I knew every inch of her." She choked.

Taylor dashed away tears. "You didn't know what her braid was for. You didn't know her aunts were witches."

"You're the one who says that!"

"You didn't know anything except that you wanted her."

"Stop it," Kelly said, her voice edged with warning.

"You had her body, but she never gave you anything else. Not even her trust."

The truth was brutal, and Kelly felt something snap. She lunged forward with a cry and backhanded Taylor into the gravel. "You lied to me — you told me everything would be okay!"

"I told you everything I knew," Taylor sobbed from the ground. "She's the one who told you almost nothing."

In her fury Kelly wanted to kick Taylor, to grind her into the dirt. Her rage peaked and she found herself on the ground next to Taylor, shivering. "Don't make this her fault."

Taylor wiped blood from her mouth. The sight of it shook Kelly and her stomach heaved. Taylor's bloodstreaked fingers reminded her of her own, in the dream when she had hurt Ursula. Why couldn't she escape it?

Taylor held her head while she was sick. They managed to support each other enough to get inside. She sluiced her face with water and drank thirstily. The water quieted her stomach. She collapsed into a kitchen chair and rested her head on her folded arms.

Taylor pressed a paper towel-wrapped ice cube to her swelling lip and joined her at the table. "I hope you got that out of your system."

"I've never hit anyone before in my life," Kelly whispered. "I — I'm sorry."

Taylor's sharp blue eyes were tortured. Kelly hadn't known her long, but she could see how the color had sunk from a spring noonday sky to a wintry sunset, in the same way her own eyes had dimmed from honey to the color of mud.

"I think I wanted you to do that," Taylor admitted. "I could tell you were at a breaking point. I baited you. I guess I think I had it coming. That and more."

"Nothing excuses it," Kelly said. "I'm not a violent person."

"You have violence in your past." Taylor was looking at her speculatively, her face taking on the austerity she had worn on Lammas Night, cloaked in her ritual robes and magic.

"If you're going to start talking about that shit, get out," Kelly said. She felt her anger blossom again.

"We've missed something." Taylor set down the ice cube. "I need to know what you saw — I don't have it clearly. I might be able to tell where she went."

"No."

"Kelly, please. I can't go on like this. It's killing Liz."

"Don't put that on me." Kelly could believe that Liz somehow was a sponge for other people's emotions, bad or good. As a child, Liz had always been the shrinking one, preferring solitude to any game. She would sometimes sleep in the depths of the closet where she said it was quieter. Kelly had wondered, when they'd both grown up, if Liz's oddness was a symptom of denying her sexuality. Now she knew it was something else entirely.

"I had shields, good ones, and I used to spread them over her. She learned how to raise her own. But they're not strong enough without me to refresh her energy." Taylor's voice broke. "When we're together I dump all this on her, but she won't raise her shields. Because she loves me. She says we swore an oath to share everything, and that means this, too. And now, when we're this far apart we're not really in rapport any more. She's just not there and neither of us can bear it."

"And yet you're here without her."

"I couldn't bring her near you." Taylor closed her eyes. "I don't have much left, but enough to tell you are radiating rage. I'm surprised . . ."

When Taylor said nothing for another minute, Kelly finally prompted, "Surprised by what?"

Taylor's eyes opened. "That the darkness isn't looking for you. I don't feel it at all. You have — *had* good shields here. But they've been depleted and without active intervention they'll take a long, long time to generate again. You're vulnerable and yet I don't sense that presence outside your gate. Why would it leave you alone now?"

"I don't believe any of that garbage," Kelly said, though a shiver went down her spine. The darkness — Uda — had found her. Rachel had been soft and so hungry for Kelly's strength. No, it was just a dream, she told herself. Only a nightmare.

"I need to see what you saw." Taylor's intensity was growing and Kelly felt a wave of fear.

"No. You're not looking around in my head."

"I didn't look hard enough before —"

"What does that mean?" Kelly rose to her feet when she understood. "You did it before? You pried into my mind already?"

"When you were sleeping, right after it happened."

"You bitch! Don't you people have any kind of rules?" Kelly towered over Taylor.

If Taylor was afraid, it didn't show. "Yes, lots of them. I've broken a fair share of them. It shouldn't surprise you. None of us are what we were. I'm certainly not what I was. I'm no cleric, no priestess. I don't even have the shields or control of the most basic initiate. You're right not to trust me because I don't play by the rules anymore." Taylor said it with an edge of bitterness.

"Is that pretty little speech supposed to make me ignore your own advice? Forget it. You're not getting inside my head, not again." Kelly felt a returning wave of illness. "I can't believe you did that." She sank down into her chair. "I don't believe it." She almost added *you're no better than she is*, but it had just been a nightmare. She didn't believe in any of this. Uda could not have been in her mind. If she didn't believe, she could forget.

"I'm sorry about Liz," Kelly added. "But I can't help."

"None of us are what we were," Taylor said again, almost as if to herself. "Except Uda, whatever she is."

"And who says being an evil, murderous witch doesn't have its rewards?" Kelly almost smiled.

Taylor looked at her oddly. "Could you at least offer me some lunch? It's a long drive home."

Kelly wanted to refuse, but her country habits of hospitality hadn't been beaten out of her. She nodded. "But then I think I'll go over to one of the other farms. It's going to rain and he won't have his tomatoes in yet." She'd feed her and get her out as quickly as possible.

She made sandwiches while Taylor brewed tea and poured

it out. They ate without speaking, then Kelly got up to tidy the dishes. She caught herself on the sink when dizziness washed over her.

Taylor's voice seemed to come from the other side of the moon. "You're going to need to lay down."

"You bitch," she managed, now realizing the tea's bitter aftertaste had been sharper than normal.

She tried to push Taylor away, but was aware, before oblivion took her, of Taylor lowering her to her bed. She had shared that bed with Ursula. The prayer filled her mind: *Ursula.*

* * * * *

"Out of the way of your betters, boy!"

Autumn didn't respond to the quick slap. The pain seemed to radiate down her chest for a moment, then faded. She lowered her gaze, stooped her shoulders and tugged at what passed for a forelock in a show of respect. There had been a time when the warrior in her would not bow, but the years — the many, long years — had taught her more than one way to survive. Survival was the only way to win.

She made way for the retinue of a noblewoman and followers. She wasn't going into that part of the church anyway. The likes of her — to all appearances a scruffy, underfed, badly groomed boy — went to the rear balcony to stand. It secretly amused her, for it seemed to her that if nobility needed to be closer to the priest, then everyone understood they must be more in need of the salvation the priest's promised.

Up among the unwashed and largely female audience she found a place where she could lean against a column and watch the choir. She didn't need to see the three priests who would officiate for this feast day. Listening was what would give her a rare moment of respite.

She had not been in Yarmouth in a very long time. Four

lives at least, four failures ago in her endless search. She was going back over old paths, once again, and hoping as she always did that something would catch her attention, would point the way to finding Ursula. The streets were as silent to her now as they had always been. Rocks did not speak. Even the sea seemed to have forgotten that Ursula had ever existed. There had been a time when she had trusted that the sea had seen and known all.

She never went into the church of the White Christ. After these many centuries, she was probably the only person who thought of the anguished figure on the cross by that name. Everyone seemed to have forgotten there had been another way before this relentless parade of suffering, retribution and divine wrath.

The exception to her avoidance of this interloper and his angry father was today. Today, before the sun even rose, began the feast of St. Ursula. The first office of the day, the Vigil, would shortly begin, and with it the first praise of Ursula's name Autumn had heard for the past year.

There was something new about the day. Today would be the first time she attended the feast day in a church where Ursula had once been a guest. That abbey had long since fallen down and the present buildings built on its ashes. There was nothing left of the place where Ursula and her companions had taken shelter while the ship that carried all of them toward her wedding day had been repaired.

But this sky, this sun, this air, and the stars tonight — they had known Ursula. To Autumn it had been five centuries of life, searching, death and life again. To the stars it had been the blink of an eye. The stars had seen them then, and they saw her now. Perhaps they would speak.

She put away the memory of the stars that had held them both the one time they had reveled in each other's bodies and minds. They had rocked safely in the light of these stars. It was painful to think about it because it only made her remember anew how it had all ended.

She turned her mind from the memory of that day. It seared in her, that final moment when Ursula had pleaded with Autumn to draw her bow, to end her life before Uda secreted her away. Her hands twisted, for she had not been able to do it. Uda had triumphed, Ursula was still gone past recovering. Despair had led her to take her own life. To think of it was to blank her mind to an ugly red. Every time she thought of it she felt as if a piece of her was lost. She would remember the past, but not dwell there. The past would not secure the future.

She had been loved by a goddess, floated among stars with her, felt the unutterable grace of a goddess's light. That first death led to this strange path of life. She searched, she studied, she practiced her magics, honed her skill with dice and blade. She played many, many parts. And she died.

Death held little mystery for her after this long acquaintance. Death led to finding herself seventeen again, and still looking for what she had lost. She had ten years in this search. Ten years of dressing like a boy and persuading no one to notice the lad who asked so many questions, read so many languages, knew so many customs, had traveled so many places.

She distracted herself from wounds of grief never healed by wondering how this celebration of St. Ursula would differ from all those in the past. The stories the priests told were laughable fabrications. Eleven thousand virgins, in eleven ships? No ship known carried a hundred, let alone a thousand. Virgins they had all been — none of them touched by a man — but it had not been love of the White Christ that had made them set aside the pleasures of a man's bed.

The contempt she felt was not new. It grew as the years went by. Contempt and disdain sometimes threatened to overcome all her emotions, but she fought it. Ursula had been compassion and pity. To lose those feelings might risk losing Ursula forever.

The music was always better than the sermons. She

42

understood the Latin, which made it easier to appreciate. The music would be different today, however. She'd noticed the elegant Norman French proclamation on the door of the church, though a person of her obvious rough upbringing — everyone ignored a dirty peasant, making a peasant boy a safe creature to be — would not be expected to read the language of the ruling monarchs. A nobleman had sponsored today's celebration, paying handsomely for a German choirmaster to train the choir of the Abbey of St. Giles. There would be a new liturgy today, new responsories, new antiphons, a new hymn. The composer was noted only as "a faithful and humble servant, scribe of the living light."

The church grew quiet. It was chilly in the dead of night air. She heard someone whisper that the day's benefactor had come in, which surely meant the services were about to begin. She cared nothing for a lord. Lords came and went. She'd seen empires rise and fall. Even Charlemange, who had taken up the exclusive standard of the White Christ in his search for conquest, had bowed before time. Everything turned to dust. Everything except her love for Ursula.

The light below increased as the priests came in with candles before and after. Vigil was the deepest hour of night and the ritual prayed for daylight to conquer the darkness again. Autumn didn't mind the night and didn't fear that dark. The absence of light was not the kind of dark she had learned to hate these many years. Midnight and its shadows were old friends.

Altar servants lit candles and the three priests were occasionally visible from where she stood. The priest's invitatory did not seem unusual.

The choir's responsory rang out — and it swept all her pasts away.

She abruptly stood on the deck of a sailing ship watching a goddess she had loved at first sight saying goodbye to her people.

A dripping honeycomb, was the virgin Ursula.

Honey and milk under her tongue, she gathered to herself
A fruit-bearing garden and the most fragrant flowers . . .
And her name in heaven was Columba . . .
Gods — gods!

She clutched the column and let the frigid stone shock her back to where she was. The music — Hilea's music. It swelled out of the choir, rose like a visible force. Profound magic seemed to be woven into each note. The longing, the emptiness, the sorrow — she knew it all so well. It had become a part of her every breath the day she had met Ursula and her companions.

She wept silently as the words gathered around her.

O pulcherrima forma . . .

Most beautiful sight,
sweetest scent of desired delights,
We long ever after you in lamented exile.
When may we see you and be with you?
We are alone and you are in our mind . . .

The words had changed slightly. Singular became plural. But the melody was the same, the same leaping, twining voices of longing.

She had heard it as a song of departure, when Ursula had left her people, a bride sold for the sake of an alliance.

The music coursed through her like her own blood. How could this be sung in the White Christ's church, paid for by a noble patron?

As far as Autumn knew, three of them had survived that day in the abbey. Killera and Elspeth were dead, but Ursula had spared Hilea and herself by pushing them through a gate to safety outside the abbey's walls. Uda had taken Ursula. In all her wanderings there had been no hint of Ursula or of Hilea. It had been hard to go on trusting that if she survived in this odd cycle of life, then they somehow survived as well.

44

And now this — this music, this magic. Hilea survived. She was alive, now.

The music worked its magic on her, and she relived her precious memories of that journey: Hilea's bawdy songs, her small features that showed her Pict blood, the magic of her fingers on her slender lute. Hilea had taken the notion of festival to heart, and there were few women she did not try to bed. They had been friends. They had laughed so much. Hilea had been the first to know that Autumn's soul was lost to Ursula.

At last, Autumn had a sign. She would find Hilea. Together, anything might be possible.

When Vigil was over she knew she would return at Lauds, at Prime, at Sext, at Vespers, even Compline. She would listen and she would learn all she could about the music and its composer. And she would study the lord, now of profound interest to her, who had paid for this music to come to this church — where Ursula had once slept — all the way from Eibingen, Germany.

A peasant boy didn't ask the name and whereabouts of a nobleman's ship. She'd learned that lesson long ago, and she got no better results this lifetime than in the past. When anyone deigned to respond it was with a quick cuff to the ears.

She wandered deeper into the Yarmouth working docks, searching for the vessel that belonged to Lord Aldtyme. Lord Aldtyme had been the benefactor of yesterday's celebration of Ursula. Autumn knew the place, Aldtyme. She had first met Ursula there. She did not know this lord, whose modesty was obvious from a retiring bearing and shadowing hoods any monk would welcome.

Not that one, she told herself, surveying the begrimed fore and aft castles of the current vessel with disdain. The ship she sought would be well appointed and in good repair. Lord Aldtyme's reputation was sound. It had been easier to find out about Lord Aldtyme than to actually get close enough to study the lord's features.

The lord in question was regarded as a man of deeds, not words, honest and generous to those who served him well. His Northumbrian farms were productive and he tithed generously to his Norman king, as had his father before him. The Aldtyme estates were not expansive, but they had survived the conquest of King William in the same family hands. The current lord was one of the few nobles left with Saxon heritage.

She ducked to the next quay, dismissed the barely seaworthy craft there and went on to the next. It was a long time since breakfast. She'd hoped to find the vessel she sought by now.

She quieted her growling stomach by considering the mystery of this lord. He was pious in public — who had a choice about that, these days? Pious in private as well, she'd heard in tavern talk between Vespers and Compline last night. A farmer monk, not a warrior, but pleasant enough when he spoke at all. One would expect such a man to be generous to his own church, but why such generosity — the sponsorship of an entire feast day — at St. Giles in Yarmouth, far from home? And why that particular feast, one more popular with women?

St. Ursula, like all the female saints, was beloved of women. Not as much as Mary, as the jealous priests had renamed the Great Mother known throughout the world Autumn had traveled. She had watched it happen, watched even the sacred winter quarter taken over by birth celebrations for this holy lord. The Great Mother was reduced from giver of all life to the motherhood of only this lord. Legions of the faithful turned to Mary for comfort and compassion. She was their Queen of Heaven, a title even these empty, jealous priests could not stamp out. The people clung to what they needed. Even after centuries of the denigration and vilification of women, they still needed Her love though they knew only Her shadow.

Ursula was Autumn's Queen of Heaven, and always would be.

She rejected four more vessels as possibilities and trudged back to the base of the dock. There were three more docks in busy Yarmouth harbor, each with nearly twenty ships. She fortified herself with as much pasty and ale as a lad like her could reasonably afford and began with the next.

The sun was in the third hour of the afternoon when she found what had to be Lord Aldtyme's ship. *Greenest Branch* was no ordinary merchant vessel. It was fortified in both castles with stations for archers, and the waist glittered with shields. It wasn't a craft of war either, for deckhands and dockworkers were busily filling the hold with bolts of wool and crates of foodstuffs from more distant shores. The ship was obviously the property of a secure and stable merchant. The name, too, had a familiar nuance.

The landward breeze lifted the family standard on the mast. It bore the same insignia she'd seen on the lord's attendants: a golden "A" woven into the pelt of a bear rearing on a field of green.

The breeze also brought the aroma of the pungent ground bark of Mediterranean trees. She had been to Italy, to Spain, to the lands of the Moors. All so long ago, so many skins ago. But her nose remembered, just as she remembered the scent of Ursula's hair.

She lingered in plain view, but no one seemed in the least interested in pressing her into service, not on this vessel. The rapid, northern Anglo dialect used aboard was no mystery to her. She quickly learned it was bound for the lord's home, catching the evening tide in a matter of hours.

She would have to make her way aboard, then. When the deckmaster came down to the dock to settle a loading dispute, she crossed his path at the bottom of the gangplank.

"Please, my lord, I must get to York and I've no time to

waste. I can work. You don't have to pay me. I know a ship, and I'm good with my hands." She added a simple, truthful suggestion. *:This one's no bother.:*

The deckmaster considered her. "We've got all the cabin boys we need, lad."

:This one will be no bother.:

"I'm willing to work." She added a note of whining youth. "I'll knot sails or do galley work. I can get up the main in a trice. I can lift, though not as much as might be needed." *:No bother at all.:*

The deckmaster had a rough but gentle soul and Autumn did not need to further prod him. "All right, lad. I'll see if cook can use you."

Cook set Autumn to cleaning pots on the deck with a paste of sand and a great deal of seawater. She kept her head down and worked, speaking little and waiting for any opportunity to study Lord Aldtyme.

Her chance came just before they cast off, when the lord's small party finally came aboard. The rising wind swept the lord's hood back. Many questions were answered by that one look. For a moment she felt as if she were drowning and her heart hammered. She'd been waiting so long for something to happen. First the music. Gods, now this.

"You're presentable enough. Clean your hands. Put on this apron and you can serve," Cook decided. He'd taken a liking to Autumn's shy ways, a liking Autumn could tell might be more intimate than she cared for.

The members of the lord's party — a scribe as substantial as fog and a body servant whose girth attested to an appetite frequently fulfilled — shared quarters next to their master. Their cabin also served as the passengers' and officers' dining room. Space was precious on board and squeezing between bunks and chairs required some agility. But the vessel's motion was as familiar to Autumn as breathing. She set trenchers at each place and quickly returned with a hearty lamprey eel stew. The florid valet was ravenous. The scribe

48

seemed too green to care. The captain and deckmaster tucked in with pragmatic speed. Rough weather brewed to the east and the night passage could be troublesome. Lord Aldtyme said nothing beyond gruff thanks when Autumn refilled the half-empty tankard.

She went to the door and glanced back at Lord Aldtyme. It would be a pity to die, now that she had finally found something familiar, but it was a risk she had to take.

She sent the suggestion with a tight focus, not wanting to influence anyone but Lord Aldtyme. *:Look at the boy.:*

She waited a moment, her gaze fixed on the lord's face.

Slowly Lord Aldtyme's head came up, and brown eyes caught her stare. They narrowed with disapproval.

:Boy? Or woman?:

The lord's eyes widened. Autumn allowed herself to blush before she ducked out the door. She lingered for just a moment, sensing a wave of confusion tinged with cautious interest. It was the response she had hoped for.

By the time she took in the sweet the deck's pitching had reached full sail. She let herself enjoy the feel of it for a moment, and wanted to dash topside with the officers when a called signal was plainly heard. Autumn thought it was notice of an increase in the weather. It would be glorious to have the salted wind in her face. She pitied the poor seasick scribe, who had retired to the furthest bed with an ewer handy. The sea was the great giver of life no one could hide from, for it seemed to her that the sea touched everything. The sea had been her truth before she'd met Ursula.

Lord Aldtyme took no sweet, instead waving her back to her duties. She was aware of the brown gaze on her shoulders. The lord's confusion had given way to desire, fueled by loneliness yet restrained by fear. She understood that combination all too well.

She scrubbed pots until her hands were raw, certain she was uncovering hundred-year old layers of burnt leavings. After that there were a few items to ready for the crew's early breakfast. The crew had changed shifts by the time she had leave to find a corner somewhere for sleep.

Weary though she was, and in spite of the lateness of the hour, she had been hoping Lord Aldtyme would find a way to speak privately with her. The lord's sudden appearance in the gangway outside the galley set her heart to beating high in her throat. A lone lantern swayed behind Autumn, but the light was too weak to read the lord's expression.

They said nothing as ocean-green eyes gazed into deep brown. Then Lord Aldtyme took her by her upper arm and hurried with her toward the private cabin across from the dining room. Once they were inside the lord struck flint to light an oil lamp. With the wick turned up Autumn could see that the cabin was small but usefully filled with a comfortably sized bed, a large desk, and a number of books wrapped carefully in oilskin.

"What do you want of me, boy?" The gruff voice hesitated before the last word.

Autumn said nothing, trying to read the emotions that flickered over her temporary master's stern features.

Habitual caution warred with reckless desire, she could discern that much easily. There were murkier impulses at play, however, and she had trouble reading them. Her own confusion made her lose her focus. She was caught off her guard as she was pushed hard into the cabin wall.

She let herself be kissed, let powerful hands find her breasts, let her legs be kicked apart. She wrapped her arms around the broad shoulders as one hand found its way under her thick tunic and belted woolen hose. She didn't resist the discovery. Her crotch was fondled none too gently. The kiss deepened for a moment, then Lord Aldtyme murmured roughly, "You're no boy."

Autumn slithered her hands to the lord's ribs, then she swept her fingers firmly over the front of the layered tunic with deliberate strokes. "And you're no man."

She had expected panic, for this secret had obviously been long and well guarded. In this situation, from this woman, she had thought fear would win, at least for a moment, but instead a strong forearm was instantly across her throat. There had not been a moment's hesitation. Autumn struggled for breath but did not panic.

"How did you know? I don't care." The weight across Autumn's throat increased. "Understand me! Your body will be food for the deep if you say another word. Do you understand?"

Gasping, Autumn nodded. The pressure on her throat let up a little. She had underestimated the determination that drove this woman. She would be a formidable ally — something she should have remembered.

"Give me a reason why I don't kill you now and throw you overboard."

"We keep the same secret," Autumn said hoarsely. "We want the same pleasures." :It has been so long.:

The brown eyes seemed to bore into her soul. Finally, the arm was removed from Autumn's throat.

"Understand me as well," Autumn said more clearly. "When I die it will not be at your hands. I am not defenseless."

Lord Aldtyme stepped back as Autumn increased the pressure on the point of the knife she had against the lord's ribs. "What are you then?"

"Searching, like you." Autumn flicked the knife back into her sleeve. "Lonely, like you."

She let herself be pulled far more gently into those strong arms. There was tenderness now, and Autumn felt a rising tide of unexpected desire. Was this what Ursula had meant by festival feelings? Lord Aldtyme's mouth was demanding and hungry, and Autumn did not want to simply endure this touch. They had gone so far from celebration of their bodies. Hiding, denying, banking the anger when priests preached that the ultimate evil was woman's doing. For the goddess in both of us, Autumn thought. After all these years she finally understood something of what Ursula had meant.

She shed her clothes, and with a fluid, unseen motion stowed her only two possessions of value in the space between the cabin wall and the featherbed that covered the bunk frame. She wanted to be unmistakably female as she went willingly to the arms that reached for her from the depths of the bed. Autumn rolled onto her back and gave herself to sensations she had not felt in so long. Her hands found their way to heat and they both gasped.

When their mouths parted from a kiss of sweet promise, Autumn whispered, "Just think of her. Let us both think of her."

Time blurred. Autumn knew they had never been friends. She suspected they never would be. But they had love of Ursula in common, that and the desire to glory in a woman's passion.

"Think of her," Autumn whispered again to Killera. "Think of her, because she will understand."

Three

Taylor lost control of her breathing as the next wave of pain seared behind her eyelids. Kelly had seen into chaos itself, had never flinched from the roiling mass of energy that had coursed from the open gate. Ursula was rising into the chaos. Her terror had resonated through Kelly, who held on and would never let go.

Taylor made herself look. Her brain stretched to comprehend the incomprehensible, to bear the blazing beauty and profanity. How had Kelly stood it? She wanted to shrink from knowledge and emptiness, from music and cacophony, but she made herself look. Kelly had never flinched.

From the pulsation of color and fury she finally saw what Kelly had never mentioned afterward.

Hands.

They came from a gate of their own and reached for Ursula, who had seen only two choices: a stranger's hands or the ravening darkness. She could not stay. Her braid was undone, the circle that had protected her was shattered. Daybreak brought a moment of strength and she had persuaded Kelly to let her go.

Hands. Kelly believed they were Autumn's hands.

Her brain's panic for oxygen finally made Taylor pull back. Fool, she cursed herself. Even a beginner knows you have to keep breathing. Let it go, she told herself. Focus. You won't get this chance again.

Given the magnitude of Kelly's rage, it was possible Kelly would kill her when they next met. Taylor hadn't understood — and perhaps Kelly didn't either — the complex weaving of peace and power that drove Kelly.

Taylor rested for a few minutes, leaving Kelly sound asleep. She concentrated on slow, steady breathing and a deliberate effort not to think about what she had seen in Kelly's memories. Her fingertips began to tingle from the extra oxygen. She could almost summon a trance that would let her sort and learn so much easier. But the spell eluded her, like a sponge had passed over that part of her memory. So she recoiled from examining what Kelly had seen, having no protection from it.

Kelly hadn't needed any, which amazed her. She herself could not contemplate the chaos — she knew no one who could. Ursula had been terrified by it. It would consume Liz in a heartbeat. But untrained, uninitiated Kelly had borne it without one moment of hesitation.

Bitterness swelled through Taylor again. Training had not done her any good in the end. The circle, the gate, it was all meant to protect the open mind from the swirl of relentless energy that enfolded all living things. Most people were so closed up they never felt the unlimited power that could be theirs. Like all power, the chaos was neither good nor evil. She had once known how to bend the energies to her own needs, but that was gone.

The chaos was a force to be tapped. Properly focused, a trained adept could mine the chaos for information, for remnants of consciousness from those who had gone before. And yet Uda's power had come from it and her brutal essence seemed to always dwell there. The mere existence of the chaos had terrified Ursula — but how could Ursula not have known it was there all along? She wore the Norn braid, which meant she had met the triple goddess and been placed on a path.

Oh, it was all so confusing. Taylor rubbed tears from her face and tried to focus. She'd learned something new. Kelly believed that the hands that had lifted Ursula were Autumn's. Had Autumn somehow reclaimed Ursula for the past? Her own dreams had only a fleeting memory of the white-haired, confident Autumn and her defiant, warrior-like bearing. She had faced Uda without hesitation and twice should have left Uda dead.

What more could she learn? She regretted slipping the sedative into Kelly's tea. Given how depleted Kelly was it hadn't taken very much to put her completely out. But she needed to know what Kelly knew. How else could she begin her atonement?

The headache was fading and she slipped into Kelly's mind again, avoiding the most recent memories because they would have nothing about Ursula. Instead, she plumbed deeper.

She was surprised by an image of Liz, much younger, huddled under a tree with a book while her cousin and neighbors played some sort of game. A boy snatched the book from Liz's hands, jeering, " 'Fraidy cat,'fraidy cat!"

Liz never said a word, but only shrank against the tree behind her, even when Kelly — as bold as Liz was mild — had the boy's arm twisted behind him and forced out an apology along with the return of the book. Her poor, poor, baby, Taylor thought. No one had understood her. Kelly had been trying to help, but her own fierce, loving protection had been as painful to Liz as the bully's casual hate.

Another memory of Liz flitted nearby, but Taylor had only lost her powers, not her training. She would not be caught by the seductive nature of another person's memories. It was all too easy to want to see just one more. She was there for a reason, even though being there was unethical in the extreme. She should focus on keeping her crimes to a minimum, as someday there would be a reckoning. Crimes such as this were always paid for in potent coin.

Ursula, she directed, and the memories flooded up. Kelly had no training and so even the most intimate of those memories was at the surface to be read. Taylor's own private moments were sequestered where only a trained adept could find them. Even more tightly sealed was information that had come to her in her offices as a minister or during her training as an adept. Those memories she would never leave open to another. They would have to be taken by force, or death.

Not so with Kelly. Ursula was joking with an Amish farmer who came to buy tomatoes. He laughed and Ursula was running from a plane's Jetway to Kelly's arms. They cried and Ursula was walking across a field crusted with silver and lavender. Kelly took her hand and Ursula was making love to her. Kelly cried out in disbelieving ecstasy, looking up into Ursula's face. Ursula looked up — there. The moment they met. The shop was small and Kelly's memories were bathed in golden light. The three aunts were there, looking as they did in the memories of them held by the chaos.

Became, becoming, shall be. Every breath was all three: past, present, future. So. This was what she might have to face. Became, becoming, shall be. Completion, beginning, oblivion.

A shop selling herbs for medicine or cooking. Aldtyme. England. From there she jumped to Kelly's memory of planning the trip. On the northeast coast, south of the Scottish border.

She covered Kelly and left a note of apology, though she knew that Kelly would not be moved by it. She drove home, deep in thought the entire journey, and her mind for the first time moved past what had happened and looked instead toward what might come to be.

Liz was waiting for her, and sensed where she had been. But they didn't talk about it. Instead, Taylor pulled Liz to her with a lighter heart than had seemed possible even that morning. She kissed Liz and hid her plans in the recesses of her mind, wanting Liz without the shadow of knowing that her anger and despair were only being masked by desire.

Liz smiled — the first in nearly seven weeks, Taylor thought. For a smile she would do almost anything. Let there be smiles and love tonight. The future was coming.

Desire came with genuine depth, and she reveled in their passion. She loves me, Taylor thought. And when Liz finally slept, long into the night, Taylor cupped her face and said a silent good-bye, not knowing if Liz would forgive her.

* * * * *

:Come back.:

Autumn ignored the voice. Darkness was welcome. She was held, touched. Hands on her body echoed between lives. She wanted to stay with the strong hands that gave comfort in a past that rocked on the sea, but gentle hands offered hope in a sweltering present. A voice she longed ever after called to her.

:Come back.:

The voice won and Autumn felt herself rising from murky depths into a room of light and heat. No ocean swelled under her, just the hard, cracked linoleum of the tiny bathroom. The dizziness was the consequence of Ursula's touch — her hand still pressed to where the dagger scar had been. Autumn opened her eyes and looked into that dark, dark gaze.

:There you are.:

Ursula's thoughts so intimately in her mind brought a confusion of memories. Autumn had not let herself dwell in them before — to remember the sweetness of Ursula's touch while this Ursula looked at her blankly had been unbearable.

:I'm here.:

But this Ursula had lost her empty gaze. The touch of her mind was deliberate, provocative.

Autumn whispered, "I can't stop if you do that."

:I know.: Then, with what seemed to be a conscious setting aside of fear, *:It has taken all these weeks for me to find my courage. Show me.:*

Autumn had longed to show Ursula what she had dreamed of, the vivid past, the love they had discovered, the beauty of their journey. It was the next best thing to Ursula remembering these events for herself. Instead, they had only their darkest moment — death, rage, despair, suicide — in common. But to show her was to touch her and not want her, and that was impossible. She shivered and memory surged like the ocean through a shattered hull. She heard Ursula gasp, but there was no stopping it now.

:This is the way you felt to me. This is the way you touched me. This is the way you kissed me. This is the taste of your mouth, your skin, your hair.: She could not stop, and she could not yet go to other memories that were less intense. She endured these memories and knew she had endured them lifetime after lifetime. For better or worse, they had to start here.

Her mind turned to her pasts, the snatched visions of earlier selves that had faced madness and ruin in mindless searching for a hint of Ursula's presence. Ursula cried out at Autumn's visions of death by fire, by her own deliberate hand, by explosions of energy that had torn spirit from mind, then flesh from bone.

:I can't stop.: Ursula's presence was a balm for all that pain, but she could not let go of it because pain had formed her purpose. They were not safe yet, and there was nothing she would not suffer — had not already suffered — to put Ursula beyond Uda's reach.

Uda. The thought brought the dagger slicing through air into Killera's chest on the dusty steps of the abbey, then into her own chest as she lay manacled to the bed where she had welcomed and enjoyed Uda's touch.

:Not your fault.:

The assurance was far away and Autumn could only answer with, *:But mine to pay for.:*

She tried to spare Ursula the agony of the dagger, but Ursula's arms gave way and she collapsed onto the floor next to her. They soared above the suffering and Autumn was at last able to turn her memories to more useful events. Ursula's shivering stilled when she saw the face that had sent Autumn spinning back to life.

Beauty nearly beyond bearing had met Autumn as she died. *:Beloved.:*

From death, life.

:That's not me. It can't be me.: Ursula shrank from the knowledge.

:It's you, my love. You saved my life that night. There's more.:

She plunged back toward her body, passing over a barrage of images she now began to realize were happening at the same time she was dying. There was a circle of gray-robed figures, a concert with a magenta-haired guitarist, then, too vivid to bear, to painful to watch, Ursula with another woman.

:Killera.: Autumn gave her the only name she knew, recognizing the strong back and hands now. A hidden door of

memory opened then, and she recalled those hands on her body as well, in another time, during a long-ago search that she had only just dreamed of.

Ursula was desperate with desire, crying out for Killera's lovemaking as they tangled feverishly in the back seat of a car. Ursula looked up, saw Autumn, reached for her, strained toward touching even as Killera gave her what she begged for.

Beside her, Ursula was crying. *:I wanted to forget. I hurt her and I wanted to forget.:*

Autumn had slammed back into her body then and it took all the control she had left to push away the shattering agony of being lifted from her blood-soaked bed.

She had learned since then how to put the pain away and that practice helped as she shifted Ursula's awareness to another sequence of memory. She felt more in control now that the worst was behind her. There was more for Ursula to know, and much that could help them.

She found the strength to move and was able to coax Ursula to her feet as well. She settled Ursula onto the bed and got the forgotten orange from the bag.

"Her name isn't Killera, not now." Ursula shivered in spite of the growing heat of the day. "That was me, though, but I don't remember when or where or her name."

"When is the Fourth of July," Autumn said quietly. Killera and Ursula had been in a late-model SUV. This lifetime was the only possibility. "Before then I didn't know what you were to me. I had forgotten *everything.*"

Ursula seemed to calm herself, though the quaver in her voice spoke of how difficult it was to maintain. "Who am I to you, then? I — I saw that we were intimate once."

The memory shuddered between them. Autumn had to take a deep breath before she could join Ursula on the bed in seeming control.

She held the orange in her hands. "Are you ready for more?" *:This will not be as hard.:*

Assent was tentative, but given. *:I must know.:*

She broke open the orange and inhaled the impossible sweet scent. The aroma drove her memory to the moment she had first been awed by Ursula's powers.

She gave Ursula her perception of that long-ago leave-taking, when Ursula had left her people of Northumbria with a blessing to protect their futures in harsh times. Hilea's voice shimmered in the air. In Latin tinged with more archaic forms, the words joined with a power that came from Ursula alone.

"When will we see you and be with you, in a garden of fruit, among the splendor of flowers? We feed among the lilies in a garden of fruit. We join with Ursula."

In the crowd Ursula's three aunts had joined the women aboard ship in opening oranges, an impossible delicacy in this place and time of year.

The juice of the orange ran over Autumn's hands. She fed Ursula a slice of natural beauty she had grown in the harsh desert climate. *:You are this to me, and more.:*

She let a slice explode in her own mouth, as potently magical now as it had been to the young woman she had been then. At seventeen she had known only the sea, the moving deck of the *Verdant Bough*, and the love of her two fathers. The day before they sailed in the harbor where Ursula would come aboard, Tain had died in a stupid fall from the sail netting. Edrigo, her other father, had shied away from Ursula's magic, preferring the reliable unpredictability of the sea to govern his actions. But Autumn had been forever found by Ursula's love and not known it.

She gave Ursula all the dreams she had, of weeks of unending sky and wind, ever blowing the *Verdant Bough* toward a wedding Ursula did not want. They evaded dangerous pursuit by pirates who wanted only treasure, and Uda of Jutland who wanted much, much more.

Her memories ended where she had begun, in each other's arms, satisfying their bodies, then exploring their minds. They sailed with grace and ease through the tunnel of light Ursula opened for them so the stars could witness the love they had found.

:You carried us.:

:It's not me. It can't be me.:

Her lips still damp with juice from the orange, Autumn kissed the corner of Ursula's mouth. Ursula was vulnerable and frightened. She had to be completely overwhelmed with memories that had taken Autumn months to sort through and bear. But this was the only comfort Autumn had to give, the fact of her unwavering love.

:I cannot comprehend the time that has passed, nor the suffering and the emptiness. Part of me does not believe it is real, but there is this as reality.: She took Ursula's hand in her own, and once again pressed her lips to the corner of Ursula's mouth. *:You are here. I love you. I loved you before I knew you existed. I will never take anything of you that you do not freely offer.:*

Ursula opened her eyes and Autumn let herself fall without restraint into the black depths. These past weeks of holding back, of hiding how she felt, of trying to let it not matter that Ursula did not remember — they were over. Ursula knew the truth now and Autumn would not pretend otherwise. She could only trust that Ursula would remember for herself, some day, and what they had shared could be theirs again. Regardless, her soul's duty was to protect Ursula from the darkness that wanted her.

It surprised her, then, when Ursula's mouth opened to hers. They were still for a long moment. Autumn thought she could end all her lives here, in this instant of happiness. For Ursula kissed her not in gratitude, not in desperation, not in a desire to comfort or be comforted. Autumn felt a momentary certainty ripple through Ursula. *:Yes, this is true. Yes, I have loved her.:*

Passion flared — how could it not? Her skin tingled with longing, but instead of feeling oppressed by it, she felt instead a delight. The scent of orange was all around her and with it was the lingering call of Hilea's song. *We feed among the lilies in a garden of fruit. We join with Ursula.*

"What is that from?" Ursula murmured against Autumn's mouth and did not seem to want to move away.

"Hilea's prayer."

"I feel . . ."

Autumn let Ursula draw a deep breath while she sought the soft hollow of Ursula's throat with her lips.

"I know this," Ursula whispered. "I remember this magic."

"You just don't remember me." Amazingly, Autumn found she could smile. She raised her head and gazed into the black eyes that were her world. "I don't mind. Not right now."

An unexpected grin lit Ursula's face. "Neither do I. Not right now."

They reached for each other at the same moment and Autumn would not let it mean more than it did. It was light, and honest, and cleaner than anything that had graced this life so far. There was nothing uncertain in Ursula's gentle touch. Autumn held back a moan and instead let Ursula's sighs come to her. So sweet, with longing creeping in.

She quivered with happiness and got lost in their kiss. Ursula's hands found her still bare breasts and raised a riot of goosebumps all along Autumn's chest. They laughed together because it was a celebration of sensation and what their bodies seemed to be made for.

Autumn saw that strands of Ursula's hair were drifting as if a light breeze swept over her, and she basked in the faint reddish glow that seemed to come from Ursula's hands. The next kiss was more intense. She held her breath to better focus on new shivers in her nerves. It had been such a long, long sleep for them. At Ursula's touch her splintered selves awoke to their fullest at last: lover, warrior, magician, beloved. They could become one woman, who was finally loved.

She held her breath so she could hear Ursula's low moan.

She held her breath until fresh air would feel as wonderful as the kiss — and found she could not breathe in.

Realization hit her just before it did Ursula. She choked, fought for consciousness. Their laughter had long faded, yet a hint lingered, changing. The morning desert light was gone and a sharp shadow lingered over them.

They were found.

Useless, Autumn thought — useless to think now of Ursula's gate, which a moment of carefree happiness had left unguarded. Idiot, for getting lost in her when you knew you were not safe.

Ursula was wracked with a silent scream as Autumn felt something steal over her, trying like a thief to pick the locks on Autumn's own gate. It wouldn't work, she told herself. She had been a warrior and would be now. There were many ways to fight.

She could not let fear of loss — her life, Ursula's love — stop her. She had died before. She had one weapon left, her will. She gathered up all she knew, the meager memories of what she had once been and all the hope of a future free of this endless battle. Dark rags of unconsciousness danced around her eyes and she let go of the light. If she failed she would not need it anyway.

:Do you think you can fight me, delicious one?:

The low voice, sounding almost in her ear, was supposed to frighten her, as was the image of the dagger descending toward her helpless body.

It was her dagger. She knew that now. Her ankle itched with the memory of it in her boot, and her fingers tingled with the desire to throw it, to see it once again buried into the black heart she had struck at before.

No — a distraction. The dagger was not her weapon here. The weapon was her will.

She turned to what she knew best. The Queen of Hearts painted herself behind Autumn's eyelids. She was love.

:She is weakness.:
Another card, the Queen of Clubs, life from earth.
:She is barren. Love cannot save her now.:
Queen of Diamonds. Clarity, victory.
:She is breakable.:
Queen of Spades, the unquenchable spirit.
:She left us, left the only real power. She is nothing now.:
Indeed, nothing. Autumn sensed a long way away that life was draining out of both of them. They were trapped in a vacuum of blue-green light, but she continued to turn over cards, all of them queens, all of them a face of herself, a face of Ursula. Even, she thought with a flash of rare wisdom, the faces of Uda as well.

:If Ursula is nothing, then why do you want her so? Does she have what you lack?: And still she turned over cards, face by face, building a wall, giving every card size and heft, thickness and weight. Ursula's gate was open, but Autumn could build a wall in its place.

:She is dying.:
Queens of hearts, diamonds, clubs, spades. Memory came when she needed it, and she could see these cards in earlier guises. She had known them when they had first made their way across Europe as prayer cards. From prayer cards to mystical tarot, from mother to queen, from cups to hearts.

As far as Autumn was concerned, reaching down into a place where she had no fear, a woman was a woman. She could even pity Uda for having lost some essential piece of this truth.

Queen, queen, queen, queen. Red, black, red, black, like the choices on a roulette table. She kept turning cards, filling the void with brick after brick of her will.

:Tissues I can sweep away. She is dying. Help her!:
And still Autumn turned cards until there was nothing but queens, red and black, with ocean-green eyes like her own. Red, black, green, the tick of the wheel. Fate danced across the cards until they spun with the wheel. The wheel grew and

Autumn could faintly discern the wind of its turning. She held it over her head and let it spread, wheel becoming dome.

:We gather, in a splendor of colors, in a garden of queens, to Ursula.:

A bright, single note that could have been from Hilea's lute seemed to sound within the dome. Autumn was neither a priestess, like Ursula, nor an initiate like Hilea, Killera and Elspeth had been. She was a magician, a warrior and a woman aching with love. She anchored the dome so that Ursula was centered below its apex, in the place where the dome's protection was strongest.

She looked up to see the dagger again, this time wielded by a hand that seemed all too real. For the first time in this life she wished for the swift accuracy of a bow.

A wave of rage, of intent and chaos came ahead of the dagger. Autumn covered Ursula with her body, her lungs aching, her mind ringing with the need for air.

She felt, rather than saw, the dagger implode on her dome of cards.

The dagger shattered as if it were glass. Autumn had only time enough to think, "A shame, it was a fine blade," before air flooded her nose and mouth and, so wonderfully, her lungs.

They were quiet for a long while and Autumn marveled at the circle she had built. It was like the one she had seen the long-ago Ursula raise to combine the energies of her companions into a usable force to mislead their pursuers and gather information. Like it, but uniquely Autumn's. She, of course, had no idea how to punch a hole in the dome and create a tunnel where their spirits could travel. Ursula had mastered the tunnel of light with ease.

"I think I shall paint my gate with cards," Ursula murmured some time later. "They are powerful things."

"It seems to work for me." Autumn was exhausted, but a tired urgency had taken root. "I can't keep this in place for much longer. We have to leave Las Vegas."

66

"But you drove her away," Ursula said. "I don't even know how you did it."

"Her, yes, but she has her agents and at least one of them knows where we are." She remembered Staghorn's fury and knew he would not be long in finding her.

Ursula said firmly, "My gate is locked again. Save your strength."

Autumn let go of her circle of cards and put away the image. She would have need of it again.

There was a discreet tapping at the door and she tensed until she realized who it was. She pulled a fresh T-shirt over her head before letting Ed in.

"Are you okay? Scylla's been whining at me to come up. And after last time, well, I thought I'd check."

Autumn scratched Scylla's ears. "Good dog. We're fine, really, but we have to leave."

Ed seemed to understand that she didn't mean for a little while. "Where can I take you?"

"I don't think you can go with us," Autumn said, though she would be grateful for his protection. She could not visit more of Uda's evil on him, and the all-too-real Staghorn had seen her with Ed. "You can safely say you don't know where we are. And we might be back tomorrow."

His eyes flicked to where Ursula was rising from the bed. "Neither of you can even drive a car. She might know how but she's got no identification. Getting on a plane without I.D. is hard these days."

Such a practical man, Autumn thought. He was right. It was a problem. "There are other ways to travel. We'll be okay. I'll let you know how we manage."

She had made that promise long ago, to Edrigo who had set them ashore in Germany, at the mouth of the Rhine. She would let him know where they were, she had promised. She had never had the chance, not in that life. In this one, she thought, I will remember.

"There's something else," he said finally. "Take a look at the garden."

Ursula crowded behind her as she stepped onto the wooden landing outside the door.

The orange tree, the flowering plants, the shrubs — they had all sprouted new leaves and colors. Where they had been neatly pruned only an hour ago they were ragged with what would have been verdant new growth. But where the leaves and blossoms were new they were also seared brown. Ursula's moment of happiness and passion had touched them. Then Uda had touched them as well.

She heard Ursula make a sound of loss and tried to comfort her. "They're not dead. Plants can grow again." From another time came a memory of Hilea's verse. "Winter's breath can never hurt them."

"Indeed," Ed said. He was averting his eyes as Captain Edrigo had, not wanting to intrude on mysteries not meant for his understanding. The sea had told too many tales of lost sailors who had not shown sufficient respect for women's magic.

"She did this?" Ursula was past Ed, most of the way down the steps. "But a garden helps everyone." She was utterly puzzled.

"She did it because it was something you loved. I think that's why she —" She stopped in time, not wanting to say more in front of Ed. "That's why she's done everything." Including me, she wanted to add. I was just a way to hurt you because someday the fact that she was in bed with me is going to hurt both of us.

But she couldn't say more, not when Ursula's distress was turning to anger. She had enough anger for both of them. "Let's get ready to go, Ursula. We need to get away from here."

"You pack," Ursula said shortly. She picked up the clippers she had kept in a small wooden box Ed had given her for that purpose.

Autumn heard the steady *snick-snick* of the clippers while she put together the few things they would need. A change of clothes, though they could buy more. The cash she'd received only that morning — already seeming like a lifetime ago — would get them away. She could make more in any casino, and quickly if she did not care about being noticed for winning. A couple of boxes of crackers and other snacks joined several pouches of dog food. Bottles of water. She assembled it all on the table and realized she had nothing to put it in. She had never left Las Vegas.

There was another knock at the door and she found Ed holding a large, sturdy leather knapsack the color of midnight.

"I thought you might need this," he said.

"It's beautiful, Ed, I can't take it."

"It was never mine to keep," he said. "In 'Nam there was a guy I liked — he was about the only thing that kept us all sane. Could dice anyone out of their pay and had me laughing when I could have died any minute. He gave it to me the night before he bought it in the same sortie that gave me this." He patted his bad leg. "He said I'd know when to give it away."

A premonition sent hard chills across Autumn's shoulders. "What's in it?"

"I never wanted to look. I didn't think I should."

Her fingertips itched. There was something she had had at the abbey and in some later memories that she did not have now. She didn't know exactly when she had lost it. Something Uda had known nothing of and Autumn had only just begun to understand might have meaning to her.

She took the knapsack and undid the catch on the front pouch.

"Are you okay?" Ed asked from far away.

"Yes," she whispered. Summoning a sense of great respect, she withdrew the small panel of yew wood from the depths that had hidden it for so many years. It was the lid of the small box the long-ago Autumn had taken away from the *Verdant Bough* when she'd left with Ursula. The box had been

Tain's, and it had contained the dice and coins he'd used to pass the endless hours of sailing.

There was no sign of the rest of the box, nor of the dice. The symbols on the lid in her hand were the same as she had painted, in a fever of preparation, on the door of the *Spirallig Tor*, the magical box she had made to bring Ursula to her safely from wherever it was that she suffered.

She had flashes of herself taking the box from her sleeve to practice with the dice and coins. Years and years of practice — she had had nothing but time.

"What was his name?"

"Jack Fontaine."

The Jack of Hearts. "You called him Tain, didn't you?"

Ed nodded. Gruffly, he said, "He was special."

"I understand," Autumn said. She did. She had believed, because Edrigo said it was so, that Moorish Edrigo had fathered her on a liaison with a Nordic woman. Her mother had given her winter-white hair and the green eyes of the northern sea. But the night she had left he had told her the truth. Tain's blood was in her veins. Edrigo had taken her and Tain under his protection out of love for Tain, but had never been less than a true father to her.

No matter what had happened to the box, this small piece was a miracle to have. She could feel it tingling with an energy she did not understand, energy that explained how it had survived a millennia and a half. It was, perhaps, something in which she could have a small measure of faith.

Their belongings fit in the knapsack and she slung it over one shoulder. "Thank you," she said belatedly. "I wish I could leave Scylla, because she loves you far more than she does me." An itching between her shoulder blades told her that leaving Scylla behind was not a good idea.

"Dogs can be replaced," he said, still gruff. They both knew he was lying, but she left it alone.

Ursula had clipped all of the dried and dead foliage away from all the plants that still lived. "I think the tree will survive," she said. "The rosemary will, but the hydrangeas are lost. Give the garden all the water you can spare and the strongest will survive." She sighed and gave Autumn a long, steady look. "I'm ready."

They walked side-by-side away from the only home Autumn had known. Scylla loped behind them, having given Ed a long, sorrowful look before trotting in their wake. When they reached the corner Autumn looked back at the dark, unmoving figure and knew she was losing something she would never find again. And for the first time she had a prescient tickle of fear: this was her last chance, her last battle. The next time she died it would be forever.

Part Two:
Feather's Breath

We meant Us.
All of Us, who died and did not,
For Ursula.
— Hildegard of Bingen, "Private Scivia"

Four

She was unaccustomed to hangovers. Taylor's tea had left Kelly with a headache so bad she wished she'd indulged in a vat of vodka. If she was going to suffer why not have had the fun beforehand?

That bitch. Even now it was hard to believe that Taylor had drugged her. All that goddess nonsense, all sweetness and purity. Serve the light, look toward the light so you won't see us stab you in the back. Nothing excused what Taylor had done to her. Her stomach churned at the idea of Taylor in her head, looking through her memories of Ursula. What could Taylor have hoped to learn?

Whatever it was, Kelly would pay her back. It was too much to bear, being treated like chaff, just something to be sifted through and cast aside. She took a shower and let the moist air ease the ache in her sinuses. She'd slept the day away, and now it was raining steadily.

She wiped away unbidden tears and wished she could do something. Anything. Another day gone, and a painful one at that. Where could a future be in this mess? Did she even have one?

This isn't you, she answered herself. You've never given up. She'd force herself to sleep tonight so that tomorrow could be faced. There were no other choices.

Her head scarcely on her pillow again, sleep seized her with a suddenness that left her heart pounding. She woke again in a panic. She wasn't alone. She covered herself. How could she be naked? She was never nude, never revealed. Who in Satan's hell was in her bed?

She pulled the bed curtains to one side and the faintest gray glimmer of a rain-soaked daybreak spread light across her companion. Then she felt the undulation of the bed, a rhythmic rocking from side to side that was abruptly familiar to her. Her panic eased; she was in a place she knew well. The difference was that she was not alone.

She remembered now, this mysterious boy-woman. The sense of disbelief that she had allowed this woman, of all in God's creation, into her bed, faded. White hair, chopped into a bowl shape like any peasant's, framed an angular face. Corners were softened in sleep. Was that a smile of satisfaction at the edges of her firm mouth?

She recalled then, the lovemaking of the night before. This slender, muscle-hardened woman had been soft where it was best, and like liquid gold to her mouth. She had been hungry and open, and had only whispered once, "More gently, my lord." Even so, she too had applied her strength where Killera had so badly wanted it. She had never known such abandon or energy in a woman, so much that it almost equaled her own.

She drew the curtains against the chill and settled back

into the warm bed. She'd carried on the masquerade for so long that she had forgotten what it felt like to hold a woman, forgotten what it felt like to be a woman.

She let her body take in the warmth. She had never been skin-to-skin with anyone and that ought to have frightened her. She had never let anyone this close. She caressed the hip nearest her, found a small, soft breast.

The light of day began to filter through the heavy curtains and the woman rolled over with a sigh. "Good morning, my lord."

A kiss of desire was her answer, and she was welcomed again into the stranger's arms. After she had nuzzled into the soft, tender throat she asked, "And what shall I call you?"

"Autumn, my lord."

"Hardly the name of a cabin boy," Killera answered. "If you're interested in a change of duties."

"These duties are most pleasant," Autumn murmured. "I am from Braden, if that is any help."

Killera didn't fight the unaccustomed smile that made her lips curve. She looked more like a woman when she smiled, so she had learned not to. "You hardly look German to me."

"I did not grow up there." Killera sensed this was truth, but she had a flicker of uneasiness, as if Autumn's answer hid a larger lie. That kind of lying was a skill Killera knew all too much about.

"Braden? Bradford? Branley? What shall it be?"

"Make it Bradley and be done," Autumn whispered. "But not here. I am Autumn here." She hissed as Killera slipped fingers between her legs. "Autumn there, too."

Killera responded to the bawdy smile with another kiss. She slid down the long, lean body to taste again what had delighted her so last night. Autumn pulled the bedclothes over them as she opened her legs. "I must keep you warm, my lord," she said with a sigh.

How could she be this happy? Since infancy her mother had been preparing her for this grand lie wrapped in smaller, provable truths. A girl could not hold the family lands, not under their new Norman kings, and her father's only son, her half-brother, was illegitimate. It was a desperate gamble to raise Killera as a boy, but her mother had impressed upon her, every day, every night, how important it was that the next Lord Aldtyme be ready to take his father's lands. Her father had died before she was born, in a Scottish border war. Her mother could only survive as regent of those lands if she had a son to eventually take her place. That left her to be Killera in the privacy of her mother's arms, and Kyler, Lord Aldtyme, to the world. She was Lord Aldtyme to reclusive Elspeth, her cousin, who knew the truth as well but would never speak of it to anyone. Keeping these lands in their family was her sacred duty to her people and her family line.

If she ever wavered in what she knew to be her duty, if she ever thought she was not strong enough for this burden, she received succor in her dreams, when her private saint blessed her.

Her half-brother was the only other person who knew the truth. He kept the secret willingly. His sons, born of a legitimate marriage, were already named as heirs to the childless "Kyler." It behooved them both that Killera saw to their growing merchant fortunes — frequently away from the estates — while he oversaw the actual maintenance and care of their lands. Some day she would simply not return from a voyage and arrive, unnamed, with gifts at a convent. She had accepted that she would spend her final years that way. Any community of women would be better than none.

That had been her plan of life. The next forty years were known. Nothing had foreseen this utter happiness, finding not only a woman who was also pretending to be male and used its undoubted freedoms with some regrets, but also one who sought the pleasures of women. She had managed two brief affairs in her life, never questioning that her bedmates must be women. Not only would a pious lord seek only women for his bed, women were what pleased her there. That the church said differently was irrelevant to the life she led for the sake of her people and lands. The saint of her dreams blessed her and gave her strength and that was all she needed.

Her previous lovers believed that a childhood sickness had left her impotent. That rumor had spread, leaving the lack of heirs of her own body unquestioned. Any mannerisms she might still possess which were not strictly masculine were also explained by this unfortunate condition. She would take pity over discovery. The lands were safe. She made the lack of a hardy male staff up to them in pleasurable ways, as fiercely and lustily as any man, and both had been well satisfied. She had ended the affairs when she feared discovery, yet both women had made it clear they would gladly come back to her bed. But it had been years since she had risked it.

And now she did so with utter abandon, letting Autumn know her secret and eager to feel Autumn's mouth on her again. How could her caution, her lifetime of secrecy, be so easily overcome? Who was Autumn that she could sweep aside years of hiding?

Autumn tasted like fire and wine and Killera soothed the shaking of Autumn's legs with the deep caress of her fingers and tongue. *A woman*, her heart sang. So sweet, so wonderfully needful. *A woman*.

"My lord? Are you ill — Oh! Forgive me, my lord, I had no idea!"

Autumn had frozen, then whatever part of her was exposed she quickly covered with blankets.

Embarrassed and badly frightened — for she might have been the one exposed — Killera snapped in her lowest voice, "Get out, Sardon! I'll summon you when I need you."

"Of — of course, my lord, of course!" The cabin door slammed.

"Damnation," Autumn said. "He saw too much of me. Wait until the captain finds out there's a woman aboard."

Killera emerged from the covers, trying to hide that she was shaking. "It would be worse if they thought I was ravaging a boy. We must think quickly, and be very careful."

Autumn nodded. "Yes, my lord. I have no desire to die before my time."

"You came aboard because we had briefly met in Yarmouth."

"Am I a tavern maid, a charwoman?"

Killera did not believe Autumn could pass for either. "No, a girl of good family from Wales. Your father died on the journey, your Norman relatives repudiated your ties — hardly unusual, that. You had no means to get home and were frightened for your virtue in such a vulnerable predicament."

Impossibly, Autumn smiled. "Any lord who honored St. Ursula seemed a safe haven to me. I did not know I would find you so attractive, is that it?"

She grimaced. "Something like that." She found she had to swallow hard. She almost told Autumn why she had decided to honor St. Ursula's feast. Autumn would not believe her. To have a saint bless one's dreams was not a bragging point. Such pride always came to a profound fall. "I can protect you if you are willing to play this game."

Her gaze direct and level, Autumn asked, "And if I am not?"

Killera let herself fall more heavily on Autumn. Could she be this ruthless? For her lands, for her servants, for all those who depended on her to protect them from the acquisitive Norman lords, yes, she had to be ruthless. Her gentle words were at odds with the hands she wrapped around Autumn's throat. "We could be happy together."

The prick of a knife blade at her side made her pull her hands back sharply.

Autumn, still seeming perfectly calm, said, "I told you I would not die at your hands. I will keep your secret — I have no reason not to. I will keep it and you will help me with my quest." Strangely, she added, "Perhaps you will remember that this is your quest as well."

Killera would have asked what she meant, but her mind turned to more immediate concerns. "I was bringing some new cloth to my cousin, and I bought her a simple gown as well. You should have it for now." She left the warm bed to go to the trunk of gifts for the gown. It was the gentle color of dried sage. It would not look so well with Autumn's white hair, but it was all she had. There was also a square of deep blue silk she'd been given as a sample of a new dye. That would serve to cover her head.

Autumn had risen as well. From her own twisted bundle of belongings she produced a cross hanging from a simple gold chain. It was a woman's ornament. Once Autumn hung it around her neck it dangled between her bare breasts. The emotions aroused in Killera were most certainly sacrilegious.

Her mind seemed to ring with desire. She swept Autumn into her arms, feverishly seeking the heat of her kisses. "You should not wear such a thing," she whispered. "For you are most certainly the devil's temptation."

"It reminds me of a gift I once had." Autumn kissed her back and several minutes were lost in delirious need.

"My lord," Autumn finally murmured, gently pushing her away. "We must think clearly. Let us get dressed."

What was she thinking? Anyone could open the door, in spite of her instructions, and heaven knew the doors on a ship sometimes opened of their own accord. Killera dizzily reached for her own clothing, suddenly hating the binding undershirt. The rest she had never minded — men dressed more comfortably than women — but after a night of her breasts being caressed it hurt to deny they were there.

Once girdled, Autumn was presentable in the gown, and the headrail fashioned from the square of silk helped to hide the boy's haircut. Finding her habitual remote scowl, Killera escorted Lady Bradley to breakfast and explained the circumstances of her masquerade. The captain and mate said they sympathized with the lady's predicament and even understood her attire of the previous day. Their eyes said they certainly understood their lord's sudden enamorment. Yes, Autumn was bewitching in even the simplest of gowns. In a more fashionable bliaut, gathered tight over her breasts and hips, she would be irresistible. Killera had never cared about such fripperies, for women had always been more to her than flowers to grace her eyes, but now she saw their appeal.

They sailed north toward home, and each day Killera grew more eager for the night. She loved the coastline of her homeland, but this journey she never looked at it. She began to believe the tale they had concocted. She even imagined that Autumn would always be the queen of her bedroom, the lady of her deck. Home approached and she thought only of Autumn in her arms. This was the future that Autumn's eyes, her hands, her body, seemed to promise.

They talked of the sea, of music, of the past and the church. Autumn was as learned as anyone Killera had ever met, and, when she was in the mood to amuse, could spin fascinating tales of crusades and courageous voyages.

They arrived in Aldtyme's small harbor with a seeming suddenness. She had not noticed the change in ship routine, not with Autumn telling her a ribald story of a sultan's seraglio as they sat apart from the crew in the cool breeze of the aft castle. One moment her mind was on the next time she would be alone with Autumn and the next the mate was barking out orders for a starboard approach to the quay.

When she scrambled to her feet she saw that her home port was graced with another of her ships. Autumn, who seemed to know so much about the sea, was exclaiming over its size and lines. Killera could tell that an entourage from the estate waited at the end of the pier. There was nothing alarming in that. Merchants were clustered as well, eager to hear what had been brought for them to buy. None of it meant anything anymore. She wanted to unload and go back to sea. Her half-brother could have it all now, this very day. She had finally found a happiness of her own.

"It's a fine vessel," Autumn was saying. "Not that the *Greenest Branch* is less grand." She pointed at the forecastle. "But that's one of the largest I've seen. Does anyone dare to molest her?"

"Never," Killera admitted. "Not with thirty skilled crew who have string and cross bows ready at hand. She's been to Rome and Tripoli and never been touched."

"She sails fast, then?" Autumn seemed speculative. "What's her name?"

"The *Verdant Bough*."

"Yes," Autumn said. She added, in her odd way, "*Greenest Branch, Verdant Bough*. It would have to be, wouldn't it?"

"Why do I think you know everything there is to know about me before I tell you? You knew my cousin's name was Elspeth, after all."

"I am a lucky guesser, my lord," Autumn said. She tucked her hand under Killera's arm.

She was lying, but before Killera could ask more pointed questions, a commotion on *Verdant Bough*'s deck drew her attention. The captain's dog seemed to want to jump ship for the pier. She saw the flash of the captain's dark skin as he grappled with it. Restrained, the beast began to howl like a wolf at the moon.

Autumn visibly trembled. "Gods," she murmured. There were tears in her eyes. Drawing a deep breath, she called out sharply, "Scylla!"

The dog's wail ceased, leaving an eerie silence.

Killera had a disconcerting sensation of coming out into light. Who was this woman? How did she know the dog's name? Elspeth's name? Her mind gathered up the little puzzles that would lead to the truth. Autumn had spoken of a quest, and that first night together had urged Killera to think of "her" — but that woman was never named. *Why have I not worried over this?* It made no sense. Where had her lifetime of caution gone?

Her grip tightened on Autumn's hand and Autumn winced. "Who are you?"

The eyes that turned to hers were shimmering with emotion. "I am who I have always been, my lord."

More truth hiding lies. "Speak plain."

"Perhaps we can discuss this later, my lord." Later, her eyes promised, there would be a prolonged time of no talking at all.

The desire was her undoing. She would know that soon. But then, with the sharp heat of Autumn's passion in her mind all other thoughts were of little consequence.

Once they were landed she was able to focus on the matters of homecoming. She greeted the steward and other managers and gave them a brief summation of the voyage and their cargo. The merchants listened with interest and began making notes of what they would bid for cinnamon, cotton, pepper and dye.

The sight of several servants in her livery puzzled her. Puzzlement became astonishment as she realized who was in their care.

Elspeth had not ventured out of Aldtyme Castle for years. Even then, her path was from her apartments to the gardens and back again. And yet she stood on the busy dockside, looking half-faint.

Killera became aware of Autumn standing behind her. She turned to discern Autumn's expression and watched — she ought to have felt disbelief, but did not — as Autumn carefully approached Elspeth.

"I know that this is hard for you."

"The alternative is unlivable," Elspeth answered.

They had never met, and yet they knew each other. Killera opened her mouth to ask the question, but Autumn was turning back. She saw the soft swell of Autumn's breasts and was lost again.

"Elspeth will be coming with us, my lord?"

"Yes." It was the only answer she felt free to give. To where — she had no idea.

"My lord, it is good to see you again!"

Killera turned from the women to greet her most able captain, Edrigo. But whatever she might have said was drowned in a joyous yelp from the dog.

Autumn was on her knees in the quayside dust, arms around the huge beast. Killera had never seen the dog anything but watchful and angry, but now it licked Autumn's face with abandon. Autumn was between laughter and tears. Elspeth looked on with what might have been a hint of a smile through gritted teeth.

Captain Edrigo had a strange expression on his face as he regarded the woman and dog. "My lord?"

"This is Lady Autumn Bradley," Killera explained. "She was abandoned in Yarmouth by her faithless Norman relatives."

Autumn disengaged herself from the gleeful dog and rose to take the captain's hand. "My lord tells me you are to take us to Germany."

Killera was stunned but her protest was lost in a memory of Autumn's hand on her skin, in her hair. "To Germany," she echoed.

"I need to go to Eibingen," Autumn went on. "My lord says that there is sufficient business to be conducted that the coffers won't be bankrupted by such generosity."

The captain only asked, "By barge on the Rhine?" When Killera nodded, he turned to give several sharp orders to nearby sailors. Killera recognized the abrupt scurrying that began to take place on the pier. They might even make the final edge of the receding tide.

Elspeth was moving toward *Verdant Bough's gangplank, waving off assistance of all kinds. The men gave way to her stillness, but near the top of the steep incline Elspeth faltered.*

"Go," Autumn said and Scylla bolted past them up the gangplank to press her heavy bulk to the back of Elspeth's knees. One more step and Elspeth was safely aboard without anyone but the dog needing to touch her. A mate waved her to a bench and she sat down, one arm around the dog.

There were so many words in Killera's mouth. They jumbled around each other. They wanted out, but one look at Autumn kept her silent. What was there to say when tonight, in their own world, Autumn would spread herself open and be all that Killera desired? She could feel Autumn's mouth on her breasts.

"My lord, I was detained. My apologies."

She turned again, feeling dizzy and overwhelmed by people and details that had been second skin to her. Her half-brother regarded her with his measured equanimity. "I'm glad you're here now, Randolph. I have a change of plans."

She beckoned to Autumn with one hand and with a flush of happiness introduced her to Randolph. Randolph, the only man alive to know her secret, looked back and forth between them with some confusion. "So Lady Bradley must get to Eibingen and I can take care of some early contracts for the next shipping year."

Randolph said in a low voice that only Autumn could overhear, "Will you be returning married, my lord?"

Killera trembled. To have such happiness had never been a possibility. "I don't know that yet." She looked down at Autumn, who had demurely lowered her gaze. Randolph would be shocked to know how passionate this suddenly fragile appearing woman really was. "If so, it would change nothing in the estate. Nothing."

"My family is gone," Autumn said. She looked frail and unworldly. Her voice very low she added, "And of course there could be no children."

Randolph gave Killera a surprised look and she nodded. Autumn was looking utterly demure and innocent. "Congratulations, my lord. This is most unexpected but my felicitations are yours."

"Thank you." She had a sudden impulse that both her business sense and the wonder of her joy pushed on her. "I would like to spend a few minutes with you and my scribe, right now."

"I'll get my things, my lord," Autumn murmured. "And join your lady cousin aboard *Verdant Bough*."

Killera could not let Autumn go without kissing her fingers. Then she barked a request for her scribe and the three of them adjourned to the nearest merchant's to borrow a table and parchment.

Be done with it, she thought. You are done with this half-life. Randolph can have it all.

"Are you sure you wish to do this, my lord?" The scribe was amazed.

"Yes," Killera insisted. "I know that God will not grant me a son and I see no reason why my brother need wait for what will eventually be his son's. I do not want the title, and frankly, will be glad to be free of administering it when my home is on the sea."

"This is most generous of you," Randolph stammered. "Even at twelve my son is young to be Lord Aldtyme, but you know I am an able regent."

"I know. Even at his tender years he will make a better lord than I." She allowed herself a rueful smile. She signed the bluntly phrased document with her sigil and name, then let the scribe salt the ink. "My lady has no home now, no family, and she loves the sea. We will be happy. It is more than I have ever dreamed possible, you know that."

She did not need to say more. Randolph understood. An impossible dream come to reality, Killera thought. She felt weak, only for a moment, as she considered a lifetime of having Autumn in her arms. Then a sense of strength rose in her like she had never known. There was nothing she could not do or face now that she was free to be who she was, at least in the privacy of her bed.

The scribe made a copy of her declaration and gave the original to Randolph.

Randolph held it like gold. "No doubt our lord king will charge me handsomely to acknowledge this, but it will be worth it."

"I hope so," Killera said. She embraced Randolph with a hearty thump on the back. She sensed she would not see him again, but what panic the thought might have brought was nothing next to the way she hungered to feel Autumn's soft flesh against her fingertips.

She saw to the last transfer of her own belongings, her books, her favorite maps and charts, and boarded the *Verdant Bough* without a backward glance. She was puzzled, for a moment, because it seemed as if this leave taking ought to have something to mark it. She smelled oranges and heard a voice, high and sweet. It was gone in the heat of Autumn's smile.

She slept that night in the satisfaction of Autumn's arms. It was like fire between them, and never enough. She craved Autumn morning, noon and night, but it was as if Autumn could not satisfy the very desire she provoked. She wanted . . . something. Her dreams became murky, empty. She longed for . . . someone. She was cold in spite of Autumn's heat. Empty, though Autumn ought to have made her replete.

She woke in a chill gray morning to the patter of rain. The bed — the world — was still and quiet.

Never, Kelly thought, never. I never held her, or wanted her, I never did her bidding. This dream was a lie, a sick perversion. Burning with lust for Autumn — impossible.

She faced the bitter day and pushed the disconcerting dream out of her mind. She could still pretend it had never happened. How fanciful, she could chide herself, to think she might have in one life passed for a man.

She trudged to the barn heedless of the rain, ready to spend the day in well-known, tedious sorting tasks. She could tell herself that that bitch Taylor had planted the dream in her head. Taylor had replaced Ursula with the lying witch Autumn — that would explain it. And none of it could change the miserable, empty present.

She could believe and not believe, love Ursula and hate Autumn, know to her core she had never been ruthless, not like Killera had become. She had never been like that in bed, not so lusty, so aggressive, so dominating. It was not her.

She could believe in peace and still plot vengeance. The best part of her had come alive when she had met Ursula. She had lost it when Ursula was taken from her. She felt half alive, and half dead, half insane and half dreaming.

It all became too much to be true, even the present. She slumped on the bench, too exhausted to move. She did not sleep, but she still dreamed that Rachel came to her again. She wiped Autumn from her mind with Rachel's body and she gave Rachel all that both of them wanted.

* * * * *

Taylor fought back the returning headache. Once they had gained cruising altitude she had felt much, much better for a while. She had experienced this euphoria whenever she flew and it helped her to bear the final loss of her rapport with Liz. Up here, above the clouds, it was very quiet. Her grief was equally muted. The shields she had developed early in life were not tested here.

The respite had ended after four hours of flight time. She ached with missing Liz, knowing Liz must be frantic. She could not summon a healing spell, nor one to make her sleep. But she still had her training and could use it.

She tuned the headphone to the channel featuring classical music and was drawn in by an Elgar sonata. A few minutes of the pleasing, balanced music, steady breathing and a constant visualization of soothing blue light around the spot where the headache pulsed helped enormously. Mind over matter, she thought. I'll just have to learn to do things the old-fashioned way.

She did not think about what would be waiting for her in England. She only knew she could not wait for knowledge to come to her, she had to seek it. If Kelly was right, and Ursula was with Autumn, that was good news. But that did not mean that Ursula was safe. That did not mean that the darkness had given up hunting. Taylor knew nothing of Autumn or her abilities, but it would take more than a warrior to protect Ursula.

She reminded herself that she was ill prepared for both this journey and any challenge she might encounter. She didn't even have a suitcase, just an old satchel with a change of clothes, passport, not nearly enough cash, and her worn Bible that had been a gift from a long-dead mentor. She would give much to spend ten minutes talking to Donata again, but she did not dare the chaos. Donata had known how to please both church and circle. Donata had never failed the way she had.

Her mind wanted to dwell there, in the years when she had attended seminary by day and taken tutelage with older, experienced women by night. All had given her a gift of wisdom and a piece of themselves to keep. It had been a successful, happy time, when nothing had seemed impossible. Such wonderful women — some had become lovers, many she had known at festival, when she attended. They had universally agreed she was strong and gifted.

Pride, she thought. You're paying the price of your pride.

Ought to, ought to, ought to have done. She ought to have sought some of them out before trying her working with Ursula. But her pride had told her she was as trained, as strong and as knowledgeable as anyone she could ask for help.

She was young to be centering for a circle of eleven, but everyone agreed she did it brilliantly. Who could truly be of help to her?

Pride, she thought, had led her astray. Eleven wasn't enough. If she had set aside her pride she would have asked the acerbic, competitive Alexis in Hershey to add her circle of twelve. Twenty-three balanced by her and Alexis might have been enough to stay intact, to bear the suffering Ursula had unleashed against the protection of the circle. But no, let's be honest, she told herself. You wanted to solve the mystery of Ursula yourself. You wanted to present what you had done alone as a testament to your prowess. You're as competitive as Alexis has ever been.

And Kelly paid. Liz paid. Ursula — of course, Ursula paid and paid wherever she was.

Now she had to make it right. Ursula had come from Aldtyme, a place that existed in the here and now. Kelly knew it in the here and now. Ursula had been raised by three women, in the here and now. Those women wore faces that belonged to ancient, elemental crones. They could be a doorway into a completely new area of knowledge, the one that had allowed Ursula to effortlessly bond with living things, that had trained Ursula to release her spirit into the physical world.

She needed a new doorway — the old ones were closed to her.

A new door, she mused. She dozed lightly, and let her mind take her to that lesson.

Only an eight-year old could ask in genuine curiosity, "Aunt Violet, why do you live with Uncle Jimmy when you love Gloria?"

Her aunt had turned ashen. Her mother had quickly closed the kitchen door, leaving the rest of the family in the sitting room.

"Taylor! That's not something for you to discuss with a grownup." She had seen the shocked gaze her mother had then turned on her sister. "Vi?"

Even then her mother had known Taylor spoke the truth. Taylor was only in trouble for — as usual — not knowing the best time to speak it.

Aunt Violet had covered her face with her hands. "I can't talk about it. Not yet."

"Vi? Gloria is engaged. To our brother, remember? And you're married!"

Aunt Violet had shook her head. "I know, I know, but something happened. We both tried so hard to not let it happen, but it did. Oh God, Lu, I haven't been able to tell anybody."

Her mother had hugged Aunt Violet then, and Taylor had sensed that a profound family shake-up was around the corner. Gloria was in love with Aunt Violet, Taylor knew that was true, too. She had just been puzzled at the way Aunt Violet and Gloria hadn't spoken to each other all day even though they were constantly thinking about each other. She had been intrigued, too, by the idea of helping the course of true love. Even at eight years old she had been certain of her right to meddle.

Her mother was saying, "She gets more like Aunt Peela every day."

"Have you thought about . . ." Aunt Violet stopped and looked pointedly at Taylor.

"Taylor, honey, could you check that all the places have glasses for water?"

She had slipped out of the kitchen as asked, knowing that

very soon she would be sent to Aunt Peela. Her mother had a way of making up her mind so loudly that Taylor could hear it. Taylor was never in doubt as to what her mother had decided about anything.

She'd never met Aunt Peela. Her father said she was the family loon. But Aunt Peela's birthday cards, all the way from Key West, had always tingled her ears on her birthday, as if a voice whispered, "I look forward to meeting you one day."

She accepted that she was different, in the same way Aunt Peela was different.

Aunt Peela had been the first teacher of her mind. A decade old for every one of Taylor's eight years, she had been less spry in body than in mind. The two weeks Taylor had spent with her were still the foundation of all she had learned since.

Doors were the first things Aunt Peela had spoken of when they were alone. The excitement of a plane trip, the wonder of the exotic plants and warm weather in February had all faded.

"Let me look into your eyes, child."

Taylor had waited, telling herself she was unafraid.

"Open the doors, child."

Once she had discovered she could make the world quiet, she had not ever let the noise of it back in, not completely.

"Your shields, child. They're fine and strong. But you don't need them right now."

A deep breath left her feeling calmer, but she had to admit now that she wasn't unafraid. She was scared, a little.

"That's all right, too. You should be frightened. You're controlling it nicely."

She swallowed hard and let go of the tightness she had thought of as barriers.

"Shields, dear. There, that's much better. The eyes are the

easiest doors." Aunt Peela had been silent for a minute. "An old soul, yes, to have shields so developed you would be an old soul."

She'd heard her mother call her that as well. "What does that mean?"

"That you've been around the spiritual block a few times more than most of us, child."

"My name is Taylor," she said with a flash of spirit.

"Of course it is. It is now, at least. Let's have something cool to drink, shall we?"

Aunt Peela's garden, tended by women Taylor learned were her aunt's friends and students, overflowed with tropical fruits. Taylor had her first homemade lemonade that day. She'd felt very grownup as she'd sipped from the tall, crystal glass. She forgot about being grownup as she sucked the lemonade off wedges of chilled papaya her aunt had slipped into their drinks.

Aunt Peela had joined her in papaya sucking after a moment. "Don't tell — but I think that's delicious, too."

"Do people like us have to care what other people think?" The question had been bothering her and no one at home could understand. She knew so much, so easily. She already knew that if she didn't know an answer on a test she only had to listen with her mind and someone else would think it.

"No, not at all," Aunt Peela answered promptly. "We can be as cheating, lying, selfish and despicable as anyone else."

Puzzled, Taylor chewed on the inside of her cheek. "Do we have to be?"

"Now that's a different question. I thought we were going to spend the next week developing your shields, but we can skip right ahead," Aunt Peela pronounced. "The intersection of morality, ethics and laws. The sooner the better. You know all this, child, you just need my help to remember."

"I don't understand."

"That's an excellent start. Admitting ignorance is the

fastest way to end it. You don't know, child, but your old soul does."

The light of the small kitchen shifted as the day waned. The light breeze moved the palm fronds outside the window. Orange-gold sunlight made the room alternately shadowed and bright.

Across the table, in the moments of shadow, Aunt Peela seemed much younger. "Your doors are open now, child. That's good. So are mine. Will you look into my eyes, Taylor?"

She looked. Aunt Peela had sharp blue eyes, just like hers.

"Look into my eyes, Taylor . . . look closely, Claire . . . look closely . . ."

Aunt Peela was taking off the net where long hair had been captured. The silver abundance was strangely braided. In Aunt Peela's eyes, Taylor saw that braid now black with youth. Aunt Peela's eyes, yes, but the face was a little different and not just younger. Priscilla St. Claire . . .

"Deeper, child, look deeper, for I am here."

:Aunt Peela?:

:More, child.:

Afraid but fascinated, she concentrated on the bright thread she could see dancing in Aunt Peela's eyes. Priscilla St. Claire, Priscilla McNaughton, Priscilla Lowell, Priscilla Standish . . . the names rolled back, the centuries rolled back. There were resting times, blackness in anticipation of light, then blazing rituals and ceremonies overwhelmed by music and joy.

:Look deeper into yourself, child. Slowly, gently.:

Even as she wondered how to begin she knew. Taylor St. Claire, Taylor Bennett, Claire Lowell, Claire . . . Taylor . . . the names wove in on themselves until they were only useful as bookmarks to her pasts. She was an old soul, constantly circling, searching, following the light and trying to find a single path in competing truths.

There were tears in Aunt Peela's eyes, but she didn't

speak of what she had seen of Taylor's past until their two weeks were at an end. They had spent a lot of time reading. Happy with Taylor's progress, Aunt Peela had carefully given her an awareness of the chaos. When she was trained, she would be able to combine ceremony, ritual and her own will to gather the light from the chaos and spread it to others. She was awed, but intrigued.

Taylor had at first been maddened by her aunt's knack for answering questions with questions or apparent non sequiturs that made sense only after she'd puzzled over them for two days. But she got used to it, learning not to ask questions until she'd considered what her aunt might answer. It saved a lot of time.

The last night they had together came too soon. Taylor liked her tan — everyone at home would still be pinched and pale from winter. She loved the fruit from the garden every day. But she had a child's life to go back to. She'd been a child many times and that particular journey was never wasted. Aunt Peela was weary, too, she knew that as well.

"And so you must make yourself a promise," her aunt was saying. "Promise yourself — for you are the only one who will care — that you will search out teachers."

"Why not you? I can come back." She slid in between the sheets Aunt Peela had turned back for her.

"I won't be here, child. The wheel is turning for me."

Taylor was struck with sadness, but that eased abruptly. Her aunt's body was wracked with more pain than respite. Death was never the end. "I understand now."

"I knew there was one last task laid to me, and this was it. Ritual will be like breathing to you, so you must look for others. They will not find you — nothing of value comes without being sought."

She snuggled sleepily into her pillow. "I have to be fully trained, don't I? I have gifts and I have to use them wisely."

Her aunt had smiled at that. "Which means no more silent help on spelling tests."

96

Taylor grinned back. "I know. That's cheating and it only makes me weaker."

"There's something else, child." Aunt Peela stroked her cheek as she pulled the light sheets to Taylor's chin. "I don't want you to be frightened. I only want you to be aware. Your soul has journeyed a difficult path and I can hear something calling to you. You'll hear it louder as you grow older. Listen for that call. You will know when it touches your mind. It will seem familiar, but do not trust it until you understand what it is saying." Their sharp blue eyes had been doors for each other until they parted the next day.

By the time Taylor was home again there had already been a call to tell them Aunt Peela had died. Her mother had expected her to be distraught. It wasn't the last time she had disconcerted everyone with calm maturity beyond her years.

Aunt Peela *had* been the first to warn her about the call she would hear. Donata, too, had said she would eventually hear it. She had always felt that call would be the sign that gave her life's work new direction and meaning. It was her pride that had made her think she had to and could do it alone.

The classical program on the headset concluded and the next program was hard rock. It ended Taylor's meditation, but she didn't turn it down. In her teens, loud music had been one way to shut out the world while she tried longer and deeper meditation. There was as much beauty in the scream of a steel guitar and blasts from a well-matched horn section as any harp or violin. She let the beat wipe her mind free of memories and regrets. For now, she would just breathe, perhaps doze.

Her body clock knew it was after midnight. They would soon be landing in what would be morning. She knew it was wisest to stay up so she could adjust to the time zone, and besides, she wanted to press on to her final destination. Once on the ground, she wouldn't waste time on sleep.

She dozed off in a few minutes and dreamed of Liz undertaking a journey, frightened, but not alone. She turned to a companion, but Taylor could not see the woman's face clearly. Liz was shaking her head, but in tears submitting to the other woman's kiss. The image wavered and Liz was standing in a circle of light, her lips pressed together as tears poured down her cheeks. Questions demanded answers but she said nothing, even when she was on her knees, even when the questions came piercing with fire.

Taylor surfaced out of sleep with a jolt that sat her upright in her seat. She had been wrong to leave Liz undefended.

Her defenses are better than yours, right now, she reminded herself. This is your fear talking. She reached to shut off the now too loud music, when the lyric — if she understood it correctly — stayed her hand. The song seemed to be wrapping up, then cut out completely as the cabin steward asked them to put away any electronic devices they were using. It was so frustrating — there had been something pulling at her in the song.

It came back full blast, definitely repeating the refrain and wrapping up. It sounded almost punk — surprising airplane fare — with a female vocalist who had a lovely voice ripped into hoarseness by the demands of the song. And yet, in the midst of an angry passage there was a sudden calm. The archaic Latin was almost unintelligible under the ramped up guitars. *Alienam viam ad te currens.* Something like, "Running toward you on a different path." Could that be a harp? In amongst all those heavy metal chords? A whispered *sonus aquarum multarum* — the sound of many waters — at the very last closed the song.

Whatever came next on the recording was muted as the cabin crew gave more instructions and began collecting the headsets.

How incredibly vexing! The song was gone. They were

landing in Manchester. She flipped through the airplane magazine, which usually listed the songs and performers. She found the listings but there were three rock programs to sort through. None of the song names made sense for what she had heard. Of the fifty or so songs, fully half were performed by women, and many of them had composer credit as well. There had obviously been some sort of revolution in rock music since she'd turned to more esoteric recordings.

Alienam viam ad te currens. The phrase played with her memory — it had to be from Ursula's feast chants, and most likely of original biblical source, like the *sonus aquarum multarum*. Before Lammas night she would have slipped into a light trance, opened her gate and cast the phrases into the chaos to see what came back. Now she would have to use more conventional methods. She shoved the program listing into her satchel and braced herself for a journey begun without knowing her first step.

Five

Using all her skills in her quest had never bothered Autumn, even those of a seductress. Her body was temporary; survival was survival. Only her love mattered. She moaned into the arms that held her, whispered, "More gently, my lord, more gently," for strong as she was, she could only take so much.

Someone murmured in her ear, "I'm sorry, am I hurting you?"

Against her mouth a hard groan. "I've never known a woman like you."

Soothing hands stroked her forehead. "Wake up, Autumn, you're dreaming."

"More . . ." Killera's voice faded away.

"My love, wake up. I thought I was hurting you. You kept asking me to be gentler, but even after I moved my head off your shoulder you were . . . Are you alright?"

Autumn swung her legs off the motel bed. She could not meet Ursula's gaze. Her head still seethed with what she had done to Killera, making Killera burn for her, ache for her. And for what? What could possibly change? She could blame it on necessity, or claim it restored her long-depleted belief in the magic of the love of women. It was respite and renewal, for both of them. The Ursula of the past would understand that at least. There was no shame in desire.

But there was shame in manipulation. How had she not understood that? This Ursula, who called her "my love" so shyly, would not understand what seemed like a heartless and continuing calculated use of the body.

But Ursula had been with Killera, too, and in this life. Gods, what a tangle. While she knew she had been a warrior in her past, been ruthless and merciless, she had not known it had been against others who had also loved Ursula. This was a new, unexpected cross to bear.

"My love, what is it?"

"A bad dream." Not all bad, because she felt weak between her legs. Vivid, memorable, sweltering. But it had been frightening at the end, when Killera's need had begun to spin out of control and Autumn had felt almost as helpless as she had with Rueda.

She had not told Ursula everything about Rueda, and could not tell her now about Killera. She knew she ought to. Scylla's tail thumped hard on the floor as if to say, "Yes, tell her, you fool."

"It's barely past midnight," Ursula said as she switched on the bedside light. "You seemed so restless I thought I would just lie next to you for a while. I thought it would calm you. I — I didn't forget about my gate though it felt good to be near you while you slept. We were safe."

"I know." Autumn would not make the mistake of under-estimating Uda's powers, but she had no reason to think that Uda could easily find them when they weren't doing anything more than maintaining their gates. Reno by bus was only the first leg in a journey Autumn hoped would render them thoroughly lost. Even so, she could not look at Ursula, not yet. "It wasn't you. It was a dream."

"Like the ones you had before? About the past?"

She nodded and prayed Ursula would not ask more. The truth wanted to be said and it was hard to hold it back. It was selfish, but after so long how could she not hope that Ursula would love her again? How could she ruin that chance by confessing that she had been easily — admittedly in ignorance of the past — seduced by the woman who was hunting for Ursula's soul through the ages? Far less excusable, how could she admit that she had knowingly used sex and desire against someone that Ursula had dearly loved? What words could she find to admit that she had found some of it pleasurable, words that would not also wound?

Surely she was allowed one secret, one part of her that was just human and flawed? She knew so little of love, of kindness or compassion. She loved Ursula utterly. Only now did she realize she had not the slightest idea how to show it or prove it. She had not known she had a guilty past to weigh against her. Secrecy was not the way and yet she could not make herself speak.

So she had been a magician, a warrior, and she had brought Ursula to her after lifetimes of struggling and madness. What could she offer Ursula now? Why should Ursula care?

Her shoulders felt cold when Ursula's hands left them. Autumn couldn't tell if Ursula withdrew because she sensed Autumn was lying or because she could feel the one way that Autumn very much wanted to show her love. It was too risky — one moment of inattention and Uda had nearly finished them both.

Passion — and complete truth, it seemed — was not yet within their grasp. She was too wise, had remembered too much not to know that they would never be at peace until they had no secrets. But her mouth would not form the words.

"I couldn't sleep. I've been thinking," Ursula said. She settled back on the bed and Autumn braced herself to turn and look.

They had no clothing to waste on modesty and Ursula was as naked as she was. The body that disappeared beneath the sheets was sinuous with muscle, but still seemed dauntingly fragile. "What kind of thoughts?"

"I feel like what happened — you showing me what we once had. That it turned on a light inside me. I feel like I can think again." She regarded Autumn with an innocent simplicity. "I was frozen. I realize it wasn't easy for you to just let me be. Thank you."

"There was no other way," Autumn admitted.

"You could have shown me our past sooner. Forced me."

Autumn shook her head. "No. I'll never —"

Ursula put her fingertips on Autumn's lips. The sheets clung loosely to her breasts. "I know, my love."

"Please," Autumn murmured. Her lips wanted to kiss the delicate fingertips. "Please don't touch me right now."

Ursula pulled her hand back as if stung. "I'm sorry."

"I'm not made of stone. I'm — not as strong as I seem." She found a weak smile. "At least not where you're concerned."

Ursula drew the covers more firmly over her breasts. "I understand." Her answering smile was full of warmth and her hair seemed to shimmer. "I am not stone either." After a self-deprecating sigh, she said, almost business-like, "So I have been thinking. Where am I from?"

"If we knew —"

"We do know. My voice tells us."

"You're English, of course. That's not exactly new information. How does that help us?"

"That's what I've been thinking about. Do you agree that we've known each other in a previous life?"

"Yes." Time for some truth. "As improbable as it may seem, I believe it with all my heart."

"We're far beyond improbable." Ursula smiled with just her eyes. Autumn swore she saw stars dancing in them. "Why can't I be from the same place as before? From Aldtyme?"

"Did I pull you from there? No." Autumn rejected the idea. "You were with Killera on the Fourth of July."

"Why can't we have been there?"

Autumn had to consider the question. Why had she assumed that Ursula and Killera had been in the United States when she saw them? She flushed. Her ears filled with the sound of Ursula begging for what Autumn now knew only too well Killera would freely give. "I think it was in this country."

"Did you notice anything that could tell us for sure?"

Autumn forced herself to play the memory again. She closed her eyes. Killera's back, Ursula's nails raking across it. Ursula's voice, pleading in a desperate way she herself had never heard.

"You were here. In America," she said raggedly.

"How do you know?"

"The car is one I've seen on the roads. I hear her voice. She's American." In this life, she might have added.

"What did she say?"

She'd held back too much truth for one night. She didn't want to say the words, but they spilled out of her in Killera's choked gasp. " 'Yes, yes, baby. God, I love you.' "

Ursula abruptly got out of bed, dragging the blanket with her. She turned suddenly and Autumn could not look away from the piercing black gaze. *:I'm sorry. I must know. Show me.:*

She had no choice. She gave up the memory again, this time with every shuddered nuance. Ursula's prowess with her mind was growing. It was a step in the right direction, Autumn told herself, even though she realized that what

104

secrets she had would not be safe for long, not when Ursula could be inside her head so skillfully. The intimacy of it was the same, better than and no substitute for sex all at the same time.

Ursula gasped and staggered to the other bed. "How could I do that to her?"

"What?"

"Make her love me when . . . when I must have loved you."

She didn't want to answer. The uncertainty of Ursula's love was costing her far more than she had thought it would. She had gone without for so long. Survived with so little hope. Now that she knew Ursula lived, she felt as if she would perish if she did not also have her love. She felt nauseous and had to speak. "You loved her."

"How can I love you both?"

"I don't know." She made herself look into Ursula's eyes. She could see that Ursula wanted to trust that she loved Autumn, but she didn't really feel it. Not yet. Maybe never. Gods, it hurt.

"Did I stop loving her, before?"

"No," Autumn whispered. "You never told me you didn't love her anymore. You told me you loved me differently. That I was in your mind."

Ursula settled on the other bed and turned off the bedside light. "I'm sorry — I can't right now."

She was crying and Autumn knew she did not want comfort.

"I understand." She did. She didn't cry, though she could have. Enough weakness, she scolded herself.

She listened to Ursula weeping and did not go to her, did not whisper words to assure her that somehow it would all work out. She did not believe, not right then, and so she could not say it. She did not touch the tears, but she still felt burned by them. She faced her most bitter fear. *She might never love you, not the same way she did before.*

She did not know what she would do, or fail to do, to

secure Ursula's love. After so many lifetimes of believing that she knew who she was, what she was capable of, after gaining the simplicity of purpose she had winnowed for centuries, all to be worthy of Ursula's love — after all that, any uncertainty of her own motives battered at her confidence. Yes, she had started this life with nothing, no memories of the past, no drive, just talents that kept her alive. But now her pasts were starting to come back and that wasn't all good. She had thought she understood who she had been: a magician, a warrior, and a woman in love.

She had done something in her past that she was ashamed of. She was now not sure she wouldn't do something shameful again. Not knowing what she could or would do, not knowing for certain what she was — what good was she to Ursula now?

* * * * *

Traveler's Aid was helpful and the old gentleman's directions to the Manchester Piccadilly train station were perfect. Taylor used a credit card to purchase a ticket to York, which would take her through London. Once the train was underway she bought a sandwich from the steward's cart. She finished it quickly, being hungrier than she had thought, and had to make herself not give in to an inner urging of a pint to wash it down.

The clack of the train had its own steady rhythm. She felt her heart keeping pace with it. It lulled her into a state of receptiveness. With little effort she could see a more ancient countryside, vistas free of cities. Here there had once been a forest, dark and brooding, hiding places where power was birthed, built and spent.

This land was old, and there were many vibrant voices in its past. Without her shields she would find it easy to get lost. A pint of ale, a good song and she would forget why she was there. Yes, she mused, she had been in this land before. Her old soul remembered, but that did not comfort her. Breath had

106

hung around her like a mist. It was cold, Winter's Dead Night. She wielded the axe. A silver flash, a sacrifice's cry.

A gasp brought her out of the fleeting memory. Heart pounding, she told herself that was another world, another time. Memories from this ancient land, but it could not be a memory of herself.

They were in York by late afternoon. The local bus for Hornsea was more than an hour's wait, so she took a short walk into the oldest part of the medieval city. She seemed to have known this place when it was new and had thought herself prepared for the narrow streets and fabled gates. But the sheer antiquity pushed hard on her ultra-thin shields and she was glad when it was time to go.

The bus to Hornsea stopped at every village and hamlet. Her headache doubled while they jerked and rattled southeast. The pain was sharp enough to leave her wincing at each bounce on the hard seat. Sleep was out of the question even though she'd been up for nearly thirty-six hours.

They approached the coastal town at sunset. The fall air was sharp but clean with the scent of the sea. Armed with directions from a helpful publican, who sold her a slice of corn and tuna pizza, Taylor decided to walk the remaining six kilometers to Aldtyme by way of a promised scenic trail across the bluffs. She was tired, but so close. She'd done nothing but sit for nearly a day and her body ached from lack of exercise. She would sleep better for an hour's walk, and there was enough light to illuminate the way. Once in Aldtyme she would surely be able to find a night's lodging. She would locate the herb shop and Ursula's aunts all the sooner in the morning.

She passed a few other hikers, but all going in the opposite direction. The moon would be full in a few days, and even as the sun set it was rising. Both lights — gold and silver — reflected off the white rocks that lined the trail. The stone distance markers slowly ticked by her as she held back her weariness. Six, then five. Four, then three. Her shoulders and knees ached. Her feet cramped. Two, then one. She stumbled on in the dark and then couldn't remember — had that been one or two behind her? Had she passed two twice?

She sat down on a rock and tried to massage away a stitch in her side. Unbidden, she remembered that disconcerting half dream of Liz letting another woman kiss her. It was fear and exhaustion talking, she told herself. She would feel better when she had some sleep and a decent meal.

She forced herself back to her feet and had to think long and hard which was the right way to go. The sun had set and the moon seemed veiled in black. She plodded onward, though her feet screamed in protest. The still air suddenly gave way to a sharp wind in her face. Every step was harder to take. She had to lean all her weight into the wind to make any progress at all.

The wind stopped so sharply she fell. Her wrist seared with fiery pain. When had she started to cry? This was madness, the entire trip. More pride, trying to do the impossible alone. Liz would never forgive her for not saying anything, for sneaking out, for going so far away that their rapport had finally fizzled out. Everyone would hate her. There were quite a few who would delight in her downfall. She was useless and broken. She couldn't even walk properly.

She hauled herself to her feet. What had happened to the light, to the moon? The wind snapped in her face again. It wasn't fair. Why was this all on her? No one cared about what she was doing. It was too hard. It was her pride putting her onto this dangerous path.

In the distance a light glimmered. She was close. Fine, she thought. Let the fates be against me. I will get there anyway.

The wind howled at her to stop, then rain fell from the clear sky. Her shoe caught on a root and she fell again, injuring the same wrist further.

Get up, she told herself.

She didn't want to.

It would be easier to go back. Go back and be ordinary. Go back to Liz and be loved while there was still time.

She got to her knees. Her ears tingled.

:Who do you think you are, child?:

:Aunt Peela? Help me!:

:Why should I? You abandoned me, you let me die alone. You didn't cry for me.:

:You were on the wheel again. There's no grief in that.:

:Selfish child, after all I gave you.:

:Don't say that! Aunt Peela, please.:

Liz was letting the other woman kiss her. The tears were gone. Her face gleamed with the light of desire. Who was the woman? No — not Alexis. Anyone but the insufferably competent Alexis.

:Is she any different than you, child? At least she can offer Liz protection and real passion. Not just that weak tolerance of your affections, based on gratitude.:

She was on her feet, though she didn't know how. That was not what she and Liz shared. Stumbling, she headed for the light. When in doubt, she told herself hysterically, go toward the light.

Her feet were dead weights. The wind buffeted her backward and the rain sapped her of all warmth. The light seemed never to grow closer.

She was surrounded by the furies of failure and despair, reminding her of her mistakes, tallying their cost and presenting the bill with visions of Liz with Alexis. Her religious training condemned their sinful acts, and fundamentalist terror drew vivid images of satanic lesbian orgies — with Liz as the featured player — in her mind. They would burn for it.

Sanctimony was warming.

No, she wanted to argue. This was not Christ's way. All she had ever done was try to hold true to his gospel based on his words, not those of others. She had given aid and comfort to so many as a minister. She would still be one if the church council hadn't insisted she break her ties with her circle. They had not truly believed the circle was about satanic orgies, but others might. What could be tolerated in a parishioner was inappropriate in the minister. She should never have listened to them. She gave it up, gave up her vestments, her rituals, her sermons, even her prayers.

:You should have stayed with them and their mediocre ambitions. They know nothing of real power. You were perfectly suited to Christ and his limiting dogma.:

:There is no limitation in Christ. Not in his perfect love.:

:What could a man ever preach about perfect love? Tell that to your circle — they gave you the same ultimatum. They knew that the followers of Christ were dragging you down and all women with them. They wanted you to stay with Christ so they could find a new center that knew what she was doing. You let them all down.:

She was on her hands and knees. The rain felt like drops of lead, pummeling her into the ground. She scraped her cheek on bracken, blinded by tears, shrieking a silent no at Aunt Peela, who didn't let up. Aunt Peela's hair became chestnut-hued, and she wore it wound around her brow like a crown.

:You've achieved nothing. She cannot be saved. The best thing you can do with your miserable life is go back. Liz might have you back, but only if you go now. Otherwise she'll go to Alexis and Alexis will touch her in ways Liz would never want from you.:

Sobbing, she ground her knee on a rock. Her wrist was swelling and the rain still fell. She drug herself forward because everything was conspiring to send her back. If everything she had ever been was now gone, she was still contrary and stubborn. Her mother had said so, and she had been right about so many things.

Her mind was willing to go on, but her body gave up all at once. She crumpled off the trail, rolling onto her side.

For a while she was only able to breathe. When her sobbing abated, she blinked her eyes free of rain and realized she was staring at a marker in the ground. She could use it to get to her feet.

Aunt Peela was old again, gasping her final, painful breaths. *:Die! It's what you deserve! Your treachery is endless!:*

Ursula's face, in her last extremity of pain, swung before Taylor's eyes. *:You're not worth saving.:*

She stretched her hand toward the marker. When her fingertips touched it, green fire burned her hand.

She became a silent, screaming stone, skipping on a cold, clear lake. As the stone disturbed the silvered surface she saw her lifetimes flicker past. She had always been searching, looking for a sign. Priestess or minister, always a servant to her faith. Lifetime after lifetime was filled with ritual and words, music and praise. But so little love . . . where was Liz in all these pasts? She had clung to the idea that Ursula was a sign but it was Liz she searched for, frantically. Ursula had only been a door to this place.

She rocketed upward, leaving memory behind. She punched a hole in the malice that surrounded her and saw the light again. Three figures rippled in shifting colors, then they were gone in a sharp, hard crash of heavy metal.

A different path.

The green fire blazed to magenta and a rising, bitter cry tore through her mind. *:Get on your fucking feet! What do you want from me?:*

She rose. She took the step.

The wind ceased in that instant, as did the rain.

Taylor swayed on her feet and tried not to pass out. She had taken the step, the last required of her.

She dully became aware of a light bobbing toward her. A woman's voice called out, "Do you need help?"

"Yes," Taylor croaked. How to explain she was soaking wet with no sign of water on the ground?

"Stay there," the woman said. "I'm coming."

Taylor waited for what seemed like a year. Finally the flashlight shone across her knees, then up to her face.

"Gods!" The flashlight clattered to the ground and threw light on the features of the woman who had carried it. She was perhaps a decade younger than Taylor and her hair, long and black, was twisted into a Norn braid. Taylor's mind tried to add more years to the woman's face, to make it as she had once known it, but it was beyond her.

As she passed out she heard the other woman ask, "What has happened to you, child?"

* * * * *

Autumn slept for a few hours but awoke before daylight. Ursula was coiled in the blankets of the other bed. She looked down at her for a few minutes, struggling with fantasies that reduced the world to the blanket and their bodies. She wanted so much. She could have gently touched, kissed the red hair that spilled like a waterfall onto the floor. She did nothing. One touch and something inside her, the guards she had always needed, would be swept aside.

There was danger looking for them and her first duty was to Ursula's safety. Nothing else could possibly matter, not the ache in her heart or the pulsing hunger deep in her belly.

Autumn let Scylla out for a few minutes as she scrubbed sleep from her face. When Scylla returned she slipped out the door with a whispered reassurance. They all needed food. Reno was a good place to pick up some cash, too. That, at least, was something she was good for.

It was a short walk in the dark to the nearest casino. Roulette was quick and simple. In minutes she parlayed twenty dollars into seven hundred. She tripled that at a second casino. She wouldn't be here again, not any time soon, and so she didn't care who noticed that she won without losing. Those ways of caution were no longer needed. Instead, she was wary of pickpockets and other thieves. She felt a tickling certainty that if they stayed long Uda would sense them through their gates, or Staghorn would track them with more conventional methods. They would never be able to linger any one place.

The sun had risen when she left the third casino, many thousands of dollars richer. It felt like play money — a means to an end in a game that could only be settled by power. As she stepped into the daylight, the sight of mountains, the very peaks snow-capped and seeming near enough to touch, struck her silent. In her past memories she had seen mountains such as these, some taller, some icier, but just as sharp, brooding and inhospitable. In this life, however, there had been only Las Vegas and the arid desert that surrounded it. Mountains were soft-edged shapes that wavered in the distance. Her eyes felt new, suddenly. Perhaps she had seen and done many things in her past, but there were still fresh experiences ahead of her.

Perhaps, said her voice of inner caution, experiences that were not so pleasant as watching morning sunlight spread gold over desert and evergreens. A chill ran up her spine as she remembered the sensation of Killera's angry touch.

She found a convenience store and regretted the necessity of feeding Scylla cheap lunchmeat. For herself and Ursula she acquired cheese pizza that would no doubt be as tasteless as it looked. Every instinct told her she shouldn't take Ursula into a more public place than the motel and the bus station. It didn't feel safe. They couldn't live this way forever, but she didn't yet know where they could be both lost and live a normal life.

Normal. It sounded so safe and yet she knew that normal was something neither of them would ever be. Part of her knew they could not run forever, either. They just weren't ready for a final confrontation.

The crowds yesterday, such as they were, had been hard on both of them. Autumn had feared discovery around every corner. Ursula had seemed to notice every discourtesy and rudeness with a wince of pain. Last night had been simply agonizing. The more they talked the less she could count on as truth. For seven weeks she'd had only one foundation on which to build: she loved Ursula without question and therefore needed nothing more to survive.

Now she was increasingly aware that she wanted more. She was beginning to realize that all her lifetimes of waiting had only been prelude. The future was now more important than the past. She would need more than memories in her future to survive. She craved love in return and knew that was selfish.

One thing was clear: she didn't understand perfect love yet. It was entirely possible that given another millennia she still wouldn't understand it. The irony might have been wryly amusing if it hadn't been so damned personal.

The more Autumn learned of this Ursula, the less certain she became of a future that had some measure of peace in it. She had not thought Uda could so easily threaten them. A moment's inattention had nearly been enough. No, they were not ready for a final confrontation, and the longer they put it off, the better.

What if someday this was all behind them, that they survived? Autumn could not think about that because Ursula's love was an unknown. And there it all was: the future was unknown only because she wasn't certain of Ursula's love.

Ursula had showered and dressed by the time Autumn returned, and was grateful for the pizza. Scylla wolfed down the deli meat and looked around for more.

"I'm sorry, girl. Maybe at our next stop. Look," she said to Ursula. "Anything could happen. You should have some of this." She handed over a wad of her winnings. "I don't know where you could go, but wherever it is you'll need money."

Ursula hesitated, but Autumn couldn't tell if it was the amount or simply the necessity that bothered her.

"It's hardly mine — think of it as a casino's. They won't miss it."

"It just seems a fair bit of money there. I don't know where to put it." She indicated her pants pockets.

"Oh." The bills were bulky. She had pockets inside her leather jacket, and nothing fell from her sleeves unless she intended it to, but Ursula had no such skill. "You'll need a jacket and a money belt. Easily remedied."

"I don't like to think of us separated."

Neither do I, Autumn wanted to echo. Not again. Even though being together was becoming personally painful, being apart was not an option she could contemplate.

"I've been thinking again," Ursula said, almost nervously. "About where I'm from."

Autumn wanted a shower but made herself listen and hoped that they would not talk about Killera. Her sleep had been murky with regret and guilt — hardly restful. "When I pulled you to join me, or before that?"

"America is a big place. With so little to go on . . ." Ursula paused and swallowed hard. "She said so little that I can't guess where she might have lived. But that doesn't make my first instinct any less likely. Why can't I have begun in Aldtyme? Perhaps that is where Kelly found me."

Autumn's head snapped up. "Kelly?"

"Kell — oh." Ursula put her hands on her temples. Tears swam in her eyes. "Kelly. Kelly . . . oh, I can almost . . ."

Even Scylla seemed to hold her breath while Ursula rocked on her feet.

"No," she whispered. "It's all fading. Her name is Kelly, now. But the only thing that came to me was a golden field, and a smell like a farm after the soil is turned."

"It's okay," Autumn reassured her. She would have made her sit down, but that would have required touching her. She didn't want to risk it, not when she wanted to kiss away the tears and lines of headache. "That was significant. The rest might come just as unexpectedly."

Kelly. It helped to think of Ursula having been with a mysterious Kelly, not the same Killera she had seduced and used without a second thought.

Scylla was on her feet, rubbing her long gray nose against Ursula's knee. Ursula scratched Scylla's ruff absentmindedly. "Kelly. I can hear myself saying her name. I wish I could hear how she answered. If she said my last name."

"It's enough for now. We know her name. And as you were saying, maybe she found you in Aldtyme. It wouldn't hurt to find a map and see if there even is an Aldtyme now. Maybe it's still a little place."

Ursula was nodding, still distracted. "There must be a library here somewhere."

A library in a gambling town? It hadn't occurred to Autumn. She knew so little outside of Vegas nightlife. Until a month ago she'd rarely seen the sun. "You're probably right. We can start there. Even if we did find it we couldn't go — not until you had some identification. But it would be a start." She went to take her shower, trying hard not to mind that Ursula was whispering, "Kelly," as if to taste the name in her mouth.

They set out an hour later, two women and a dog. A casino gift shop provided a warm suede jacket and waist pack for Ursula. A cab ride later they were at Reno's main library. The reference librarian explained that an Internet search would find almost any town worldwide and provide detailed maps and listings of businesses in a few minutes. No terminals were available, however, so they followed her directions to an Internet café, something neither of them had known existed.

"Sometimes I feel like I never left a world without electricity," Autumn muttered. The café was all angles, metal and plastic. Several tables were occupied with people hunched over small keyboards. It might have been the dark side of the moon for all the affinity Autumn felt for it.

The clerk sold them a little card to give them thirty minutes on a computer. They settled in front of one. Autumn shook her head morosely.

Ursula stifled a laugh. "This is only faster than books if one knows what one is doing."

"What were we thinking?" Though Autumn saw little amusing about their situation, it was nice to hear Ursula sounding lighthearted, if only for a moment.

"Just point and click, the librarian said."

The middle-aged man at the next table overheard their muttered whispers. Autumn saw him start to roll his eyes, but then he seemed frozen by the sight of Ursula's smile.

"Our first time," Ursula said to him after a steady, considering look that seemed to measure him with her eyes.

He nodded and seemed to shake himself. "I could give you a few pointers."

"Thank you so much." Ursula indicated their computer as she vacated the chair in front of it. "We've never done this before."

"What are you trying to find?" He pushed his wire-rimmed glasses back up his nose as he clicked rapidly with the mouse.

"A small town in England on a map."

"Yahoo," he said oddly. His fingers tapped merrily. He was grinning at Ursula. "What's it called?"

Ursula spelled it for him. In a few moments they were looking at a map of Aldtyme, Great Britain, U.K. A few clicks and they were zoomed in enough to see that it consisted of a dozen short streets and a small harbor.

"You've been super," Ursula told him. "Is there a way to get the names and phone numbers of residents?"

He kept looking at Ursula as if she reminded him of someone. It made Autumn nervous. "Looking for your ancestors?"

"Something like that," Ursula said.

"Well, there are sites that can give you that kind of information, but you do pay through the nose. At least that's what I've heard. I've never done it myself. Now a listing of businesses in the town is free. That's easy." A few clicks later it was there. He sent the list to the shared printer.

"How can I thank you," Ursula was saying.

"It was a pleasure." He blinked as if he'd found himself in unexpected light while Ursula gave him another long, considering look.

"Go home early tonight. Your kids do miss you," she said, finally.

He went back to his own work with a nervous smile at Autumn, who tucked the list in her pocket as she favored him with a level stare. "Let's make some phone calls," she said to Ursula.

"There's a pay phone here."

"No." She glanced at their helper, aware that he continued to listen. How could he not be intrigued? "There are more private places." She was thinking of the soundproofed phone booths most casinos had, especially popular with patrons who didn't want anyone to know they were gambling.

They sat outside a fast food place. Scylla was delighted with two hamburgers, lettuce and all. Ursula sipped a styrofoam cup of tea as she scanned the list.

"Fishmonger, harbor, green grocer, teas, herbs — none of these names seem familiar."

Autumn read the list over Ursula's shoulder, though it was hard to concentrate with the scent of Ursula's hair right under her nose. If she'd ever seen more of Aldtyme than its docks she had yet to remember. Hadley & Sons Fish, Grosvenor's Bakery, Aldtyme Harbor. Other businesses were sensibly named after their trade: wool, tea, groceries and so on. But the list wasn't that long.

She felt hopeful, suddenly. Wouldn't the only grocer in a fairly remote town know everyone? Or the person who sold everyone their tea? "Let's start with the grocer, then the tea place. And just ask for you. And see where that leads us."

"We could ask for my aunts — from the previous time. Those names might be around." Ursula shimmered briefly with a reddish glow.

"Don't do that," Autumn cautioned. "It might be all she needs to find us." She had a sudden itch between her shoulder blades and got to her feet.

"Sorry," Ursula said. The glow faded. "I forgot."

"We need to go. Now." She fought the urge to crouch because she didn't want to alarm Ursula. Every nerve in her body was on alert, ready to fight or fly.

Ursula didn't question. They walked quickly toward the casino strip, then Autumn caught her breath. "No. We can't." Her stomach was knotting the closer they got. Scylla was pressing hard against Ursula's legs.

She studied the side streets available to them as the ground began to rumble with the impending arrival of a train. The tracks ran parallel to the main casino strip. "This way."

They hurried through the alley and into the train terminal. Passenger service was available and Autumn quickly bought them month-long passes — no tickets to leave a trail. Scylla resentfully settled in a large cage that was loaded into a car where pets traveled. They could visit and bring her food and water.

When the train began to move Autumn felt marginally better. She studied a route map displayed in the narrow foyer of their car. "I'm sorry," she murmured to Ursula. "I just felt like we had to leave. Let's go for a while and then hop off to make those phone calls. In a while. A few states, maybe."

Ursula didn't answer directly. She raised her fingers to trace the outline of the Great Salt Flats, which they would soon be traveling over. "A wasteland of salt," she murmured. "So far to the west."

She was so pale that Autumn put her arm around her waist. Every nerve in her body seemed to burn. Pleasure, gods, pleasure that was all pain. She wanted to bury her mouth in Ursula's throat, to share kisses that would make the past irrelevant. "Let's find a place to sit."

Ursula shook her head. "I'm okay. It's just — we're going the right way."

"The right way to get to where?"

"Paradise. That's all I can think of. Paradise."

* * * * *

"Taylor went to England without saying a thing to me. I knew she was planning something, but this — why? What did you tell her?"

Kelly wanted to hang up on Liz. She was busy. She needed to get back to the barn. She had work. Something . . . yes, it was work. Essential. "I didn't tell her a damn thing. I told you, she put something in the tea and rifled around in my head."

"I know, I still can't believe she'd do that."

"You don't know her very well then, do you? All I know is she better not come back here."

Liz's voice grew thin and plaintive. "What could she have found out that would send her there? I know that's where she went. I couldn't stand not knowing so I checked our credit card statement online. She bought a British Airways ticket yesterday morning. I'm sorry about what she did. Part of me doesn't believe she did it. But I have to know — what was in your mind that sent her there?"

"You should have asked her."

"I . . . we're not like we were. Since that night it's been so hard to maintain. I've lost my connection to her."

"What do you want from me, Liz?"

Liz's vexed sigh was plain through the phone. "My dreams are all a haze. Nothing is very clear except how much it hurt to be around people. Taylor didn't have the dreams until the very end. So whatever made her go must have come from you."

"Like I care."

"This isn't you," Liz said more gently.

"It is now. You can thank your girlfriend. I'm more me than I have ever been." With Rachel, Kelly thought. Rachel was the only one who understood. Rachel could see inside her, wanted everything that Kelly could give.

A small voice, growing more dim with each trip to the barn, reminded her that Rachel was a dream, a fantasy, a substitute.

"I know you're angry. Don't you think I know how much you're hurting? I, of all people, really know. You understand that, don't you?"

"It's not my problem," Kelly snapped. "Taylor helped you out with that. If being around me hurts too much then by all means, don't come around."

"Oh, Kelly, this isn't you. I don't believe it."

"Get used to the new me. Sure, I had dreams about some mysterious past. They were lies. What happened in them? Nothing but a load of guilt and crap dumped on me." The memory that had constantly reminded her that she had hurt Ursula, in this life, in the bed not twenty feet away, was getting very faint. Ursula should have stopped her.

She was tired of stop and no and holding herself back. Even Autumn — no, she thought. Not real. Rachel — no, not real either. But Rachel never said no.

"Ursula didn't blame you for anything, you know that. She understood. She even said it was her fault. She was the one who should have protected you."

"It never happened." Her stomach twisted. She couldn't remember the last time she had felt like eating. "They were Ursula's dreams. Her fantasies. They spilled on to me because I loved her so much, but she —" She never trusted me, she wanted to add.

121

She reined in her thoughts sharply. No, she would not be angry with Ursula. This was Autumn's fault, cheating, lying, manipulative Autumn. She wasn't going to tell Liz about those dreams, about Autumn like a bitch in heat, ready to do anything as long as she got what she wanted. Even Autumn told her to stop. Like all the other times women had said no to her, she didn't think twice about being the one in the wrong, the one who wanted to go too far. Only Rachel understood.

Rachel's a fantasy, she told herself, but realized Rachel as a fantasy was more truthful than Ursula's dreams.

"Kelly? Are you there?"

"No," Kelly said. "I'm not." She hung up.

The phone rang again almost immediately, but she shrugged into her rain slicker and crossed the muddy yard to the barn. Being angry was exhausting and a small part of her wanted to take the afternoon off. She'd been through a lot yesterday, but the compulsion to go back to the barn was too strong to fight.

Rachel was waiting, sitting in her demure Amish gown and cap.

Kelly felt a now-familiar tingle as she crossed over what had once been a circle in the barn's dirt floor. Rachel was rising now, unlacing her gown. *:I'm glad you came back.:*

It was intoxicating. Kelly no longer knew what was truth or reality. What she knew was that Rachel never said no, never used her.

Was it flesh or fantasy that she held, touched, stroked? She swept the cap from Rachel's head and let the coil of chestnut hair fall like a rope around Rachel's shoulders. Rachel was ready with a fire that matched Kelly's own and her eyes gleamed with a blue-green heat. Like this morning, she did not care if Kelly couldn't wait for clothes to be removed. She was all the more eager if her dress got torn. She would beg and lustily say how much she loved it. She never merely tolerated the force of Kelly's love.

A whirl of light, a ringing sound. Kelly went to her knees and let Rachel wrap her in her arms. *:You need me now, don't you? You shall have me, all that you want.:*

Kelly had said no to Rachel only yesterday. It seemed a lifetime ago. She could not find the strength again. There was no other reality, not any more. Rachel took all that Kelly needed to give. When she asked for something in return Kelly could not refuse. It was such a simple thing. Easy, really. Kelly had always protected Liz, had always helped her. Now should be no different. Were she not so angry and wounded she would have helped with all her heart.

Rachel only wanted Kelly to do what she ought to have done.

She promised in her mind while her hands and mouth reveled in Rachel's unending passion. Rachel never said no. She never said stop.

Kelly woke on her back on the floor again. The glow of the fall afternoon poured through the doors. Her body felt coiled with pent up energy. She thought, without alarm, that she would explode soon if she didn't find some way to release it. These dreams, these fantasies of sex that she would never act out — they were the result of a frustrated libido, that was all. Rachel was a dream. She would never be rough with a lover. That wasn't her way. That's not who she was.

She heard an answer to her thoughts, and a laughing murmur shushed her conscience. *:Take what you need because it makes you stronger. You must be strong to honor your promises.:*

Ursula was missing and Liz needed her help. She was still livid with Taylor for her tactics, but it was time to get past that.

:Honor your promises.:

Her promise? Yes, she had promised Ursula her perfect love and perfect trust, that was it. She had to honor that by doing what she could to find her. If that meant helping Taylor, so be it.

She made up her mind and from all around her she felt a sense of peace and well-being, like she had when Ursula had been here. Ursula would be hers again.

:Yours, again. You will take what you need, this time.:

"I'm sorry I hung up on you." Kelly signaled for her merge and kicked the Explorer into high speed on the turnpike. "I think I know where Taylor's going."

"So do I. I'm about to leave for the airport. I got family emergency leave from my job." Liz hesitated for a moment. "I know I can manage, but I have no idea really what to expect, given the past and all. I have — I have a bad feeling about what's going to happen to her — oh!"

Liz's sharp hiss of pain caught Kelly by surprise. "What is it?"

"I don't — no. I can't . . . It's gone, she's gone. Kels . . ." she said weakly. "A different path . . . the road twists again. The past calls tomorrow . . . a raven, the axe . . ."

"Liz, what in hell are you talking about?" The childhood nickname disconcerted her; Liz hadn't used it in years. She veered across two lanes to pass a truck, then eased up. This timed section of the turnpike would earn her a speeding ticket if she wasn't careful.

"I have to find her now," Liz whispered. "Will you help me?"

Liz sounded like she had so many times in the past, before Taylor had come into her life. Apparently, Taylor's protection *was* gone. "You know I will."

"I didn't know which path was true. Now I do. I must go," she repeated.

:Remember your promise.:

"I'll help you get there. Where can I meet you?"

Liz told her the airline and flight in a quavering voice and agreed to wait at home for Kelly to pick her up. A quick call confirmed another seat was available though the price was exorbitant. As hard as it was she took her foot off the gas and reasoned herself into a calmer frame of mind. She'd locked the house and barns and left a note for the nearest neighbor that she'd be away for a while. Now she was doing something, finally, out of unchanged love for Ursula and compassion for her cousin. She was keeping her promise.

The glare of oncoming cars flashed in her eyes. She flinched from the light.

Six

From far away: "Wake up."

It might have been a voice from a thousand years ago, or from a thousand light years away. Taylor floated in a place that seemed unanchored in time.

She knew the voice. It was familiar behind her eyes. She lifted a hand to be sure she had eyes. She felt unbound in consciousness, free of restraints that she had endured lifetime after lifetime after lifetime.

"It's the circle, child. The mother of all circles."

Her voice was a croak. "Where am I?"

"On the surface of a vast satellite of rock, spinning

through space and time. But that's not what you really meant, is it?"

Taylor wanted to laugh. The owner of the voice was sassy. She had already forgotten what it was that had kept her tight within her own walls. Unknown, uncomplicated, unrestrained joy crept into her heart. It was welcome. So very welcome. She opened her eyes. "I was hoping for a more precise answer."

The room was filled with the soft, golden light of morning that spilled through the open windows. The moss green walls were hung closely with paintings and photographs. Doilies covered a multitude of small tables, all crowded with thimbles, photographs and porcelain figurines.

"It's not all mine — this house has had many occupants. You have known some of them, over the years."

She found she could turn her head, though it hurt, and felt no surprise. She'd known that face with many, many more years showing in it. "I know you, too."

"That goes without saying."

"Who lived here before you, then?"

"Ursula, for one."

Taylor went rigid with surprise. She could accept that Aunt Peela was living yet another turn of the wheel, but that she knew of Ursula? Of course, she told herself. Aunt Peela is here, in Aldtyme, where it all began. Of course she knows. She can tell you what you don't know.

"All my lives have brought me here, to be Priscilla Muldoon and Ursula's replacement as the center of the outer circle. I watched her go, though none of us knew what would come to be without her with us here."

"How was she here? Where am I, exactly?"

"You're within the grace of the goddess's own circle. That's why you feel so strange."

Taylor considered how easy it would be to lapse into euphoria. Her body ached from her walking ordeal, but her mind was nearly giddy with relief. Something was missing — holy Mother.

She closed her eyes and dropped what was left of her shields.

Nothing.

She took what little power she had and cast out.

Nothing.

"There is no chaos here. There never was. Let us pray there never shall be."

"Can you — I can't even sense it beyond the shields. But I'm not functioning at full strength."

"I noticed, child. But even if you were you'd sense nothing."

Taylor began to understand why Ursula took for granted that a circle was always open, was always functioning. The mother of all circles, Aunt Peela had called it. She could believe it.

Aunt Peela rose from the depths of the armchair. "You need some tea."

Taylor tried to rise and fell back wincing. One knee was neatly bandaged and her wrist was tightly bound. She ached as if she'd crawled on her hands and knees all the way from Pennsylvania. Tea would be welcome. Breakfast would be even more so. "I don't understand."

Her aunt's voice floated back from the kitchen. It was easier to think of her as her aunt without looking into a face younger than her own. "You will. You're in a bad place, child. We can help with that."

"Ursula — she grew up here?"

"Yes."

"You know she's missing?" It was her most urgent question.

Aunt Peela came back with a tray of tea preparations. "Of course she's not missing."

Taylor sat for a moment with her mouth open. "But — she was taken away from us. Something broke our circle and took her."

Aunt Peela seemed not in the least surprised. "Yes."

"Aren't all of you worried? "

"We have no reason to worry. Drink your tea, child."

"Aunt Peela . . ." She was whining like an eight-year old. She managed to sit up and reach for the steaming china tea-cup on its delicate saucer. "I'm the one who lost her. I failed her. I need to make it right somehow."

"Ursula's journey is not about what you need."

Taylor choked on her first sip, feeling suitably chastened. "I'm sorry."

"In this place you must be honest. You're here for your-self."

"For answers, yes, I guess for answers I need. But I can't forget what I owe her."

"You only owe her what she needs that you can give. Nothing more, nothing less." Aunt Peela dropped a sugar cube into her own tea and gave Taylor a piercing glance. The doors of her eyes would have swept away any remaining doubts Taylor might have had about who this young woman really was. They were Aunt Peela's eyes.

Feeling like she'd been caught cheating on a spelling test, Taylor sipped her tea in silence. Clearly, she told herself, you have no idea what forces are at work here. You never have. You thought you had found a way through Christ to know the goddess, too, and, well, you were wrong as usual.

She frowned. Christ on the Mount, giving comfort and peace. In her mind such forces transcended gender. His face, as she had always envisioned it, transformed, became ever more gentle. The body grew more slender, the hair fell in waves of red.

She shook her head, then stared dully into her tea cup.

The bitter aftertaste was not what she'd slipped into Kelly's tea. But she recognized the flavor from her training. If it weren't already in her blood she would have been afraid. Fear was slipping away. These herbs would take her to the soul's crossroad: completion, beginning or oblivion. She hadn't come here for this, hadn't known the cup when it was before her. "I guess I deserve this."

"It must be done, child." Aunt Peela took the cup out of her hand.

If her shields hadn't already been down they would have been by then. She felt a flicker of distant panic, then remembered that the chaos did not exist here. This circle didn't merely keep it at bay, it negated it completely. She didn't need shields to protect her from the chaos, but she was beginning to suspect she might want them to protect her from what was about to happen. No, she contradicted herself. That is fear talking. All the doors must be open.

This place existed on two planes, she could sense that now. She was about to leave one for the other. Returning was not guaranteed.

Outside of this little house people went about their lives, most unaware of the paper-thin barrier between their reality and this sacred place. The chaos could not enter here, which meant that Uda could not either.

But Uda had to be here. She wore the braid. Taylor couldn't just assume Uda did not exist. Evil existed. Ursula had made the mistake of thinking evil had no power in the face of perfect trust and perfect love. Ursula had been wrong. This one lesson Taylor would remember.

She saw that her hands were glowing. It took enormous effort to speak. "When will you take me?"

"At dusk. The day is yours."

Hers to meditate on her past, to examine her conscience, to add up her accounts and decide how she might settle them. She would fast as well, and hunger would tighten her focus. It would also make it easier for the forces at work in this place to deal with her. Panic fluttered again, but it was so very, very far away.

"She has chronic pain syndrome," Kelly explained to the customs official. It fit Liz's appearance — strained, distracted, every movement considered.

Liz gingerly took back her passport. Tears swam in her eyes. She gave whispered answers to the perfunctory questions, then Kelly gathered up all their bags and managed to get one arm around Liz's waist.

She knew how to get to Aldtyme from Manchester; she'd done it last year. Liz bore the cab ride well, but the cacophony of the train station left her sagging with anguish. The train was little better. Kelly didn't mind the ticking rhythm, but Liz held her head in her hands, at times moaning quietly.

They were in London by noon, but Kelly could not imagine continuing on to York with Liz in this condition. "We're getting off here, for now," she told her, and she claimed their luggage. Porters, cabs, a modest hotel room for the night — it was just money. Money was meaningless. She was keeping her promise.

Liz made it into the hotel room under her own steam. Kelly had remembered it being very quiet. "Better?"

Liz nodded as she crumpled to the floor.

"Not there, come on," Kelly murmured, lifting her cousin easily to the nearest bed. "You need to sleep."

"I've lost my edge," Liz tried to joke. "I used to know how to bear this, that or it's worse than it was. But we can't stay here. We need to find Taylor. She's — I want to be with her as she walks." Liz's eyes were already drooping.

"We're not going anywhere until you can manage. You hardly slept on the plane." Kelly stroked Liz's hair for a moment. "I'll go for a walk, find out about buses from York to Hornsea and bring you back some dinner."

Liz was asleep. Kelly let herself out and walked aimlessly, feeling as if she was searching for something she couldn't yet define. Afternoon had turned toward evening by the time she returned to the hotel with sandwiches and drinks.

There were two women in the elevator with her, standing close together. The one in the black leather jacket held their room key. She gave Kelly a look Kelly couldn't really decipher and firmly wrapped her arm around the other woman's waist. They exited and Kelly shook her head free of images of what would happen when they reached their room. She was on fire. Her stomach hurt. She felt trapped.

Liz was steady enough to eat a little. "We have to go on."

"Even if we left now we couldn't get a bus."

"Can we rent a car?"

"Have you ever driven on the other side of the road? I nearly killed myself last year, about ten times." It was the truth, as well as a good excuse. She wanted to stay in London for the night. Liz did not need to reach Aldtyme until morning. It was for Liz's sake that they would stay here. She was keeping her promise.

"I forgot about that," Liz said. "I am feeling a little bit better."

"A really good night's sleep might get you back under control."

Liz seemed to be staring into her own soul. "I wanted to be there tonight. I tried to change things, to get there in time." She shook her head. "That's not the way it works."

Confused, Kelly asked, "What did you mean about the axe?"

Liz's gaze riveted on her. "What axe?"

"On the phone, you said something about a raven and an axe."

"I wasn't thinking very clearly. It felt like something had ripped off the top of my skull and poured acid into my brain."

Kelly could tell it was an evasion. She stared at Liz, wondering if she could read her thoughts more closely. No, she thought, you don't believe in that. You don't believe it's real. It was just Ursula.

Unbidden, her mind pressed toward Liz's.

She had a puzzling vision of Liz bound to a pillar, surrounded by sharp-fanged inquisitors, then something shoved her back inside her own thoughts. If Liz had felt anything it didn't show as her head drooped again.

"This is the way it must be, then," Liz murmured. More firmly, she added, "You're right. More rest will do me good. Can you get my suitcase open? I've got some sleeping pills and painkillers I haven't needed in a while."

A half-hour later Liz was deeply asleep. Her face was still twisted with the memory of pain. Kelly was glad she had come. It had been an easy promise to keep.

It was nearly dark. She sensed now that she was longing for the night. Let it come, she thought. Let me join with it.

Aunt Peela helped her stand up. Taylor's sore knee and sprained wrist no longer hurt. Night was claiming the little town as they left the cottage. She passed an orange tree impossibly bearing fruit, spreading its branches over a garden bursting with herbs. She smelled chervil and fennel, then the tang of white broom. The aroma put her momentarily in the circle she had raised for Ursula. She had traced the interlocking pattern in the dirt with a long brush of white broom. Ursula had walked behind her, the supplicant seeking help.

She was walking behind Aunt Peela, who now carried a bundle of white broom.

A very long way away, from deep inside or the other side of the moon, she heard herself screaming. She could not give this up. It was who she was. It was who she had always been. Her soul knew nothing else. She could not let them do it.

Still she walked, numb to the disbelief that her path took her over a picturesque cobbled sidewalk, past cars and people hurrying home. Ritual to her meant careful preparation, study, and contemplation of the most minute detail. This walk to her destiny could have been like any evening stroll, except for the tea working in her blood.

After closing a garden gate carefully behind them, Aunt Peela led her through the opening of a box hedge maze. The pattern of their twisting path began a low buzz of pressure inside Taylor's head. This was magic like she had never known. All she understood of ritual would not be enough to survive this. They would break her, like she had broken Ursula.

Vengeance was not the way of the goddess. They would not destroy her because she had destroyed Ursula. A judgement would be coming, however, and the demand for recompense. Meditation and self-reflection had showed her how often she had given in to her pride and vanity. She had violated Kelly's mind not once, but twice. Motives were meaningless. The bill for her crimes was now due.

Tendrils of power rose from the hedge itself, twisting over her shoulders and hips, enclosing her.

:You have tried so hard, but how little you understand. From the beginning you've only forgotten.:

What beginning, she wanted to ask. Her mind was naked. Her memories spilled forth from the private places she had always kept locked, where loving Liz, her secrets of initiation, confessions heard, all she had never expressed to anyone had been long guarded. She heard Liz gasping her name, saw her dying in her arms in the abbey. She had walked so many circles, been the center of it so many times, balancing energies she had never truly understood. What beginning had there been to set her on this path?

Taylor . . . Claire . . . priestess . . . minister. She had only ever been those things. Her soul was old, but it knew nothing else.

They stopped at the steps of a gazebo. She had to shield her eyes from the roiling light that surrounded the structure.

134

Another circle then, a circle of high power within the mother of all circles.

It was a place of endings and beginnings.

Her soul was old. It knew nothing else.

No, she thought. I don't want to do this. But her thoughts were nothing on the edge of this place. The tea, meditation and hunger had prepared her for what was about to happen.

She wanted to rage against it. To cling, because it was her right to be who she had always been.

Aunt Peela went lightly up the steps and was no longer visible once she crossed the threshold of the waiting door.

Taylor went up the steps because her feet would not stop. At the very threshold she paused.

Three maidens, no, crones, no, maidens, waited. They were weavers, no, unravellers. They were the chaos and yet they were clarity. They could grant completion or dispense oblivion. The Norns, the triple goddess, the faces of past, present and future — who was she to approach such deities?

She would not go in. It was her right to say no.

"Who comes to this place?" They spoke in unison, their voices like music and drums.

"I am Taylor, a daughter of the old ways."

"Why do you seek this circle?"

It was her right to say no. They could not force her.

But she said the words. "To find a new path."

She stepped over the threshold.

:Take what you need. You deserve it.:

Kelly showered and changed her clothes. She wasn't used to all-black attire, but the button-up shirt and close-fitting slacks suited her mood.

She walked a dozen blocks to escape the hotels and bars that could have been anywhere in the world. The tourist district eased into the London she had explored less than a year ago, at the beginning of the trip that had led her to Aldtyme and to Ursula. Finally, she turned in at a corner pub filled with locals. She surveyed the room from the door.

She did not believe in what she did next. She did it any way, lying to herself that it wasn't really happening. She told herself she was making it all up.

It could be just heightened intuition. She'd always had it — enough to make her family nervous at times. That's all it was now. It was a skill, a strength. She would not apologize for using it. She would celebrate all her strengths tonight.

She let her gaze wander over the crowded bar and where her eyes went her mind went as well.

A beautiful, elegant blonde was thinking about sex with the man next to her. She was also wondering where her husband was. Her gaze slid to a mousy brunette with an aristocratic nose. That was more likely — she was thinking about the blonde's legs. Kelly paused, taking in the brunette's surface thoughts. She was glad she hadn't moved any closer when she realized the brunette was thinking not about the blonde's legs as a pathway to her sex but rather how she could get legs like those. Envy, not lust.

She drifted in and out of dozens of women's surface thoughts. Alcohol and the night had most of them thinking about sex of one kind or another, but always sex with men. She was in the wrong part of town, perhaps.

She faded back into the dark and walked until she found another pub, and from that one to the next. She felt stifled and frustrated. One woman — she ought to be able to find one woman who was looking for what Kelly needed to give her. She only wanted to find one woman.

In a strange city, approaching midnight, she should have felt frightened. But she felt only calm and confident, certain that she could handle anything that might happen. She risked poorly lit alleys and walked unmolested past street corners where huddled groups transacted business. No one seemed to notice her. Or perhaps no one felt they ought to take notice of the tall, broad-shouldered woman in black, moving quickly and with purpose.

She slipped into the next pub she came to. The crowd was thinning. She quickly scanned the room and experienced a hard, pleasurable jolt in her stomach when she paused in the petite redhead's mind. The redhead was here looking for a one-nighter. With a woman.

She rested in the other woman's surface thoughts, enjoying the swell of arousal. At that moment she could tell the difference between what the woman was here for and what she was fantasizing about. She wanted a woman to pick her up. She wanted to have sex. Her fantasies went much farther than that, tangling with images of leather women on motorcycles carrying her off in the night, of being blindfolded at an orgy where women's hands never left her body. These thoughts were insubstantial. They stopped at specifics. It was the mood, the thrill, that this woman was after.

She was looking for mystery but only a little danger.

Kelly had never been that way for anyone, had never known that this mood could be part of her. She felt Rachel's body in her arms and was weak with the idea that tonight the woman would not be a dream.

She remembered, too, Ursula's body in her arms. Soft, fragile, sweet and unreserved — she loved those things, too. She was still that woman, who could be tender and gentle, who had never intentionally hurt anyone in her life.

Taylor, she remembered. She had hit Taylor.

There was a moment when she realized where she was and could see where she had been. She felt like she had boarded a ship and looked back at the dock, watching that reality grow small and distant. The ship headed for dark waters. And for that final moment she knew no matter how hard she tried she could not leave that reality behind. She could not leave that person behind, not forever — it was also who she was.

The moment was gone and she was adrift in obsidian

waters that could hide so many secrets.. The redhead was the shore she would find.

:If you serve all that the goddess stands for, why do you resist what we must do?:

Taylor could barely speak over what seemed like an endless, deep throbbing of a gigantic heart. The gazebo was a vast cavern of echoed energy. "She gave me a mind. She gave me free will."

The Norns answered with memory. Or did she answer herself? All her mistakes played to her guilt. Ursula screaming in agony, Kelly a mountain that could never break and was broken. She had abandoned Liz, tried to do it all by herself.

She had never asked for help. She accepted assistance. She was not fit to be a center, not with her arrogance and pride.

It was all she had ever been. She could not let go.

:Did you think to ask us for power?:

"No. I came in search of Ursula."

:Did you think to gain understanding without sacrifice? Why do you resist what we must do?:

"The goddess gave me a mind," Taylor answered again. "She gave me free will."

:Became. Becoming. Shall be.:

She shuddered with fear. She had not been wrong. She was to be changed. She said no, she did not want to be here, no, she did not want to be changed, no, she did not consent. She said it over and over.

And learned, when she felt the gentle but persistent hands at the nape of her neck, that she did not mean it.

She would be unmade. It was the only way to begin again.

Her name was Wendy. She wanted Kelly to stand closer, to tower over her a little.

Kelly stepped off the barstool and moved just close enough

for Wendy to feel her body heat against her silky, bare arms. Their conversation had been mundane but the chemistry was unmistakable. "Just today. I wasn't sure what London nightlife was like."

:I'm dying for her to touch me. Gently, but like I'm hers.: "What part of America?"

Kelly put one hand on the small of Wendy's back, a light touch that moved slowly around to her hip. "Pennsylvania. A little place called Paradise."

:I want to take her home. At last, someone I want. That sexy American accent. A sexy dyke to take home.: "I spent my life looking for Paradise and here you live in it."

Kelly studied the soft contours of Wendy's lips and she let Wendy see her doing it. "Paradise can be anywhere we make it."

:Everyone would see if she unbuttoned my blouse, but I almost want her to do it anyway. I don't care if everyone knows how much she's turning me on. I want her hands on me. I want her to ask me to leave with her.: "Even here?"

Kelly would have never said anything like it, except she knew it was exactly what Wendy wanted her to say. "Here? No, but at your flat it could definitely be Paradise."

:She's picking me up. She's going to fuck me. Oh my God.: Wendy's lips parted and Kelly angled her head as if she would kiss them. "I know what you want," she murmured. She tightened her grip on Wendy's hip until she felt a pure thrill of excitement course through Wendy's mind. Less gently, more possessively. "Let's go."

Was this what Ursula had endured? Pain needled through Taylor's shoulders and down her spine. She wanted to cry out, but she would wait until she could no longer bear it.

:This was created with powerful but small magic. It is unmade easily.:

Her outer braid was undone and the hands had firmly begun work on the first of the inner braids. The pain was there, but she could tell it did not begin to compare to the agony that had left Ursula screaming in the dirt of Kelly's barn floor.

:That was the goddess's own work.:

Taylor needed to know. *:Was I right to undo it?:*

:There is no right or wrong.:

It wasn't an answer she could understand. Of course there was right and wrong. There was service of the light and service of the darkness.

:Can either exist without the other?:

Taylor knew the answer was no, but it was irrelevant. She had a choice of which to serve. She served the light. The goddess, the mother of everything and all she represented in the souls of humankind, she was the light. All flowed from the mother.

:Look deeper, child.:

She had celebrated the light and explained it to others through all her lifetimes. That was her purpose, to radiate the light outward to others.

She felt a comb at the nape of her neck. It was a long, long forgotten sensation, that of a comb running through her hair. She could feel the strands across her back now.

She had forgotten to do something. When she had raised the circle for Ursula she had let some of the magic come from Ursula herself. She had been surprised when Ursula had taken off her robe and stood naked for her ritual. But Ursula had been right. She felt the hands begin on her second braid. Her own hands went to the buttons of her shirt. She was being undone, so let it be utterly.

When she was naked they spread her hair over her back again and this time she felt the fire of it in every nerve. The second braid was unraveled and her skin was hot with distress. Nothing like Ursula's pain, but it was enough to bring a moan to her lips. The old skin would be burned away. It was the only way to start again.

She could bear the pain, she found, if she remembered Liz's touch. It was solace and purity. Liz's image fled when she finally stood in the center of the vast circle, naked, unbraided, and ready. The comb passed carefully through her hair — no remnant remained of the braid that had symbolized who she was through all her lives.

They would braid something new into her in an act of perfect love. She would become a different kind of servant. This was her perfect trust.

Became, becoming, shall be.

She gave the kiss of peace to her aunt. She knelt before the Norns. She was their clay.

:Did you think to take power from us?:

Naked, her soul utterly exposed, she felt the first surge of power, as inexorable as deep ocean tides.

She prostrated herself, feeling dirt under her. It only then occurred to her that her crimes were large and she ought to beg for mercy.

:Look.:

The irresistible compulsion to raise her head reminded her she was nothing in this place.

She was in a glade surrounded by ash and alders that had never known a saw. The grove was closed at one end by a magnificent tree of a type she did not recognize. It's branches stretched over her, sheltering, hiding. A mammoth root had burst upward in the middle of the grove, creating a table. A table — an altar.

She was standing next to the altar, an apple in one hand. She tossed the apple to one side. "I will not be Eve for you."

The surface of the altar flickered as if a body writhed on it. There was an axe in her hand, long and double-bladed. The sharp edges were spotted with dried blood.

She let the axe fall to the ground. "I will not play this part either."

:You have chosen.:

The altar became a bed with Liz gasping under the weight of a woman Taylor did not know. Liz's accusing gaze found hers. Liz said, "I knew I would find you. I knew I would lose you, too."

"No!" Taylor had not chosen this, to forsake Liz and their love that had brought them together over centuries. The goddess had given them that love. She could not turn her back on it. To do so would be to profane it. She willed the vision away and the grove disappeared. She was in darkness.

:Nothing comes without being sought. Nothing powerful can come without a test.:

She turned toward a flare of light — a figure in a blue cape trimmed with white bears stepped out of a spiral of green and blue.

She saw the face.

She saw the dagger.

:Do you really know what perfect trust is?:

She was afraid. She had said no. She wanted to run.

:Then go.:

Not this, not this, not this — it wasn't going to be completion for her. Not a new beginning.

Oblivion.

:Then run.:

She wanted to retreat as the regal figure approached her. Chestnut-hair coiled on her brow like a crown. The dagger was held in the crook of one arm, a queen's scepter.

She was not aware that she wasn't breathing. She was not aware that terror had cost her control of her bladder. Her eyes streamed with tears.

Completion, beginning, oblivion.

Became, becoming, shall be.

:Run while there's still time.:

She stared up into the haughty face, frightened to the

point of tunnel vision. Her blood was cold while her head felt hot enough to melt. She saw the dagger move. It was lifted.

The cruel clarity of Uda's intent possessed her mind. *:The lamb, always the lamb.:*

I am what I am, Taylor thought. I am what I will be.

She lowered her head and stood ready for the blow. Oblivion, then.

Her hair was lifted from her neck. To make the blow easier, to make it quicker? She didn't know.

Oblivion, then.

The dagger was cold fire and it burned.

Wendy's mouth was hot and hungry. Kelly pressed her hard into her door, feeling the kiss like fire in her arms and legs.

:How did she know I wanted it like this? I don't care if she fucks me right here where anyone could see us.:

Wendy was arching hard up against her. Kelly's hand firmly stroked between her legs. She was welcomed there with the promise of heat and wet when Wendy was naked.

:I want her to tear my clothes off. Rip them off my body and take me, hard and completely.:

Kelly felt a moment of uncertainty. True desire or fantasy? The more aroused Wendy became the more difficult it was to tell the difference. The difference would matter to her, for a little while longer.

"Open the door," she said huskily, when at last Wendy needed to breathe.

Once inside, Kelly swept Wendy up in her arms. She kissed Wendy as she carried her to the bedroom, a deep, thrusting kiss that was a promise. She spread Wendy out on her bed, then let herself fall heavily on top of her, pinning her down.

:I could get lost in her. She's as strong as I need. God, I can hardly breathe.:

She gave Wendy more air, then kissed her again, this time gently, sweetly, for reassurance. "This is what you want, isn't it?"

"Yes," Wendy groaned. Her mind shimmered with the pure blue of Yes.

That Yes tore into Kelly, setting her nerves ablaze. She straddled Wendy and ripped open her blouse, stripped off her skirt and hose, made her naked, spread her legs open.

The pure blue of Yes never wavered. She wrapped Wendy's hands around the spindles in her headboard, seeing in Wendy's mind that they had been used that way before. "Keep them there," she ordered. The pure blue of Yes never wavered.

This is what I am, Kelly thought. What no one has ever wanted me to be. What I wouldn't let myself be. This is as much love as anything can be, because it's what we both want.

Like a ripple in the air around her, she felt the chill of certainty in her shoulders, her hands. *This is the goddess in both of us.*

She was inside Wendy and Wendy was crying with pent-up passion. She clung to the headboard and let her hips answer Kelly's strength. *:I've always wanted it like this! Always!:*

Pure blue boiled toward white. Wendy's body reached for its pleasure point and Kelly felt, at last, the rising of her own tide. She let Wendy's resounding Yes guide her. She was driving Wendy to heights Wendy had dreamed of but never experienced. She knew what Wendy wanted. Her head began to swirl with the giddiness of the power she had over Wendy. She had always known what they all really wanted.

Wendy was trying to talk, but her words were incoherent. Her mind went to searing white, her body responded with a clasping tightness that tried to suspend itself in time, to stay there in the moment of complete ecstasy. *:Never, oh my God, never. The best . . . oh my God. I can't believe what she did to me.:*

She knew what Wendy wanted, had brought Wendy to this incredible place. Wendy wanted more even than this. Her fantasies cried for more, for all night, for every No to become Yes.

She moved against Wendy's tightness, ignored it. She could raise Wendy up again. She was strong enough to do it. She was powerful enough to make Wendy love her for it.

Was it minutes or days, hours or weeks? She pushed into Wendy and felt a hot, heavy, addictive pleasure in it. Her gate was open and she tumbled through the chaos.

She became a stone, skipping across the still surface of a silver lake. She faced down the bullies, and Liz cried. She walked a plow through rocky soil. When she rested Liz was there to give her water. She was dressed in men's clothes as she sailed into a new port in a new world. She had left the old world and what she had become there. Women danced for her, danced for her customers. Faceless women cleaved to her, let her show them what they wanted. She stopped her ears to their cries, left them to their tears. Liz knew it all. Liz suffered enough for both of them.

Autumn was crooning, "Love me, my lord," then alluded to a quest to find their past. And she skipped again, further back, into the past, into the crow's nest, into Ursula's arms. She could make Ursula love her again . . . she was strong enough to make her do anything. She should never have regretted that moment. She gave Ursula what she . . . deserved.

:No!:

Was that cry her own? Or Ursula's? It seemed so far away, or so long ago. Ursula hadn't said no then. She'd never said no. She hadn't believed she needed to. Ursula had never really known her.

Wendy's hands were on her shoulders, pushing desperately against Kelly's weight.

Kelly surfaced to a sound like the crack of a whip. Disoriented, she felt Wendy's palm smack across her mouth again and only then, not knowing how long it had been, did she see that the pure blue of Yes was gone.

The echo of Ursula's voice was faint. "My moon blood," she had tried to lie.

:Mother's grace, gods, what have I done?:

Wendy was sobbing as Kelly tried, and failed, not to hurt her any further as she pulled out of her. "I'm so sorry," she repeated, and she kept saying it even when Wendy curled into a fetal ball.

She tried to touch her gently, to show her it had been an accident. She stroked the red hair that spread limply across the pillow. She hadn't hurt her on purpose. She hadn't wanted the night to be like this, and she hadn't enjoyed having so much power.

And part of her knew she was lying.

Wendy suddenly kicked out with an angry curse, catching Kelly in the hip. She thumped to the floor and kept rolling, scrambling for the door. She needed the heady, clear air of home but found none in the dankness of the large, ancient city's early morning. A cab took her back to the hotel and she found Liz asleep, her hands clasped around the back of her neck. Liz would never know what had happened.

She could forget it happened.

She scrubbed the blood off her hand and would not look at herself in the mirror.

Seven

The *Verdant Bough*, well-watered and provisioned, had no need to cling to the coast of any land. She struck out for the open sea and trimmed tight to the wind that blew them south, toward the continent.

Autumn reveled in a long-absent joy as the bow plunged and rose. In the early mornings, while Killera still slept, she would creep out of their cabin to haunt the deck or share a quiet word or two with the captain.

It was clear that Edrigo did not remember her, not the way that Scylla did. His wariness of a woman on board quickly faded. They were soon exchanging stories of strange customs and lands. With Scylla at her feet she told him all she could of coasts he'd never seen and gave him names of faraway families who were known, like Lord Aldtyme, for honest dealing and even-handed rewards for those who served them well. It was painful, to speak with him as a stranger, but his presence brought back memories of carefree days and unconditional happiness.

When cook's helper brought up the first bowl of meal, Autumn would slip below again, wake Killera with a kiss and they would share breakfast.

She knew, as she went through the daily routine, that Killera was thinking this was forever. Every day would be like the last, that she had found a way to be happy with what life had dealt her. Killera didn't remember Ursula, not really. The joy she sought in Autumn's body, her yearning for a shared, even-keeled life, was — Autumn was certain — the echo of the peaceful world Killera had once known. The mind didn't remember, but the spirit did.

That life was gone, as shattered by Uda's designs as Ursula herself had been. None of them could have anything like happiness unless Ursula was found. When her conscience chided her for the way she planted desire in Killera, kept her from questioning what they were doing, and shushed away distractions she had only one answer.

It was all for Ursula.

She did not let herself wonder if Ursula would understand or forgive crimes such as these.

She had not been able to persuade Elspeth to come above deck the first several days, but by the fifth she agreed, looking more like the Elspeth from that first voyage. Being away from land and crowds was obviously good for her.

Killera greeted them on the aft castle where the captain spread his maps and calculations. Elspeth stumbled on the steps when she first saw her cousin and Autumn sitting together. Killera rose to steady her, then sank down next to Autumn again.

Autumn sensed the questions in Elspeth and knew she would have to be cautious. Killera's questions she could handle more easily. Though she was sorry for the necessity of distracting Killera with passion, it worked. Getting to Eibingen was all that mattered. Killera had never met the composer of the new chants for St. Ursula's feast day, but it was a woman, an abbess as famed for her visions as for her music.

Hilea, Autumn knew. It had to be Hilea. That this abbess also wrote unstinting praise and equally beautiful liturgies for the White Christ did not deter her. It was Hilea. Hilea had probably forgotten as much as Killera had. Autumn would help her remember.

She was wise enough to ask herself why she remembered so much when Killera and Elspeth did not. She was not wise enough to even guess at an answer.

"My lord?" Elspeth's voice was hesitant and hoarse from lack of use. She looked closely at Killera's face and murmured, "Of course."

But Autumn she regarded with puzzlement, as if her presence in the crook of Killera's arm simply did not make sense. Elspeth was too fragile to question or control, Autumn felt. Distracting her with passion would not work. "The sea seems to suit you."

"Yes, I feel much better. It's so quiet." She sat gingerly on the end of the deck bench that was sheltered from the wind at their backs.

Quiet, with the wind howling, the sail throbbing, the sea marking time against the hull? Autumn asked, with seeming nonchalance, "You've not been to sea before?"

Elspeth shook her head, but without conviction.

"Not that I remember," Killera said. Her arm tightened around Autumn's waist.

Autumn had been focused on Elspeth and what she might need to do to keep everything appearing as normal as possible while she got them all to Eibingen. For a moment her light control of Killera wavered.

"Of course I seem to know so little," Killera added. Her

grip went beyond affection. "You always seem to avoid my questions."

:She is desirable.: Autumn added a mental image of how they had been that first night, discovering they were women, reveling in their bodies and the glory of their passion. She felt Killera relax again.

"Is Ursula there? In Germany?"

Elspeth's innocent question shattered the fragile hold Autumn had on Killera's suspicions and awareness that she was being used.

"Ursula?" Killera grasped Elspeth's arm. "What do you know about her?"

"Let her go, my lord." Autumn succeeded in turning Killera's attention back to her.

"We're going to Germany to find Ursula? She's a saint, she can only help us in our dreams."

"I know, my lord," Autumn soothed. So that explained Lord Aldtyme's patronage of the feast. Ursula was in Killera's dreams. "We all dream of her, don't we? Ask for her guidance? She was a virgin, wasn't she, just as you and I are?"

Killera's grip was bruising. "Tell me what you know. Everything you know about her. I — I only . . ." Her gaze was suddenly unfocused and her grip loosened. "No."

"My lord —"

"No, it's not supposed to be you. How could I? What are you doing to me?"

"Calmly, my lord." Autumn desperately sent more memories of them together, texturing it with what she re-membered — so vividly — of Ursula's hair and skin. *:Ursula would understand. Autumn is merely a substitute. Ursula would understand that I felt the goddess move in us both. Ursula would understand.:*

"Calmly? Gently? You go too far — I am what I am." Killera's voice was rising. "I won't take instruction from you. What are you? Who are you?"

:She can be Ursula for me.: Autumn was desperate. Killera

150

could easily order them back to England. She felt this chance to find Hilea slipping through her fingers. She was aware of Elspeth looking on with faintness as Killera's anger lashed out.

:*She can be Ursula for me.*: Autumn would sacrifice her body if it kept her on this path. :*She can be all that Ursula ever was for me.*:

Killera seized her then, anger and fear fusing into want. Autumn could feel the leers of the sailors nearby as Killera kissed her mouth and shoulders. No one, especially Elspeth, had any doubt why they went below-deck, not with Killera half carrying her there.

The lantern clacked rhythmically against the cabin wall as the sea and bed churned. Autumn slowed Killera as much as she could, and then stopped herself. She was doing no small damage to Killera, she knew that, and at least, in this small way, she could give Killera some measure of joy. She kept her eyes tightly closed and offered no resistance.

Neither of them was anywhere near the goddess.

Clack, clack . . . it grew more rhythmic and the rocking of the sea changed to a thumping under her back. Autumn rubbed her face with her hand and cast out momentarily. Ursula was there, still asleep in the train bunk below her.

Gods — how had she ever justified using Killera like that? Using herself like that? For a moment, as the train hurtled through the night, she knew that the Ursula she loved would never accept that kind of price.

"I think it's safe to say there are no casinos here. Good thing we don't need more cash." Autumn scanned the down town district of Denver. Vegas was about gambling, about winners and losers. This place felt different, as if more of it was under the surface than what she could see with her eyes. The air was crisp and heady, though, after nearly twenty hours of the stale train. Mountains rose around them, crusted with green and dotted with white.

At first she'd thought they should get off the train in one of the many quiet nowheres it stopped, but it had occurred to her that they were more likely to be noticed in a small place. A luminous redhead that everyone seemed to look at twice, a brooding black-clad woman with stark white hair barely a half-inch long all over her head, and a dog — not quite the usual traveling group. The first truly large city they had reached had been Salt Lake City, but they'd arrived after ten p.m. Leaving the train for the night had been an option, but staying aboard they had been able to sleep without feeling pursued. When they'd awakened at daybreak, there had been time to visit Scylla with food from the dining car, have a meal themselves and freshen up before disembarking.

Autumn felt reassuringly lost in the faceless crowds. Their first order of business had been a market that carried dog food. Poor Scylla had been pathetically hungry for a proper meal. When they passed a small park she had run herself until her tongue dragged on the ground, followed by a romp in a patch of dirt. She now carried herself like a dog without a care in the world, albeit a dirty one.

"There will be phones in a large hotel, won't there? Where we can make several calls?" Ursula had chased Scylla for part of the fun at the park, and her face still glowed with the enjoyment of the exercise.

"I would think so." Autumn ushered Ursula into a steel and glass box. At least in Vegas they made interesting hotels.

"Ma'am!"

Autumn turned at the sharp call obviously directed at them.

"No pets." The doorman waved at Scylla.

"Sorry." They went back outside, uncertain what to do.

"In a large city like this, there's probably a law against

leaving her unleashed," Autumn muttered. She glanced at the well-kept street. "And in this part of town they'd enforce it. Plus now you look like a stray, girl."

Scylla looked up at her as if she understood. Autumn wouldn't have been at all surprised to learn that she did.

"Let's find a small hotel," Ursula suggested. "Maybe we won't have to be so far from the door."

"I have a better idea," Autumn said. She walked back to the doorman, waiting until she had his attention. "We wanted to go inside for a while, use the phones, grab a bite to eat. I don't suppose you could keep her behind your desk here?" She held up a neatly folded twenty.

"Is she dangerous?"

"Only if you are." She wasn't joking, but the doorman's attention was on the twenty. The bill changed hands and Autumn told Scylla where she needed to stay.

Scylla looked after them mournfully, but settled calmly behind the doorman's desk.

"It's no life for a dog," Autumn said.

"This won't be our life," Ursula answered. "It can't be."

Autumn didn't ask, "But what if it is the only way you can be safe?" Ursula had no idea, really, of what they were up against. For that matter, neither did she.

The phones presented their first difficulty — they took only coins or credit cards. Autumn asked for change at the front desk, and the clerk suggested she buy a calling card at the gift shop.

"There's a whole world out there I just never took any notice of," she told Ursula.

"I think I know what you mean." Ursula shrugged self-deprecatingly. "When I saw the price scanners at the grocery store with Kelly I was amazed."

Autumn waited, but Ursula turned toward the phones, not even realizing she'd recovered another memory. Autumn let the moment pass. Later she might be able to prompt Ursula about it. From a grocery store to the name of a city wasn't that far a journey in the mind.

Was that what they were doing? Trying to find Kelly again? Autumn resisted the very idea. Kelly hadn't done such a good job protecting Ursula. Autumn had saved her from Uda just in time.

Her reluctance had nothing to do with what she had done to Killera, with what she did not want to face, and did not want Ursula to know.

Ursula sat down at the phone with her list of businesses. "I think you're right, the grocer first."

* * * * *

Something had been taken from her. In the moment of waking Taylor could not remember what it might be. At first, in the awareness that oblivion could include the feel of moss under her cheek and pebbles clenched in her fingers, she was grateful to exist, to think.

She felt the ringing echo of No in her bones but with painful clarity recalled her submission to the will of the goddess, working through the Norns. She had refused a choice, though she did not understand it — the apple or the axe.

She turned her head, then sat up with a gasp. She put her hand to the back of her neck, feeling a cool breeze on it.

Memory surged, of terror, of the dagger. She'd felt the cold fire on her neck. It had taken her past, then, not her soul. Her hair, unbraided, had been cut. What she had been she would never be again. Another memory threatened to overwhelm her, that of Uda severing her braid in the abbey as a prelude to killing both her and Elspeth. This could be a prelude as well, but to what? If her death had been wanted she would be dead. The idea of Uda being in that sacred place was incomprehensible. That vision of Liz — that, too, was something she could not understand. Liz would never re-

154

proach her by taking another lover. That was not Liz and she knew Liz perhaps better than she knew herself. Didn't she?

She had lost her past. She smoothed the back of her neck and wondered if it was weak to hope she had paid all her debts now. She wanted to mourn, but only moments ago she had been grateful just to exist. She would remember the past — she had no choice. But she could choose not to dwell there.

She'd thought she understood that lesson, but only now did it have the bittersweet poignancy of loss.

How long had she been out? Shadows said it was noon. She was famished. It was a wobbly start but she got to her feet and took stock of where she was. She knew it immediately. She was on the trail into Aldtyme, next to the last marker. She had taken that final step right here. She had been returned to the point where her changing began, but she did not know why. Well, she was too hungry to go anywhere but back into the little town.

She took the step again and ended up flat on her back on the trail.

It took a moment for her to realize what had happened. She had rebounded from the circle that enveloped Aldtyme. The circle had let her in before. Now it was closed to her.

:*Even they no longer want you.*:

That voice — it wasn't Aunt Peela. She recognized it now. She slapped it out of her head with an intensity meant to sting and heard only a distant laughter. Well, she'd gotten some of her powers back, and that was good. Her shields were intact and the chaos — with that taunting, hateful voice — was no danger at the moment.

She gave herself a few minutes to wonder why she was kept from returning to Aldtyme. She had been changed, her braid taken. She didn't believe she was supposed to do something to earn her way back — she had been given no quest that she could recall. Was she being exiled, was this further punishment for her weaknesses and pride? It was the more likely answer.

There was no way to know. She could sit there all day and wonder, getting hungrier and hungrier, or she could get off her butt and walk back to Hornsea. She was so hungry, she'd even welcome tuna and corn pizza again.,

She turned her back on Aldtyme, having learned nothing about Ursula. A different path, she mused. Time to find a new way.

She was abruptly aware of two figures on the trail in the distance, walking toward her. They were hazy to her eyes but she felt her heart stir. One was slight with wheaten hair reflecting the day's bright sunlight, the other tall, broad and powerful, with hair only slightly darker, but short cropped where the other's was long enough to lift in the breeze.

She saw them, and this new path was so much easier to embrace. The distance between them closed and if she'd had the strength she would have run. She grinned across the last few feet that separated them, but it faded as she realized that Liz wasn't smiling.

A quick glance at Kelly didn't find any happiness there either.

Liz's eyes brimmed with tears, then she ran her fingers through Taylor's hair, brushing the short ends. "I wanted to be with you. I couldn't make it in time."

Liz had already known? It made no sense. She caught a hand in her own and kissed the palm. To her shock, Liz pulled away.

Oh, selfish, she thought. Liz was in agony. "When did you lose your shields?"

"Yesterday, just before I left home."

"I'm sorry, so sorry. It was probably because I — because I went in there." It would be hard to explain what she meant by "there" but even as she began, Liz was nodding.

"I know. It's my turn."

Kelly, who had been staring at the rocks along the trail, said sharply, "What?"

"It's my turn to go in. You went, and found Ursula. Taylor went and was changed. I must go now."

"Honey, what are you talking about?" She had at first thought that Liz was like she had been when they had first met, anguished, withdrawn, flirting with madness. But there was more than that now. She stared into Liz's eyes, wanting to look into her mind, to help if she could, but it was only then that she realized she lacked the power. She had shields but it was as if the muscle that let her touch minds with others had been cut out of her. For the first time in her life she had to ask what another person was thinking, was feeling. "Can you tell me?"

"No." Liz swallowed hard, then angrily brushed away a tear that spilled over. "I've never told anyone. But I know this path now. I must go." She shuddered.

Kelly was the one who put her arms around her. "I don't think that's a good idea." She turned to Taylor. "We left London this morning. I had to carry her half the way here from Hornsea. She wouldn't wait for the next bus or try to hitch a ride. She insisted we be on this trail as soon as possible."

To meet me here, Taylor thought. She knew I would be here. It was a testament to the strength of their bond, of course. But what was it that Liz had never told her, that had been hidden during all the ways they had opened their minds to each other? "How can I help?"

"You can't. You can't go back, so I must go alone."

Increasingly discomfited by Liz's awareness of things she had no way of knowing, Taylor could only nod. "How did you know?"

"I know this path." Liz took a deep shuddering breath, then gently pushed Kelly away. "I must do this by myself now. You must both go home. She is coming."

"Who? Liz, what's going on?" Taylor had thought she had no more to lose, no more to pay, but what was this? A Liz she

157

did not know, a Liz who was scaring the crap out of her. "Who is coming?"

"Ursula." Her breath caught with a choked back sob.

The truth came to Taylor like a thunderclap. All the love between them was founded on half-understanding, half-awareness. Their love was true, a gift from the goddess, yes, but there was more to Liz than she had ever known. "You see flashes of the future, don't you?"

Liz closed her eyes. She didn't say yes. Or no. She swayed and it was Taylor who caught her, pulling her close in what was a stranger's awkward embrace.

"I didn't choose this," she murmured in Liz's ear. "I would have chosen nothing that cost me you."

"I know." She felt Liz's lips against her neck. "There is more at work here than our choices. I love you. That will not change."

"But you're leaving me," Taylor said, close to her own tears. "How far into the future can you see?" She wanted to ask if Liz would come back to her, but she was afraid of the answer. She had never been afraid of anything with Liz before.

Liz gently disentangled herself from Taylor, saying nothing. The effort not to speak was obvious in her clenched lips.

"Do something," Taylor said to Kelly.

Kelly smugly asked, "Aren't you the one who thinks everyone should do what the goddess tells them?"

No help there, she should have known. But she didn't know anything. Kelly was blank to her, so was Liz.

Liz was walking toward Aldtyme. She wasn't looking back.

"Do something," she said again, desperate. What was happening? What had broken so quickly? She was helpless, for the first time in her life not knowing what was going on around her. This wasn't a spelling test she would fail, this was her life, her love, the only thing that mattered now. "Liz!"

She ran after her, still calling her name. Liz couldn't know she was delivering herself to the Norns, who held past, present and future in their hands. What would they make of Liz, who was tangled in all three?

Liz stopped next to the marker. She needed only one last step. She looked over her shoulder at Taylor, but just before Taylor might have touched her she took the final step.

Taylor cannoned into the circle's protections. Up became down, a spinning of blue, green and white. A dark mass slammed into her.

Eight

"It's going through," Ursula announced. She was perched on the kiosk's stool with the business listing clutched in one hand and the phone in the other. "I — I hardly know what to say."

"Just say you're hoping to find someone who knows Ursula."

Ursula gazed up at her with her attention on the phone. "What time is it there?"

"I don't know," Autumn admitted. "They're something like nine or ten hours ahead of us, I think."

"No one is answering."

"Damn."

"Wait — Hullo? Yes. Are you there? Sorry about the connection. Look, this may seem a bit off, but I'm trying to find someone who knows Ursula and anything you can tell me will help."

Autumn listened to Ursula's accent deepen, then realized Ursula had fished a pencil from her pocket to jot something down.

"Can you tell me Ursula's last name? I'm calling all the way from America. Oh, of course I understand. I'll speak to Miss Muldoon, then. You've been super."

She hung up and Autumn realized she was trembling. "Are you okay?"

"Yes, I'm just excited. I felt like I ought to have recognized the voice." She dialed the new phone number, next to which she had written "P. Muldoon."

"Hullo? Is this Miss Muldoon? She's not? When do you expect her back?" Ursula listened intently. "No, I won't be here. You sound American, you sound like . . ." Ursula abruptly dropped the receiver and put both hands to her forehead with a grimace of sheer agony.

Autumn grabbed the phone. An excited voice jabbered in her ear. "Hello? Who is this?"

"Liz — what happened to Ursula?"

"She's a little overwhelmed," Autumn said carefully. Liz? Surely not . . . "This is going to sound strange, but can you tell me what Ursula's last name is?"

"Columbine. Ursula Columbine."

"Columbine," Autumn echoed. Ursula was staring at her with both pain and knowledge in her face. "My name is Autumn —"

"I know." Liz's voice was calm and even. "I knew she was with you. I just didn't know where."

"Who — who are you?"

"Liz Shepherd."

"I know this is very strange —"

"No, no, we've all been hoping she would contact us. Why did she wait so long?"

"She's had some problems with her memory." Autumn wasn't sure how honest she could be with this stranger who seemed to know a great deal. "How do you know Ursula?"

"She's my cousin's lover . . ." There was an awkward pause. "I mean, she was. Kelly."

Autumn choked back a gasp. Ursula was already in too much distress. She didn't want to add to it by showing her shock. "Liz," she repeated, feeling dizzy. Whispered, "Elspeth?"

"Yes. What are you planning?"

The question was asked in stereo. The voice in her ear was steady and firm, the voice in her memory subdued. Wide-awake, in the instant between one heartbeat and the next she stood toe-to-toe with Elspeth on *Verdant Bough*'s forecastle.

"I don't know what you mean," she said in answer to Elspeth's question.

"I can sense . . . you're desperate, you're excited, sometimes you're euphoric, but not when you're with her. Then you're determined no matter what she does. Sometimes I can tell that you like it. And she's . . ." Elspeth dropped her voice. "She's having these wild bursts of love, but she's so angry, so angry with everything, including you, for what it's been like all her life. She suffers so much. I try to stand it. I try to take what I can."

"I don't understand." Autumn watched Elspeth's misty golden eyes fill with tears. "What do you try to take?"

"She radiates, she's like a star. It has to go somewhere. That's the only thing I think I'm good for. There isn't anything else, except the dreams —"

"Dreams?"

Elspeth's distress gave way to irritation. "Don't pretend. You have them, too. That's why we're going to Germany, isn't it? Because of dreams?"

Autumn shook her head. "They're not dreams to me. They're memories."

Elspeth looked at her for a very long moment, then she

shook her head. "I believe you, though I don't understand." She swallowed quickly, then said in a rush, "I saw your face in my dream, I see it in the past and the future." Her hand clutched Autumn's arm. "Please don't tell anyone. I shouldn't have said that. They'll burn me —"

"I will never tell anyone," Autumn murmured. "Never. What am I doing in the future you dreamed about?"

"You're dying," Elspeth whispered. "You are always dying."

The words knocked the breath out of her and the next thing she knew she was being shaken. Ursula, her brow furrowed with distress, was jostling her arm.

"Come back," she whispered. "I need you, please."

The ship was gone and Autumn felt adrift and undirected, like a kite whose string has been cut. Half her brain was adjusting to the rocking sway of a vessel at full sail while the other was coping with the intricacies of technology and the awareness of danger at any corner.

"Are you there?" The voice in her ear sounded anxious.

Autumn tried to give Ursula what she hoped was a reassuring smile. From Ursula's expression she could tell she had utterly failed. She gripped the kiosk door with one hand out of Ursula's sight and hoped the world would right itself in a minute. "I'm here," she said as steadily as she could manage.

"What are you planning to do now? Kelly and Taylor will be at Kelly's by tomorrow evening. They're expecting you then or shortly thereafter."

Autumn didn't know who Taylor was and why she mattered. If she focused she could hear the clanging of a ship's bell. "How do I know you're really Elspeth?"

There was another long pause, then, "You and I were in the second boat. You should be able to tell me between where and where."

Autumn's heart thumped painfully. "Between the *Verdant Bough* and the shore in Germany."

"It *is* you," Liz murmured. "I knew you would be there for her."

"A dream of the future again?"

There was a long, long silence. Just as Autumn was thinking Liz had hung up, Liz said, "I don't remember telling you about that. I've never told anyone, not even Taylor."

"You don't remember telling me. I've only just recalled it myself. You didn't tell Ursula about it?"

"How could I when I don't know if the dreams are what shall be or what might be." Liz's voice was losing all the animation it had had. "What are your plans?"

"We are still pursued. By more than dreams or darkness."

Ursula suddenly pitched forward, her head on Autumn's stomach.

"I must go." Autumn grabbed the listing and pen from Ursula's hand. "Give me the phone numbers for Taylor and Kelly." If nothing else at least she would have this much information.

Liz rattled them off. "Taylor is more likely to check for messages. It's a habit."

Ursula was conscious, just exhausted. Autumn had to ask Liz one more question. "I'm sorry, but who is Taylor?"

"That's right, you wouldn't know. The abbess, Claire."

Of course, thought Autumn. The picture was almost complete. That answer begged another question. "Do you know where Hilea is?"

"No. There's nothing of her anywhere."

"Just her music."

"Of course," Liz said automatically. "It has survived."

"Where does Kelly live?"

"Paradise," Ursula murmured. "In Pennsylvania."

Liz echoed Ursula's words. "How long will it be until you can get there?"

Autumn knew she should be relieved that some contact had been made with Ursula's past, but was horrified at the idea of facing Kelly, who might remember the past Autumn and Killera had shared. "We're moving pretty slowly." She did not want to say how. "Probably about forty-eight hours. But you have to understand — everyone has to understand. My first priority is protecting Ursula. If I get the feeling that a reunion is not safe we won't show. We'll think of something else."

"I understand. Would you tell Ursula that her aunts have gone beyond the gate?"

"What does that mean?"

"She will know." Liz sighed. When she next spoke her voice was flat. "I have to go. I was waiting for this call, but it's time now."

Autumn wanted to ask what Liz knew about the future. Was she dying, still? But Liz had already hung up and Ursula needed her. She went to her knees and pulled Ursula's head to her shoulder. "It was a shock, coming back all at once."

Ursula nodded against her neck. "I remember everything now. I told her I loved her, though I knew I loved you. I made her prove she loved me so I could leave her."

"Was there another choice?"

"I could have died in her arms, at least then she wouldn't have known that I used her to set me free."

"It would have been a lie." Autumn put her arms around Ursula's shoulders. They both had so much guilt for how they had treated Killera.

"Truth didn't serve her very well."

"Let's get some fresh air," Autumn suggested. "It'll do us both good."

Scylla heeled the moment they stepped onto the sidewalk outside the hotel. The world stabilized and Autumn didn't have to feign her steadiness any longer.

"We have to go to Kelly," Ursula said after a minute of slow walking. "I have to at least tell her I'm sorry. She's never forgiven herself for . . ."

"For what?"

Ursula shook her head. "It's nothing. Just between her and me. I made it worse."

Autumn was little practiced at jealousy. In the ten years she had in this life she'd felt mostly contempt for other people and herself. Jealousy was what this emotion had to be, she thought. It was irrational. It distorted her focus. She could easily forget to maintain the guards she always had on watch for danger. Emotions were dangerous. She had no context for controlling them. Not yet — she still had so much she had not remembered.

She had found her love. They had found Ursula's memories from this life. They were headed for a reunion with women who had suffered and died for belief in what Ursula had represented in the past. It was a future she had never envisioned, rich with the promise of knowledge, finally, and understanding of what the tapestry of their joined pasts meant.

But all she could hear in the swirling, dizzy recesses of her mind was Elspeth's voice saying of the future, "You're dying . . . you are always dying."

* * * * *

"What did any of that get us?" Kelly didn't want to start a fight with Taylor. That hardly served her purposes. She had kept her promise to Rachel by helping Liz, but she had nothing to tell Rachel when she returned.

Taylor would say nothing about what had happened to her, though Kelly could tell she was vastly changed. It wasn't just the bad haircut. She was also bruised. If Kelly hadn't seen it she would never have believed that empty air had flung Taylor to the ground like a rag. Liz had never looked back. Liz's decision, the revelation of her insights into the future had stunned her, stunned them both.

"I don't know yet." Taylor alternated between staring out

of the airplane window at the unbroken floor of puffy white clouds and chewing absentmindedly on her thumbnail.

"They told you nothing, nothing at all?" It wasn't the first time she had asked that question. She had asked it in many different forms as they had made their way back to Manchester. Purchasing open-ended return flights had allowed them to book as they pleased. Money down the drain, Kelly thought. For a moment she worried about her farm and her finances, then the pang eased as she thought of what waited for her when she got home. She had kept her promise.

"I told you — nothing, nothing at all. Except they're not worried." Taylor went back to gazing out the window, this time chewing on her thumbnail at the same time.

Kelly tried for sleep, and quickly found herself lost in competing memories. Rachel, wild for anything, Wendy in ecstasy. She circled between them, knowing what they wanted, giving what they yearned for, delivering on their fantasies.

She easily pushed away the memory of blood on her fingers — she had no guilt over that. She knew what they all wanted.

Even Autumn had wanted it.

She thought for a moment, as the plane rocked gently in the air, that she was falling asleep and would dream about Autumn and the *Verdant Bough*. Instead, she felt the light touch of Rachel's mind, as if from far away.

:You have done well. She will be yours, again.:

Kelly wanted to answer, but she had a curious sensation of falling. Rachel was very hard to hear.

:Learn what you are. You are finally ready to know.:

The last time she had learned about her pasts she had skipped like a stone across the surface of a silver lake. This time she plunged into cold, as if the lake swallowed her.

She could not hear Rachel at all, but she was in this place because Rachel wanted her to learn. Learn what?

She turned at the sound of laughter. She was in a garden. Scattered figures in white robes sat in quiet contemplation

167

while others gathered around a figure in gray, listening carefully to something read from a thick book.

She wore gray as well. She was speaking of the plants, the berries, the age of the tree that gave them shade from the sun.

Kelly smiled. She had loved this place. This was who she was: a listener, a teacher, a woman who loved nature.

Then it all changed. She answered questions, quieted the novices until they all agreed that a nap was what they mightily desired on this one day of rest. Then she slipped away for a walk, not for the first time. She was followed, not for the first time. Five minutes walk brought her to the tight copse where she would be sheltered and warm — not for the first time.

Their bodies collided. Novice Ruth, Novice Margaret . . . it didn't matter. Whoever it was this time was there for what they all desired to learn: what they wanted, how they liked it. Fragile white limbs flashed in the sunlight. It was all ecstasy, for both of them. It always became tears on their side. That was what she taught them. No pleasure could be bought without some payment in pain.

:The burden of fire is upon you.:

They told their friends, who sought the same lessons. An afternoon in the sun, an hour in the less comfortable storeroom off the cloister house, none of them cared where. Only the most delicate did not at one time or another come to her for tutelage.

:The blood of Ursula is upon us. Now let us all rejoice.:

When they drove her from the cloister, left her in sackcloth and ashes, a marked beggar in the streets, it was punishment for her unnatural acts. Unnatural not for her weakness for women, but for her strength in loving them. Most of the sisters had their particular friends, after all, but she was the only one who could lift a woman up to heights that rivaled the rapture of Christ. Her final transgression, as they had called it, had been with the particular friend of the abbess herself. If Sister Patience had just kept her own counsel there wouldn't have been such uproar. Like all the others it had been yes, yes, spectacularly, vibrantly yes. Sister Patience was the only one who did not forgive her for not listening when yes inevitably became no.

:Let dreams vanish in the distance.:

She begged in the streets and fought for survival, blinked, and was in a new time of velvet and doublets, hose and lace ruffs. A woman of means, but solitary. A teacher again, for the innocent who wanted to learn. This time she did the casting out of those who displeased her.

:The ghosts of darkness transfix our enemies.:

This time she saw herself coldly meting out pleasure, when properly asked. She felt no guilt, no shame. There was a flash of Liz's face. Liz saw it all.

Something was pulling at her to rise from the cold. Rachel? For only an instant she remembered that Rachel was not real.

:Enough, you've learned enough.:

But there was more to know, and she pushed Rachel's voice away so she could have it all. The stone melted into a boisterous and noisy bordello where women danced in ruffled skirts, showing their legs and fine muscles for the price of admission. She oversaw it all, took in new girls to work for her, but only after she had trained them. They were no longer virgins, pure of men — when had that ever mattered?

Out of nowhere, a gun. *:My daughter was the last you'll have!:*

It exploded against her temple. She fell into oblivion with a cry that became the caw of a seabird. She was sailing again, this time with the rumble of an engine below her feet and hidden by men's clothing. Pressed with the masses she fled the old for the new, to try again. She left what she had become in the depths of the sea.

She had only been seeking a way to be strong and not afraid of strength. To push the limits of desire and not the limits of pleasure. She only wanted to be who she was, without apologies. Frustration, mistaken passion, the thrill of power had led her astray. But it wasn't all just her — she had learned to use from Autumn. In all that she had learned to be, some part of it was from Autumn, including a violent death that had finished that world for her.

She found land, a place of quietness. Liz helped her, Liz who had seen it all. Liz guided her to peace and she tried, often failing, to make the world easier for Liz to bear. Together they broke soil and recreated the magic of the goddess: birth, growth, death, regeneration. She believed, again, that love could be strong but gentle, that power did not mean pain.

All that lacked was the completion of her soul. She had found that again, finally, in Ursula.

:Milk and honey under her tongue. Nothing but lies in her mouth.:

She'd thought she'd found it, until Autumn took Ursula away. Ursula had loved her. She did not want to remember that she had hurt Ursula.

:Peace is a sham. Gentleness is thrust on women to keep them weak. You were gentle with her and she made you prove your love anyway. She lied when she said she loved you.:

No, Kelly thought. No. Yes.

:I will give you the woman she ought to have been for you. She will only know Yes.:

Kelly trembled.

A thread of magenta flashed into the cold depths of her pasts. Her mind blazed with a single note of pure gold. *:Where are you?:*

She opened her eyes to find Taylor's sharp blue gaze looking as if it were burning a hole through her brain and into the back of her skull. "I was asleep," she muttered.

"What's going on?"

"Nothing," Kelly snapped. "I had a bad dream."

Taylor was plainly not convinced, but Kelly shifted so she faced the other direction, ignoring the fire in her shoulders

170

and hands as she recalled the way Rachel never said no, the way so many women had moved under her and liked it.

She would not remember the blood on her fingers. She would not heed the scream of the avenging bullet through her brain, nor would she dwell on what she had done to bring that kind of wrath down on herself. It was not her fault alone. Autumn had a price to pay.

She had learned enough. She knew what Taylor — so weak and useless — had never grasped.

Strength was its own permission. Whatever she could take was hers.

Part Three:
Garden of Queens

Glory to God.
If there is no God?
The never ending symphony
— Lea Battle "Symphony of Regret"

Nine

"Ursula, Ursula, is that you?"

The voice from her past tore through the veils in Ursula's
mind. Her temples pounded like drums as knowledge — so
much of it unwanted — poured into her again.

She heard nothing Autumn said to Liz. She struggled instead to keep her senses above a rising tide of grief — gods,
was there anyone she hadn't hurt?

Later, as they waited on a cold platform for the next train
from Denver to Chicago, Ursula accepted the simple and un-
judging warmth of Scylla against her knees.

She couldn't speak, though she knew Autumn had many
questions.

She didn't want to listen, not right now.

They were going to Kelly's, that was all she could take in. That, and the fact that Autumn didn't seem any more eager than she felt at the prospect. But she had to go. She had to say she was sorry and accept Kelly's judgement.

Once aboard it felt as if the rhythm of the train never stopped, a steady clack-clacking that could induce relaxation or madness. Ursula was torn between both.

With memory came skills. So easy — so simple to read strangers now, to tell what Autumn was feeling in spite of her tight, well-controlled shields. She knew if she opened her gate that she could go almost anywhere with her mind. She sensed that if she tried, the darkness would find both of them. Nothing had changed from the way it had been at Kelly's. She was a prisoner of the darkness. These past weeks with Autumn had been mere respite.

She felt shattered by memory and frustrated because she could not use her talents. She sensed that even if she could, it would not make her the person she had been. For as much as she might know now, and as much as she could do, she could not recall anything more substantial than memories of the woman who had left her home for love with such hope. She remembered working in Kelly's gardens, but the purity of her happiness there was beyond her comprehension.

She could not be what she had been. She did not know what she would become. These faces were hidden to her as they had never been before.

Whoever she was, whatever was coming, it was at Kelly's expense, at Taylor's and Liz's — and Autumn's. At such a price could she have any reasonable hope that the future held a moment's peace, a heartbeat of happiness?

She studied Autumn's profile, that beloved face, the exquisite shape of her head, those shoulders that had borne so much and yet she knew were soft and supple. Autumn was in the cabin's only chair, staring at some distant point above Ursula's head. Her body vibrated to the rhythm of the train.

It reminded Ursula of the way Autumn had moved on the deck of the *Verdant Bough*, swaying with absolute grace no matter how the sea undulated.

It had been better to be insensible of the past, to remember nothing, to go where Autumn said, to do what Autumn told her was necessary. Anything was better than the pain in her head and the guilt sapping her will.

She had abandoned safety but not guarded against danger. Kelly paid for her folly. She had not wanted to see her demon, then quailed when it finally came for her. Taylor paid for her cowardice. She escaped into numbness and Autumn suffered from her withdrawal. Was there a place where she could exist without costing others their dreams, their hopes, even their lives?

Who was she to inspire more devotion from others than she could find in herself?

For she did not believe she was a goddess, nor had she ever been. She was too flawed, far too human, and she had made too many mistakes.

Autumn was expecting explanations, but said nothing. Ursula knew she would not ask. It was a small relief — she could not have borne sharing her memories with Autumn, not when for those months between the Vernal Equinox and the Fourth of July she had told Kelly every day she loved her, gone frequently and blissfully to Kelly's bed, her love full of lies.

Fear of the darkness did not excuse her. She hadn't known until Lammas Night, when Taylor's circle had stripped her of her training, what the darkness really was.

Even now she had only a primal, inescapable fear. She would not go back to that place, never again. She would accept obliteration first, by any means.

How far she had fallen . . . in this weakness she would feed the darkness anything, anyone, to spare herself.

She stirred on the lower bunk where she had stretched out, her hand going to her unbraided hair. She had all her memories and skills back, all without the power she had thought was invested in her braid. What had the braid really given her? In the end had she been freed or bound?

Autumn abruptly spoke, her voice hoarse with all too obvious feelings. "Liz said your aunts were beyond the gate."

Ursula nodded. They were at the goddess's hand, safe there. "I understand."

"Do you remember everything now?"

"Yes. Everything." She wanted to take Autumn's hand, tell her that she remembered their love, at last. She wanted to say that she loved her, that the siren song of longing that had pulled her across the continent, across the wasteland of salt, so far to the west, had been quieted, finally.

How could Autumn believe her, now? She'd said the same useless words to Kelly, or most of them anyway. There was only one way to prove it — to both of them — but rapport was too dangerous to attempt. And she could not bear for Autumn to see the doubt and guilt that had taken over her once pure and orderly mind.

Autumn nodded and swallowed hard. The flush of gooseflesh and shiver of recalled pleasure that swept over Autumn was echoed in Ursula's skin. It was a rapport of a kind, and more painful than not. "I think I'll check on Scylla." Autumn was out the door in a flash, leaving behind a jangle of bleak frustration.

Ursula turned off the light and curled against the pillow. She imagined that there was only one bunk, to share such a small space that Autumn would have no choice but to hold her tight and close. They could lose themselves in each other, completely.

Let that be their ending.

Let it all finish in a blaze of passion.

You can't offer her that, she told herself angrily. Once you took her to the stars. But you have gone too far from that place. Seven weeks and more you spent not even thinking, letting her do all the worrying, all the protecting. You'll never be able to offer her anything but shadows now.

She had lost her certainty that trust and love brought happiness and harmony. The pounding headache that had unleashed her memories had become a steady drum of indecision and torment.

What good are you to her? You don't know who or what you are anymore. What good are you to anyone?

She had thought she wanted to remember the past. She'd hoped the past would deliver the future. Now she just wanted to forget. She had never meant to hurt anyone and yet, looking back at all she could recall, at all she had ever known, she could not see the face of anyone she hadn't hurt in some way.

So many faces, streaming an ocean of tears. The ocean refuses no river. As the train rattled into the night her regrets became a flood.

* * * * *

Killera noticed immediately that Autumn did not love her new attire. When they'd taken to port at Dardrecht on the coast of the lowlands, Killera had insisted that Autumn look like the noblewoman she claimed to be. "They are not as comfortable as they are becoming?"

Autumn yanked at the tripping double skirts of the deep blue bliaut gown. The girdle pulled the garment tight across the hips, sharply outlining her figure. She pulled a cloak over her shoulders in spite of the fine day. "No, my lord," she said sharply. "And you know it."

Their journey by barge up the Rhine was begun with laughter, hers at least. Autumn was so rarely discomfited. Killera thought that was a good sign. Autumn had been a little distant these past few days. Not while they dallied in bed, no, that was as intimate as always. But she seemed to have run out of tales to share. Since parting with the captain and his dog she'd been even more cross.

If she let herself, she would dwell on the idea that Autumn was obsessed with finding the composer of St. Ursula's feast chants. That was why they were traveling to Eibingen. She tried to care, but could not find the strength to do it. Everything would be fine, a voice in her head seemed to say.

Elspeth was taking rest in one of the tented pavilions. The motion of the barge was less violent than a ship's, but the side-to-side roll was at first unsettling. It did not seem to bother Autumn, however. Nothing seemed to bother Autumn. Nothing except women's finery.

They were being pulled up the Rhine, from lock to lock, from barge-hold to barge-hold, in a long line of narrow, shallow-hulled vessels of a variety of sizes. Some carried passengers like themselves, while others hauled awkward, heavy cargoes, moving cannons and marble blocks intact with lowlander ingenuity. It was slow progress and would be two days to Cologne and another two to Eibingen where the Nahe and the Rhine joined to flow to the coast. It would take the same time by horse, if one wished to ride the horses to death and did not stop to sleep. They could be made comfortable on the barge.

Comfortable enough, Killera thought, as she settled into the featherbed on the floor of the pavilion she shared with Autumn. She leaned over Autumn to kiss her gently.

"My lord." Autumn's hand rested on Killera's forehead. "My lord. It is time to listen and to speak."

Killera was suddenly afraid as she had never been before in her life, but was helpless to do anything about it. She collapsed onto her side as Autumn shifted out from under her. Her hand never left Killera's forehead.

She asked the only question she could form at that moment, the question Autumn had never answered. "Who are you?"

"I am Autumn. That was never a lie. You ought to remember me, but you don't."

Though her arms and legs wouldn't obey her, her eyes did. She gazed at Autumn and tried to understand.

"You've dreamed of Ursula all your life."

Her fear deepened. How could Autumn know that? Then she felt a snapping in her head, something hot and wrong. She shuddered, wanted to cry out, but could not.

:You have only had dreams. Let me give you memories.:

Her breath caught at the vision of Ursula standing on the gangplank of a ship older than those she knew, and much smaller. She had seen Ursula like this in her dreams. She thought it was the saint guiding her to the sea, helping her understand that her happiness was there.

The music flowed over her, the same from Autumn's memories as in her dreams. She had heard that music in her sleep since she was a child. She had heard it in her mind years before it was written down — with subtle differences — in Germany. The only explanation that had made sense was the saint's desire to help her through the burden of her life, to remind her that although she denied her sex she still had the power of a woman inside her.

Autumn was playing the music in her head, the same music Killera had heard so many times between sleeping and waking. The saint laughed, blessed all that she touched.

The saint was touching her, looking at her with fondness and love. This memory could not come from Autumn. It seemed to rise from within her. She was sharing a bed with a saint, defiling her with lust — stop, she pleaded, stop. Mother of god, the pleasure of her skin, the sweetness of her mouth.

:Ursula, a dripping honeycomb.:

She was aware that Autumn was breathing hard now. Her eyes were slits and her face contorted with concentration.

The rest came in a flash, some from Autumn, some from her own memories. How could she have lived then and again now? Resurrection was reserved for the son of God. Such grace was not granted to women.

:She was not a mere saint. She was a goddess. She touched us all. Then she was taken from us:

They rode into an abbey and in minutes Killera saw her cousin perish in a stranger's arms. All went black when the evil one plunged Autumn's dagger into Killera's breast and studied her eyes all the while she died.

From Autumn there was more — this was madness! How could it be real? And yet it resembled nightmares she had borne alone in the night, with no one to hold her or kiss them away. She had not needed such reassurance, for if she was nothing she was strong.

With a grunt of fierce intent she managed to lift her arms slightly. She pushed against Autumn just enough for Autumn's controlling hand to slip from her forehead.

She had only a moment, she knew. She rolled on top of Autumn and covered her mouth with one hand. She pressed her other arm across Autumn's throat.

She had a vision of Autumn crying out her pleasure. Ursula begged her for more.

Unbidden, from the well of her past, came another memory. She soared through the sky in the crow's next of Ursula's ship and angrily took the pleasure of Ursula's body, not caring that she hurt her, somehow believing that she could force Ursula to love her again.

The memory of Ursula's blood on her fingers shook her long enough for Autumn to seize control again.

:What did you do to her?:

:I never meant to hurt her. She could have stopped me.:

Autumn took the memory, all of it, the sensation of

Ursula's flesh tearing, Ursula's disbelief, Killera's anger and profound regret and guilt. *:How could you?:*

:Because you took her from me!:

"Then hurt me." Autumn's black eyes bored into Killera. Her little knife was in her hand, the tip pressed just below Killera's eye. Killera could not even blink. "But don't think that you will win. I have lived too many lives to lose to you now. You will help me, you will do as I ask." The fury in her eyes eased. "I know that in some ways I am no better than you, but at least I have held true to the only thing that mattered. *I did not forget her.* I will find her again."

Killera closed her eyes to shut out Autumn's unrelenting regard. She did not want to believe that these memories had happened and in nightmare after nightmare, when she raised hands to the saint for blessing they were streaked with blood. "I will help you," she said hoarsely. "For what I did to her."

The past came close, then, because she believed. Ursula, the saint of her dreams, had been real, had loved her. What had been real once could be so again. In the darkest, loneliest hours of her life the saint had been there. Killera could not believe the saint would ever forsake her.

"You think to give her a choice between us. She loves me," Autumn said with certainty. "She will not have forgotten that either, no matter where that she-demon took her. We're going to find Hilea. She had a magic of her own."

"Hilea?"

"You've forgotten everything, haven't you?" Autumn eased the pressure of the knifepoint. *:She is the music. She is the Voice.:*

They were at the rail of the old *Verdant Bough*, joined in a spell of Ursula's crafting with power surging from Hilea's voice. The chant wove a blessing over the land, a blessing that would not be forgotten.

Hilea, she thought, Hilea who could make a sailor blush, a nun forget propriety and a goddess laugh with delight. The past was real to her now, and she remembered that Hilea's

Pict features had been sharp yet delicate, and her small hands on her lute moved as lightly as a spider web on the breeze.

They had been together at festival many times, bonfire nights begun with Hilea and ended with Ursula. When the many claims on Ursula's time and energies left Killera feeling lonely, Hilea found a tune to pass the hours.

"I will help you find her, then," Killera said. "She was always my friend."

"As I never was," Autumn answered. "As I never shall be, I suspect." Her knife disappeared and Killera pushed her roughly away.

"I'll not share a bed with you."

"Fine, my lord." Autumn took the top blanket and wrapped herself into it on the floor next to the featherbed. "I've slept in fields, in trees, in thickets and mud. This is better than any of that. I would that you remember, my lord, I am not defenseless. Though I sleep, you cannot take me unawares."

Killera did not answer with the curse that rose in her. She would be done with this vixen, this witch, soon enough. Humiliation and loss surged through her. How could she have thought herself in love with this creature? There was nothing of love between them. It had all been a lie, a manipulation. She had given up her titles and doubtless the respect of her captains for desire of a witch, a madwoman.

Liar, cheat, thief, she mused. Liar in her mind, a cheat every time she said, "gently, my lord," but mostly a thief. She had stolen her honor and pride, her love in the past. She would try to steal that love again. She could try, Killera thought. Try.

"Who's a thief?" Taylor didn't ask the question until Kelly had finished what she wanted of the mediocre airline dinner.

Kelly looked as exhausted as Taylor felt. She'd lost her

ability to tell what Kelly thought or felt, but her basic intuition told her Kelly was a mass of contradictions. Rage gave way to regret, arrogance to guilt. She could only imagine how hard it had been for Liz to be near her.

Liz, she thought with an ache. It had been twelve hours since Liz had left her, starting a new journey. She did not understand why, either. It twisted in her stomach, as if she'd been betrayed, knowing that Liz had hidden something from her.

"Is this a trick question?"

"No, you said it. You said it just before you woke up. Liar, cheat, thief."

Kelly's hands tightened on her cup of coffee. "Thanks to all of this shit I have a lot of bad dreams. Let it go."

"Talking about it might help."

"Not to you. You're part of the problem."

Okay, Taylor thought. I deserved that. "Is there any way I can say I'm sorry that will help?"

"No, not right now."

"I understand. Maybe, given time."

"If we have any." Kelly closed her eyes. "I'm tired. I'm in a bad mood. Read the magazine. Do the crossword. Just let me be." Kelly slipped on the headphones and fiddled with the channel selector.

Taylor bit back a gasp as she remembered the song from her flight to England. She donned the headphones as well and turned to the first of the rock channels. At least the music would stop her pointless worrying about Liz.

Forty minutes later the cycled recording reached the spot where she had tuned in, so she switched to the next channel. After three songs she heard the opening bars of the melody that had seemed so familiar. The tones were harsh, angry, devoid of tenderness. Mindless male voices chanted, "running, running, running." Though she didn't really care for it she could not stop listening either. The circular nature of both the main melody and the words kept her interested. She recog-

185

nized, then, that there was a simple spell in the music, an almost unconscious one.

When the woman's voice finally joined them, soaring hoarsely over the cacophony, Taylor shivered. Here was more power. Only now could she recognize it. That power had gotten her back on her feet, when the green fire had burned her hand. Though the opening of the song was punkish and less than tuneful, with the woman's arcing words it became a ballad about trying first one way then another to reach a distant love, goal, hope. She noted the lack of pronouns, so common in much music written by women these days, and tried to keep up with the nuances of shifting words: paths, tracks, trails, roads, voyages, journeys. The synonyms flowed artfully throughout the circular melody, never strained and always adding a dimension of meaning. A path to a new love became a voyage to a new spirit. Life was all journeys.

It was over before she realized it. She concentrated to discern the harp and the Latin buried deep in the closing bars. She hurriedly flipped through the listings in the magazine. There was nothing with a name that fit the imagery of the song, but the song after it was a jarring version of a favorite she knew well. Therefore the song she wanted was listed just before it.

"Futility" was the name of the piece, composed and sung by Lea Battle. What was futile — hope, dreams, love? Or the journeys, or life itself? She would have to listen to it many more times, she felt, to discern the composer's intent.

Lea Battle — the name was unfamiliar. Taylor could not help a pulse of excitement as she turned over what she knew. Lea Battle used imagery from the Ursula chants. Hildegard of Bingen had composed the chants. Liz said they reminded her of music composed by Ursula's bard, though Liz's memory of the music was vague at best. The bard had been Hilea . . . Lea Battle.

Duh, she chided herself. Moron. Gods, you're as slow as a corpse sometimes.

She knew she had changed, then, for she'd never had a self-deprecating perspective on herself before. Ignorance ought to be her watchword. She should just always assume she knew nothing. Aunt Peela had said that was the first step to learning.

So. She almost said something to Kelly, but given Kelly's mood she would wait until they were on the ground in a few more hours. Lea Battle was probably having the same flashbacks and dreams that plagued them all. They needed to figure out a way into a rock star's world.

Given what else faced them, it seemed like the easiest task on the list.

"You're crazy." As they strode out of the terminal, Kelly could not believe it was raining again. It was early in the season for another storm. "Some punk headbanger is Hilea?"

"That's what I think. Let's go buy the recording. I think you'll believe me then."

"As if. I'll bet this Battle woman learned that stuff at music school, that's all. I hate that kind of music — it's so pretentious. Ursula wouldn't like it either. "

"That's expansive of you," Taylor said in her smug, superior voice.

"Shut up." Kelly unlocked the Explorer and slung her backpack into the back seat. As usual, she couldn't look into the backseat without reliving Ursula tangled with her there. She shook the rain out of her hair and let the wet drops shock her out of the memory.

"I'm serious." Taylor buckled up. "I want to stop at a music store."

Fuck, Kelly thought. She headed for the big outlet strip mall between Philly and Norristown. At least it wasn't far out of their way.

The volume inside the music store was painful. The caterwauling that passed for music was unintelligible. Even she could tell it was mediocre caterwauling, too. The clerk, unwashed in this lifetime, snapped a button on the stereo deck behind the counter. No relief there — the next piece was much like the last.

Taylor had to holler her request at the multi-pierced girl slowly restocking the shelves. The girl looked Taylor up and down, frankly skeptical that Taylor knew what she was asking for.

Kelly came up behind Taylor and stared at the girl over Taylor's shoulder. She was older than she looked at first glance, hiding mid-twenties hopelessness under a layer of teenage makeup and angst. Her brown hair and slender stature were attractive, but her blue eyes were jaded and dull.

The girl's mouth parted slightly and Kelly couldn't stop herself from reading the girl's explicit thoughts. *:Now there's someone who could ride me to tomorrow.:*

She found the CD Taylor asked for while giving Kelly her complete attention. When Taylor walked away with the CD, she shouted, "I'm Diamond. I'm here almost every night."

"Diamond?" Kelly let her skepticism show. She wanted truth.

The girl's eyes widened. "Jerri," she said.

Kelly's palms went damp as she realized with someone like Jerri it would be a long while before there was a No.

Taylor was receiving just enough bored attention from the clerk at the counter to pay for the CD. Kelly's temples throbbed as she grabbed Jerri's hand and pulled her to an aisle out of Taylor's sight.

She captured Jerri's face in her hands and kissed her hard. Jerri kissed her eagerly back. The tongue stud disconcerted Kelly, though she ended the kiss thinking it wasn't a problem — it wasn't Jerri's mouth she was ultimately interested in.

"Shit, baby, keep that up and you can do me right here."

Kelly smiled, cool and distant. "Some other night, maybe."

"I don't do this all the time," Jerri suddenly stammered. "You're just my type, you know?" She ran her hands over Kelly's shoulders and back and arched her pelvis against Kelly's thigh.

"I don't know if you're my type, though," Kelly said in her ear. "You'd have to prove yourself."

Jerri shuddered and pulled away. There was no need to read her surface thoughts. Everything was in her eyes. "Whatever you want, baby. I will do anything you ask me to do."

Kelly walked away without another word, aware of Jerri's frustrated arousal. She might come back when she got the chance. Jerri knew what she wanted. Even if she didn't, Kelly was sure she wouldn't mind learning.

"Where'd you disappear to?" Taylor peeled the wrapping off the CD once they were outside. She wasn't paying much attention to Kelly, which was just fine.

"Just looking at something."

"Looking at that teenager with the bad attitude?" Taylor seemed to be teasing as she struggled with the numerous security stickers that kept the CD closed.

Kelly didn't say anything more and hid the smirk she felt as she recalled Jerri's deliciously bad attitude. Taylor had no idea what real power was.

In the car Taylor slipped the CD into the player and advanced the tracks. "Just listen for a minute."

It was as feverish and pounding as the music in the store had been, but Kelly had to admit that a lot of skill was at work in the arrangement of the male chants and squealing guitars. It was music she never would have chosen for herself, but it was better than the garbage that had been blasting inside. Better than a lot of the soft jazz crap that passed for interesting these days.

Then Lea Battle began to sing.

A vacuum seemed to tear her head open. Gods, gods! The longing swept over her, the yearning for a return to something she believed was her happiness. The voice rose hoarsely, as if

189

clarity had no place in this song. She saw herself on a horse, riding into a church, not as ancient as the one where she had died. She dismounted and helped Autumn, tantalizing, seductive, treacherous Autumn, to the ground.

Her mind was riven by hot pink light, a blaze of rage that made her own hardly seem worth nourishing. Lea Battle sang of quests undertaken, journeys survived, all for nothing. Kelly understood the song now. After all, what was the fucking point? Why did she care what anyone thought of her? She was what she was, and if she wanted to drag someone like Jerri out back of the store and fuck the daylights out of her, who should stop her?

The voice soared above the bitter, empty music. There was no point to anything. No matter the path she chose she would never get what she wanted. So why not pick the way that gave her meager satisfaction? She shouldn't have left her old way of life, the old world. She'd had what she wanted there — students, lots of them, money, and hands that had never touched dirt. The sound of many waters was a tidal wave that left her cold. She needed to feel warm again.

Her hand was on the door. She was going back inside to get Jerri when the song ended.

"Gods," Taylor murmured. "It was even more powerful the second time. What an incredibly beautiful, hopeful piece."

Hopeful? Kelly looked at Taylor, stunned.

Taylor's eyes were closed. "In spite of everything, to get up out of the dust and begin again, to follow a different path if you have to, to go after what your heart desires, be it love or rapture — whatever gives you bliss."

Kelly pointed out, "It's called 'Futility.' "

"A little nihilism?" Taylor opened her eyes and looked curiously at Kelly. "Yes, I suppose. You heard it, too, didn't you? I only know Hilea's voice from Liz's memory of it."

Kelly had to admit it. She was too shaken to hide the truth. "That was her voice."

Taylor stared at her for a few minutes, but when Kelly

said nothing more turned her head with a sigh. "Can I use your cell phone to check my messages?"

Kelly handed it over. Perhaps some urgent business would take Taylor away. She didn't want to bring Taylor to the farm now. She didn't want to make plans or discuss options. All she wanted to do was dump Taylor somewhere and go home, back to the barn. She didn't need Jerri, she had Rachel. She could have them both. Why not?

She had just put the car into reverse when Taylor clutched her arm so tightly Kelly winced.

"What?"

"Gods, gods — Ursula spoke to Liz! Liz was right, she's headed here."

Kelly's heart leapt and she felt virtually unknown tears start in her eyes. Her love, her love was found. The relief was overwhelming. She turned off the engine and rested her head on the steering wheel. She needn't walk any path at all — time had taken care of it.

Taylor was listening intently, then punched at some keys and listened again. "I had to listen to it twice. Liz says that Ursula had a memory lapse. She's with Autumn — you were right. It was Autumn who pulled her out of the circle."

That bitch, Kelly thought. A true thief. Her love was found and being held by Autumn. Being bedded by her no doubt. The memory of Ursula with her in the back seat faded to a torment of Ursula with Autumn, never saying no. Autumn was making Ursula want her the same way she'd made Killera want her. Any love Ursula felt for Autumn was a lie.

"They're on their way, but won't be here until late tomorrow night, most likely. Liz said that Autumn was adamant though — they're still being pursued and if she thinks it's not safe they won't show. So I think we wait by the phone."

Oh, joy, Kelly wanted to say.

"So where's the nearest train station?"

"Philly or Harrisburg, about the same. I'm going to guess that a train on the way to Philly is stopping in Harrisburg first." It didn't seem possible. Ursula was coming home. But she was bringing that witch with her. What could she do?

"I know you don't like me much right now," Taylor was saying. "But I think we can wait better together. Maybe we can pass the time trying to figure out how to get a hold of Lea Battle."

"She'll think we're crazy."

"Perhaps. But I have a feeling that a message titled '*O pulcherrima forma*' or just 'Ursula is found' might pique her interest."

"Most beautiful sight," Kelly mused. "Of desired delights."

Taylor looked at with an odd but triumphant smile. "You can't keep saying you don't believe any of this, not now. You know that's Hilea on that CD. When are you going to stop fighting what's happening to you — to the rest of us?"

"Why can't anyone just let me be what I am? You believe what you believe and leave me alone. I'm not some mystic and I don't want to be part of some chanting idiocy in the woods." She wanted Ursula, not the rest of that crap.

"But that's who Ursula is."

"Don't start that. You're the one who convinced her to try things your way. Look where that got us." She started the car again and backed out of the parking space. It would be dark before they reached home. She would check out that all was well in the barn and then sleep for twelve hours. The less time spent talking to Taylor the better.

The rain rushed under their wheels and over the glass that reflected the light of oncoming traffic. She was going home and Taylor be damned. Home would welcome her with loving arms so they could prepare for Ursula.

Ten

Autumn hurried Ursula off the train when they reached Chicago. They needed to change trains to head for Harrisburg, which was just as close to Paradise as Philadelphia. Scylla had to be reclaimed from the pet car and she was anxious to fit in a walk for all of them. It had been a long, boring twenty-four hours, and sleep had eased little of the waiting. Even talking didn't pass the time. They were both keeping secrets now.

"I know we've got two hours, but by the time we find a place to eat and let her have a run it'll all be gone." She tipped the porter who unlocked Scylla's cage and the three of them set out for the street.

It was late afternoon. Autumn saw a diner marquee in the

next block and led them in that direction. She abruptly longed to be back in Vegas, headed for Marge's Diner where the food was simple and there was always a bone for Scylla. She missed Ed and his staunch loyalty and his ability to boil any situation down to a few words and decisive action. Was this what it felt like to think of a place as home? To miss people and places? She had never considered anywhere her home except when she'd been on the sea.

She could not sense anyone with any intent toward them in the vicinity. They had Scylla, too. A medium-sized dog was a deterrent to most harassment.

As they passed a narrow alley she saw in a heartbeat she'd been too confident. The gun was aimed at her for a moment, then quickly shifted to Ursula.

Ursula froze with fear. Scylla growled sharply and the gun jerked in her direction.

"Down, girl," Autumn said calmly.

"That's right." Staghorn waved the gun toward the alley. "In there where we can have some privacy."

Ursula and Scylla went into the alley first, then Autumn, walking backward to keep herself between them and Staghorn. His gun hand was fine — the other was bandaged. She wished now she'd burned them both.

"You hurt her and your mistress won't be too happy with you," Autumn countered. *He will have nothing of you. He never has.*

He looked momentarily puzzled. "I followed your trail through Reno. Talked to some people, watched some tapes. I wasted a lot of time at the bus station. The train was a smart way to go. You've got a bundle right now and I want it all."

"What do I get in return, Staghorn?"

"You get to live."

She knew then, in spite of what he said, he was going to kill her if he could. Her body would be his trophy with his brother cops and the murkier organizations he kept company with. He would show them what happened to uppity women who refused to fall in with his plans. Or it could be as simple as Uda wanting her dead. No matter the reason she disliked the potential outcome.

In every life that she could recall she had been in danger. She had defended herself. She even knew the heft and details of the jam-prone Baretta he held. It would be a mistake to count on it jamming when he pulled the trigger, however. But she'd never had to protect anyone but herself. Worrying about what would happen to Ursula, what she would do to interfere, was taking the edge off her instincts.

She now knew so much about covert coercion of the mind, too, more than she had ever wanted to know. He *was* Uda's tool — she was staking her life on that. But it was entirely possible he didn't know it. The night she had met Rueda, not knowing who she was, Staghorn had been there as well. Analyzing it now, she did not see that the two of them were coordinating anything that had happened. But Staghorn's harassment had pushed her into Rueda's arms.

She hadn't sensed him nearby, tonight, which was a first. Someone had shielded him at some point. That person could be nearby, and the thought was terrifying. She couldn't fight Uda, not right now. She wasn't ready.

She dropped her hands to her pockets.

"Hold still!"

"You want the money, don't you?"

"Autumn, he can have it. Just give it to him. It's not worth it."

Damn her, Ursula was fiddling with her money belt. She didn't realize what Staghorn said he wanted and his real goal were two very different things. "This is no ordinary thief. He's going to kill me and give you up."

Ursula's hands froze. "I don't understand."

"Look at his face. You've seen it before."

Staghorn reached in his pocket for his handcuffs. This was

good if he meant them for her. He'd relax and she'd be out of them in a heartbeat. But he knew that his cuffs could not hold her — no, they were for Ursula. "I haven't decided if I'll kill you for sure. You can still get out of this. Come back to Vegas and we'll see what works out."

"It can't be," Ursula whispered.

"It is." She wished for her bow, her dagger. She could silence him in a heartbeat and no one would hear.

"Now? There are people like that now?"

Gods, Ursula was so naïve. She just didn't want to believe. "There are. Even more so."

"Shut up. So what's it going to be, Autumn, dear? Are we partners?"

"You'd never trust me."

"You break faith with me and she's dead. After I give her to some friends to straighten her out." His laugh was cruel and it grated down Autumn's spine.

"No," Ursula said quietly. "No. It has to stop somewhere."

Staghorn didn't get the chance to ask what she meant. There was a flash of vibrant red light. Scylla howled, backing toward Ursula.

Autumn had his gun out of his hand before his finger could tighten on the trigger. She felt cold. She broke his arm just below the elbow and centered as she spun around to smash the gun into his jaw, breaking that as well. He reeled backward with a muted cry, vanquished.

She wasn't out of her crouch before Ursula shoved her aside.

Her hands were glowing red. No, Autumn thought, Uda would find them now. It was too late. Ursula pressed her hands to Staghorn's temples and he went limp.

"True justice comes from within," Ursula said. Her voice had an odd echo. "You know what you've done. You can atone. There is freedom if you can seize it." She bowed her head.

"Ursula, we have to get out of here."

Ursula moaned suddenly. "Great mother, so many? So many?" Tears spilled from her eyes, splashing over his face. "Such filth — gods, it's unbearable."

"Don't waste tears on that kind of slime." Autumn didn't know if she could touch Ursula when she was like this, but they had to leave. It was probably already too late.

"She did this to him, part of it. She twisted him to this, but he knew it was wrong."

"He's a murderer who preys on the weak, a coward. He always has been." Autumn risked a hand on Ursula's shoulder only to have it shaken off.

"No, no, that is only part of it." As she grew calmer, Ursula's voice took on an even deeper resonance. "He might never have acted on his feelings if she hadn't urged it on him. She ruined him, but he still knew it was wrong."

She drew back, her face like a gallows. "True justice comes from within." She rose, her movements deliberate. "It is done."

Autumn was still afraid to touch her, but she took her hand anyway. It was like ice. "Back to the trains. We'll get on anything that's about to depart."

Staghorn didn't move when Scylla nudged him with her nose. Her tail went down and she backed away, ears flattened against her skull. Autumn hesitated. Her instincts urged her to get help, to tell someone.

"Leave him," Ursula commanded. Her voice rang like bells. "He is done."

A new kind of fear took over Autumn. She looked at Ursula and did not know her. She had never seen this woman in any dream, cold and remote, seemingly without compassion or mercy.

She wiped the gun and put it in his cooling hand. She did it in self-preservation, but hiding her responsibility left her nauseated.

Once they were out of the alley, with Scylla growling over

her shoulder as they hurried down the street, Autumn tried to push away her fear of what Ursula had done. They plunged into the station again. "This way," she pointed.

The train at the top of the marquee was headed for Boston. Good enough, Autumn thought. Then she made the mistake of looking at Ursula. She stumbled in disbelief.

A faint reddish light still clung to Ursula, and Autumn realized that she *did* know that austere face. She had seen it during her journey after Rueda had stabbed her. Beautiful and haunting, Ursula was wreathed in the essence of the goddess who had sent her back to life. She had been graced by love, by the joy of reunion. But there was no love in these eyes, no compassion or hesitation, only a frightening, composed Knowing. The body was Ursula's, but something else possessed her.

"It was his choice," Ursula said distantly. "She urged him to the lives he led, but he knew it was wrong. He will begin again. *Tabula rasa.*"

Autumn couldn't take it in. "I — what did you do?"

"He chose oblivion."

Autumn started moving again. There were things she didn't want to know. She had not just witnessed a goddess at work, meting out divine justice. Yes, she reminded herself, she had killed in her past, to survive, for vengeance, to protect others. Death — particularly her own — was almost a friend.

Ursula had done more than take a life. She did not want to be afraid of Ursula's touch. Staghorn's crimes were great, she knew that, but with every dream, with every day, she knew her own crimes were large. What would happen to her when that goddess looked into her soul? No, she did not want to understand. She only wanted to love.

The porter at the luggage car where pets were kept was just about to lock it up, but a substantial tip had Scylla back in a cage. Scylla curled into one corner, her tail still between her legs. "I'll bring you some food soon," Autumn promised as she filled the water drip.

There was a sleeper free and Autumn paid the extra cost over what their passes covered. They needed privacy to recover their wits, or at least she did. She locked the door and couldn't turn around. She could think of nothing to say that would not reveal that she was humbled and awed, but most of all just plain scared of what Ursula could be. She could not look at that face again. She didn't think she was meant to.

She didn't turn until a stifled sob rose behind her. There was only a woman there and with profound relief Autumn went to her, held her and kissed away her tears.

"He'd done such terrible things." Ursula buried her face in Autumn's shoulder. "I didn't know — I'd never seen that kind of cruelty. Elspeth and Claire, that was *nothing*. It was quick for them. He loved to watch women die."

Autumn recognized the shudder that washed over Ursula and got her into the tiny bathroom just in time. "It's just reaction. A lot of big things have happened to you in the last couple of days. It's okay," she kept repeating.

When it seemed like Ursula would not be sick again she helped her rinse her mouth and drink some water. A hot shower seemed like a good idea. When Ursula seemed too drained to manage her clothes, Autumn helped her undress and stand in the small enclosure. Within minutes she was as wet as Ursula was. She shed her own clothing and held Ursula in her arms. The water was as hot as she could stand it. She prayed for it to wash them both clean.

Ursula's hands were on her hips. "I need you," she murmured. "I need to feel like a woman again."

The shudder started in Autumn's knees and traveled upward. "We can't, my love." In a fever she kissed Ursula's neck. Water cascaded over them with a sound like pounding waves. "We can't."

"Hold me, then. Don't let go of me."

Autumn said she would not. For the next few hours she kept the promise. Eventually they both slept, entwined on a single bunk, breathing as one.

A week earlier and Autumn knew that Killera would have protested their being separated by the rules of the abbey at Eibingen. There were women's quarters nearer the cloister while men were guested on the far side of the larger house for Benedictine monks. After Autumn's revelations on the barge, Killera did not care that they would be separated until the supper fare.

She and Elspeth were to share a narrow cell. "I'm sorry you can't have more quiet," Autumn told her.

Elspeth pulled off her headrail and Autumn was struck again by how lovely Elspeth's hair was. A beautiful color of ripe wheat, several shades more fair than her cousin's. She wished she could help Elspeth somehow, but she did not want to hear any more about dying. "I am feeling better here. The walls are thick and the worship very still. I might stay, if my lord is really determined not to go home again."

"I can't be sure of that."

"I know. Your path and my cousin's diverge here."

Elspeth's calm assessment gave Autumn a shiver of foreboding. "What about your own?"

Elspeth bit her lip. "There is a light, alive, here, and there are no ravens. But they are never far."

Unable to understand, and unwilling to try harder, Autumn finally asked, "Will you come down to supper later?"

Elspeth nodded and Autumn left the tiny room to explore. Somewhere, deep in the cloister, where a woman such as her was not allowed, the abbess dwelled. She questioned a novice busy tending the garden, using a little suggestion to help her talk. The abbess was indeed there, but she was at present

200

seeing no one. She was consumed by the living light, *lux vivens*, the force that revealed God's word through the abbess's hand. The living light sometimes visited the abbess for a day or for weeks. It was God's will.

There were many doors with locks bound in heavy brass. None of them were a problem.. No lock kept its secrets from her for long. But this house of women was in the shadow of a large, grand abbey of men. Any trouble she might cause would come under the purview of the men to resolve, of that she had no doubt. She did not want men deciding she needed to be questioned by the local lord's reeves. After all she'd done to Killera, she would not bring any more scrutiny than necessary onto Lord Aldtyme.

She could perhaps commit a small transgression, sufficient to bring her into contact with someone closer to the abbess than the novices and tightly-shuttered sisters who kept charge of the guests. It needed to be something that required admonishment, but not the attention of a priest.

She went to get Elspeth for supper and they dined near the fire, well above the salt, the highest-ranking visitors for that day. The meal was modest, and after their trenchers were removed Autumn pulled her most valuable possession, even before her knife, from her skirts.

"I've never shown you these, my lord," she said. "They are quite amusing."

She opened the small box that had been Tain's, the box that had always been with her. She died with it, she found herself alive with it. Its journey was as long as her own, perhaps longer. It felt ancient in her hand, though none of its years showed in the polished surface. Inside were six dice, three of red quartz and three of black obsidian, all with green spots for counting. She swept them into her hand and shook them between her cupped palms. She closed her eyes, shook again, then let them fall to the table. "Black," she said quietly.

She felt rather than heard Killera's gasp. Only three dice had fallen to the table, all black, and her spread hands were

201

empty. She cupped her palms again, shook, and let the red fall. This time she said, "All ones," before they came to a rest.

"Stop," Killera hissed. "You cannot dice in a place such as this."

Autumn opened her eyes. The clatter of the stones on the wooden table had attracted the attention of other diners, many of whom mirrored Killera's shocked expression.

Elspeth, however, regarded her steadily, as if she understood that this was not just an ill-bred mistake.

The sister who had directed the serving of the meal had also noticed. She was approaching with a considerable frown.

"This is not seemly," she admonished.

"I meant no harm," Autumn said. *:Take them from her.:*

"You should not have brought such evil games here."

"It's only to pass the time." *:Take them from her.:*

"Time better spent contemplating the way of the Lord," the sister pronounced. "Since you find them a temptation, perhaps they are better held by the prioress."

The prioress would do nicely, Autumn thought. She assumed the air of a penitent. "Perhaps you are right. May I take them myself, so I may give my apologies for having brought them?" *:This one could use a dressing down from the prioress.:*

"That would be best. I have no wish to handle them myself."

Autumn excused herself from Killera and Elspeth and followed the sister to the hall that separated the common rooms from the cloister.

The prioress's offices were at the entrance to the cloister, and served as the public gateway between the outer and inner worlds. The sister went in first, then emerged a few moments later. "The prioress will see you now."

Autumn slipped Tain's box into her skirts as she went in. The prioress's hair was veiled, but nothing obscured the sharp, intensely blue eyes. She might have been in her late twenties, but middle age had not taken true hold.

Of course, Autumn thought.

They stared at each other as they tested one another's shields.

"Who are you?" The prioress rose from her desk, alarmed. "What have you brought into this place?"

"What you have been missing." She took a deep breath and did not know if her call would be heard. *:Elspeth, I need you.:*

"We are complete here. There is nothing we lack."

"I speak of you, sister," Autumn answered.

The prioress shook her head, maintaining an almost regal distance. "I am in the hand of God. I want for nothing."

"Contempt for the world rises above all things," Autumn quoted.

"I am not in need of scriptural teaching." The prioress waved her hand at shelves filled with bound manuscripts. "There is nothing you can offer me, child. But I have no doubt that there is much we can offer you."

There was a quiet knock at the door. Had she not been hoping for it, Autumn might have missed it. "There is nothing so astonishing as thinking something full only to find it unchanged, yet empty."

The prioress's patience was waning as Autumn opened the door. Elspeth peered at her anxiously.

"I had not thought this was here for you," she said, and she pulled Elspeth into the room.

She could not get clean. Ursula lathered her hands with the coarse bathroom soap and scrubbed again. Autumn had woken them when they reached Cleveland. After a half-hour's wait they boarded a direct line to Harrisburg.

No amount of distance could make her forget what her hands had done.

How had she known how to do such a thing? She hadn't

taken his life, but obliterated his soul. Without it the body had died. Who was she to judge another human being like that?

She reminded herself she had not been the judge. She had shown him his true soul, mired in the pain of others, lined with burnt flesh and bloodied instruments. She had forced him to look, to comprehend. Once done, she gave him a choice: oblivion or a new beginning, to try, one more lifetime to rise above the love of the suffering of others.

He'd chosen oblivion because he did not see another way to be free of the whispering darkness that assured him that whatever he could do he ought to do, simply because it was within his power. He was corrupted, with a mere spark of compassion left. He spent that last bit on himself and embraced the eternal void.

She dried her hands and still felt sticky. How could anyone look into a murderous abyss and feel clean? If that is what goddesses did, she wanted none of it.

Autumn made no comment on her frantic movements. The train lurched and slowed. "We're coming into Pittsburgh. We have a forty-minute wait. I was going to take some food to Scylla."

"I'll wait in our seats," Ursula said. She reached for the soap again.

It was not quite eleven and they would reach Harrisburg around two in the morning. What day was it, she wondered abruptly. She realized she had no real idea. Third week of September, somewhere around there.

She dried her hands once again and fought the urge to reach for the soap. Her eyes were hollows, her skin looked sallow. Until she had left Aldtyme, the mirror had showed her perfect health, clear eyes, and an upright posture. She had regained some of that feeling working in Autumn's garden. All that she'd gained had fled again, and so quickly. When she thought about her life in Aldtyme she just couldn't connect to it, as if it hadn't really happened. Which was the real her? The one sheltered in that place, cradled in the wisdom and protection of her three aunts, completely untouched by the world, or this haggard, exhausted and overwhelmed wreck who knew guilt, regret, and now the sick reveling in death?

The others, they all had need of her. But how could she help them when she did not know who — or what — she was?

She went back to their seats because the next time she washed her hands it would be skin the brown paper towels scrubbed away.

Her mind had begun to churn through Staghorn's most treasured images — all of them foul — when Autumn dropped into the seat next to her. "Scylla's okay. She really needs a good run."

"Sorry that didn't work out." She looked out the window, reliving what had happened instead. She had held his soul in her hands.

"It wasn't your fault." Autumn briefly rested her hand on Ursula's. "You're not telling yourself that it was, are you?"

Ursula shook her head. "I just wish — it wasn't just him. If there was a settlement to be made he wasn't the only one who owed."

Autumn's mouth went to a thin line. "Sooner or later that bill will be settled up as well. It's inevitable."

Ursula would have said more had they been alone. Today she had seen again how fierce and potentially deadly Autumn could be. Threatened, she became something elemental, primed with the essence of her life energy. That ruthless energy was something outside Ursula's world. Soon Autumn's ferocity would be reunited with women who had faced the evil before, and had fought bravely when they could. But all had been lost. How would this time be any different?

"What day is it?" she asked instead.

"The twentieth, I think."

"Today? It'll be midnight soon."

Autumn nodded. "Yes, then it'll be the twenty-first."

She wished Autumn would touch her again. It had felt so healing to lie in her arms and just sleep. "We won't get to

Harrisburg until the dead of night. Should we call then or wait until morning?"

Autumn said quickly, "Wait."

"It'll be the Autumnal Equinox," Ursula realized. "Perhaps we should call."

"Why? We're not planning to do anything that . . . that requires a special day. Are we?"

Ursula didn't like seeing hesitation in Autumn's eyes. It had been there since Chicago. She's allowed to be afraid, she told herself. She's only human, too, you know. Autumn hadn't been frightened of Staghorn, though. She'd moved decisively against him. Her fear had come later. "No, it's just auspicious. If Taylor is there we might be able to use the day's blessings, that's all. It's more auspicious before daybreak than after."

"Is it worth waking them up in the middle of the night?"

"We'll be so close," Ursula said. "I just want to tell her I'm sorry."

Autumn seemed to be biting back stronger words when she said, "I don't know what it is that you did that was so wrong."

"I lied to her. I lied about you, I lied about who I was."

"I would think you're even."

"It doesn't work that way — why do you say that?"

"Because of what she did." Autumn looked furious, now. "What she did — what do you mean?"

"I know about what happened." She lowered her voice. "In the crow's nest. I know about it now."

Ursula was appalled. "How can you? I never told you."

"You're not the only one who knows."

She studied Autumn in silence for a long while, her mind churning this puzzle and trying not be hurt by Autumn's secrecy. Finally, she said, "It was my fault. I could have stopped her at any moment. I chose not to."

"That doesn't excuse her."

"I let something evil touch us when I could have prevented it. That's my responsibility."

"I won't ever agree that you were in any way responsible."

"How did you know?" Autumn turned her head away without answering. "Tell me."

"I can't, not here."

It was extremely awkward whispering to each other when nearly everyone else around them was trying to sleep. The only people who knew what had happened in the crow's nest were Kelly, Liz and Taylor. She had told Liz and Taylor about it, as part of sharing the past. Like her, Kelly had dreamed it. It was not something Liz would have blurted out to Autumn on the telephone earlier. So how could she know?

No, she thought. No, that's not quite right. The other person who knew was Killera, because Killera had done it.

Autumn had not been sleeping well. She often awoke murmuring something, as if she'd been speaking in her dreams. In Reno she had been saying, "Gently, my lord, gently."

She hadn't wanted to ask about Autumn's sudden pattern of nightmares. It seemed so personal. She had been afraid of what she might learn when she had weakly craved blissful ignorance. But now she had to find her courage. "You've been dreaming about Killera, haven't you?"

Autumn's quickly masked look of chagrin and fear answered the question. She struggled for a moment, then muttered. "Yes."

"Why didn't you tell me?"

Again, Autumn appeared to struggle. Ursula realized she was trying to lie, but as always, only truth came out. "There are things I don't want you to know. Not yet."

"Ignorance can make me weak."

"Gods, I hope not."

Ursula shrugged. "I won't force you."

"Thanks." It was said with a dry edge.

"I didn't mean it that way."

"I think you did. I know you could. I just — give me a little time. I have a lot to show you. It doesn't flatter me."

Ursula couldn't imagine Autumn doing anything that

compromised her honor. She couldn't even lie. She had to be careful about how she won in a casino, because anything that seemed like a cheat made her ill. "No one leads a perfect life."

"I know." Autumn sighed. "When we are next alone. I'll tell you about it. And about how I got the scar." Her hand rested briefly between her breasts.

There was more there than she knew. Fine, then. She would wait until Autumn could tell her. She was not a goddess who just sifted through a mind and forced a decision of justice. She would listen. She would not judge. How could she judge Autumn? She wasn't the one who had struggled, lived, died.

That was the larger puzzle, perhaps, then. She didn't remember dying, not once. She didn't remember birth, or even early childhood. Her aunts had found her at the age of six, so they told her, and there was no reason not to believe them.

She took Autumn's hand and held it tight. Words came unbidden. She whispered, "With great desire I have longed to be with you, to sit with you."

Autumn, her eyes black as the night outside, black as eternity and the rock of time, answered, "And so I ran to you by a different path."

It didn't hurt to touch her now. It was as if they had passed a threshold of joined need and awareness that allowed a touch meant as comfort not to be torment as well. She put her head on Autumn's shoulder and let the train rock her. A few hours until this journey ended. There would be a beginning.

The prioress was frozen in place. Her blue eyes would close for a moment, then reopen as if to take in the sight of Elspeth anew.

Elspeth moved like she walked underwater, slowly, outside of time. "I knew," she faltered. "I knew I would find you."

When she was near enough to touch, to breathe in, the

prioress finally moved. Her arms were around Elspeth and their kiss made Autumn's heart sing. For a moment she felt purified. Something good had come of what she had done. It did not redeem her, but at least she could take comfort in it.

She left them to their eager reunion and set her hand to the lock on the outer door to the prioress's office, ensuring that anyone coming in would at least have to knock. Then she slipped through the inner door, the one that guarded the cloister, and locked it behind her with another deft touch of her hand.

She heard the music, then, a voice singing, far above her.

A locked grill closed off the stairway that would lead upward to the voice. She touched it gently and the grill noiselessly swung open.

She walked the newly cut stairs and listened to the voice that sang like living light, intense with the force that worked through her to pen the verses and responsories of masses for all the sacred hours, commissioned by bishops, lauded by popes, and singularly familiar to Autumn.

"The burden of fire is upon you," the voice sang in Latin, melancholy even as it rose in clear brightness. "The blood of Ursula is upon us, now let us all rejoice."

The door was slightly ajar, and through it Autumn heard the scratching of a quill. She further opened the door and saw that the abbess's back was to her. Her headdress was askew, revealing short brown hair. The abbess repeated what she had just sung, then wrote vigorously on the parchment before her.

Having come this far, Autumn paused, and sought for the best way to interrupt the abbess's work.

The abbess put the pen down. "I've been expecting you. I did not know I would have to wait so long."

Autumn held to the threshold as Hilea turned to face her. So long sought after. Not the dearest face of her heart's desire, but close. An empty place was filled and unfamiliar tears came to her eyes. "I have looked for you, over and over. For any of us."

"And what have you found?" Hilea's appearance had not altered in any way since that day in the abbey. She was just as petite, just as unbowed. Her eyes, however, didn't sparkle with the merriment that had been so much a part of her. It seemed as if it had been a long time since they had.

"Never Her. I don't know where she is."

"I don't know where she is, either. I've tried a lot of ways to seek her. This way," she indicated the desk, the abbey and the world outside. "This way is no more successful than the rest, but at least I have my music and Claire, who understands me, a little."

Autumn left the doorway and crossed the room, hands outstretched. "Tell me this is not a dream. I've had too many of those."

Hilea abandoned her desk with a grin more like the woman Autumn had known. The sensation of warmth and familiarity from their clasped hands left Autumn feeling weak with relief. She had carried her burdens alone for so very long. She let Hilea draw her to the fireplace, where low cushions waited.

"You don't look like a sailor anymore," Hilea commented.

"I suppose I don't look much like a bard."

"I'd have known you regardless. Your voice, too."

Hilea's eyes were brightening by the minute. She touched the gown. "Very becoming. I suppose you'd not consider getting out of this beguiling garment."

Autumn let the deep and hearty laugh rise from her stomach. "All this time and you haven't changed at all."

Hilea snickered. "I have, I just feel who I was coming back, being near you. I haven't felt this merry in a very long time. Other pursuits, while refreshing, don't have the same satisfaction as festival once did. I searched for that kind of experience in all my travels, but it has left the world, I think. Heaven forfend that women enjoy the way they were made." Her grin grew wicked. "I do have the occasional lapse, every thirty years or so."

"You know who I wish to be with. I'll find no substitute." Her face burned for a moment as she remembered that first night with Killera. It had been blissfully healing.

"But you've tried," Hilea suggested knowingly. "Yes, and recently."

"It was a means to an end," Autumn admitted. "I'm not proud of it."

Hilea studied her. "From the look on your face I would say it wasn't all labor."

Autumn knew she was blushing and recalled, now, that Hilea had always been able to disconcert her. "As you say, at the beginning it recalled happier days."

They regarded each other kindly as Hilea brushed Autumn's cheek with her fingertips. "What are your intentions here?"

"That we look for her together."

Hilea sat more upright with her hands in her lap. "I knew that was what you would say. This is the first place I have lingered so long, and I've arranged it to my liking like no other. I'll be building another house, across the river. More secluded. I hope to do more than I have been able thus far — to pen more for my heart. To practice things that would brand me a heretic."

"Your heart was in what you wrote for Ursula. It was what drew me here."

Hilea drew a long, pleased breath. "I had so hoped that it would call up the memories within any who once knew of her or the old ways. The seeds are there."

"Yet it speaks eloquently to the White Christ," Autumn reminded her.

"As a minstrel friend of mine once told me, anything to get them into the tent." She chuckled. "Of course his trade was parting people from their money. Mine is to shine the light we all knew into the darkness that seems to shroud these times."

" 'Tis dark, isn't?"

Hilea put her head on her knees. "So much forgotten by so many. People crowd in the streets for a sign of God's love. They find it in a stained cloth, a bit of bone in an old graveyard. So many have forgotten that you don't have to look hard at all. The divine surrounds us. It is a blue sky, the shimmer of daybreak, a broken eggshell."

Autumn nodded. "She tried to teach me that. I told her the only truth I knew was the sea. I have to believe she can be found. I feel her with me, as do you. Killera dreams of her —"

"Killera?" Hilea paled.

Autumn had been so enraptured by talking to Hilea in this way that she had forgotten all her news. "Yes, she is with me. Elspeth, too. I found them both and I take it as a sign."

"Gods, Killera." Hilea put a hand to her hair. "*Deo gratias.*"

"Here, but — it will take some explaining."

"And Elspeth?" Hilea's eyelids fluttered for a moment and she grinned widely. "She has met Claire, yes?"

"Yes," Autumn grinned. "Yes. Don't you feel it?"

"Gods, yes." She took a deep breath and some of her color came back. "It's been a long time since I felt that. It was fantasy to think I might feel it again."

"I know what you mean," Autumn murmured. "It was a relief, at the beginning, to feel that way for a while."

Hilea was adjusting her headdress. "I hate to interrupt them, but I'm eager to see Killera."

"That's a bit of a problem. Unless you can have a man brought in here."

Hilea whirled to face her. "What?"

"Killera is a man to the world, to hold her family lands. Lord Aldtyme —"

"The one who hired the abbey choirmaster to teach the Ursula liturgy in Britain. I wondered . . . with the lord being from Aldtyme. It was Killera all the while. To think I almost went myself." Her cheeks stained with red. "What might have been?"

"The question of many lifetimes, I've found." Autumn rested one hand on Hilea's slender shoulder. "We're here now."

Hilea frowned. "And?"

"And now I was hoping you would have figured out something to do."

"I'm doing it," Hilea said. She waved her hand at the parchments. "These are all spells, all seeking. I know of no other way."

"Perhaps if we were all together. In the past your prioress knew the old ways."

"And knows some of them now. I'd not thought to initiate her more deeply — she follows her own path. But she and I were going to observe the equinox, after Vigil was complete. We have only each other to mark the seasons in something like the old way." The frown dissolved. "We've raised only the most basic of circles, to keep our workings secret, but with all of you — we shall try something more grand."

Autumn was helplessly grinning. "It's auspicious, is it not, that Lord Aldtyme's party arrived this day?"

Hilea abruptly looked nervously excited. "Lord Aldtyme could come to the prioress's office without scandal, I suppose, though some of the sisters will talk of nothing else for months." She gave her headdress a final tweak. "I've not had such fun in centuries."

Eleven

The ringing of the phone roused Kelly from sleep. She heard Taylor answer, followed by an excited, "Thank all the gods. It is a relief to hear your voice. Where are you?"

Kelly swung out of bed, surprised she had been able to fall asleep in spite of her exhaustion. She'd spent the day chopping wood, at first out of simple necessity. She'd let such chores languish. As the day progressed, however, she noticed every time she picked up the axe that Taylor would leave her alone. So she'd chopped all day and only had to contend with Taylor when she was stacking.

Her surreptitious, hopeful trips to the barn had been empty of Rachel's presence. She'd worn herself out physically but her mind was taut. Sleep had been a surprise.

"You're up — you heard?" Taylor looked as if she'd stepped out of the shower on a bright, sunny morning.

"Yes. I'm glad it's Harrisburg. It's easier to find your way around."

"They're waiting inside the station. It's gotten quite chilly out."

"Weird weather for September," Kelly said.

"We usually use the lightest robes." Taylor abruptly stopped.

"Robes for what?"

"It's the Autumnal Equinox. This is the first year since I was twelve that I haven't been involved in an observance of the season turning. The equinoxes are the days of perfect balance, when night and day are the same length. We'd be meditating now, all the other work done."

Kelly heard Taylor swallow hard but didn't look at her. "Look, why don't you go? I'll fix up something hot to eat and get some tea made. I don't think anyone will be going to sleep when you get back."

"Don't be nervous," Taylor said softly.

"I can't help it."

She got Taylor the map that showed the train station, all the while feigning a shy reluctance. Once the Explorer's taillights disappeared over the last cattle stop, she hurried to the barn.

This time Rachel was there. Kelly had known she would be.

"You have news." Rachel rose, fiddling with the lacing of her gown.

"Yes," Kelly said breathlessly. She took Rachel in her arms to kiss her hungrily. Did she feel more substantial tonight? Or was she using the memory of pliant Wendy to make Rachel more real?

"She is coming here tonight? Wonderful news. You are so happy."

"Yes, I can't quite take it in." She kissed Rachel again.

Rachel was easing her gown off her shoulders. "There's more."

"Tell me, quickly. I will need much of you tonight." Rachel leaned into Kelly, a curve of skin and desire.

"Hilea survives."

"This I knew. In what form?"

Kelly told her, not questioning why Rachel asked, nor heeding the faint trickle of conscience that spoke of betrayal.

"By all means, find her. I've known she had vast protections, but nothing of their construction. When you find out you will tell me, won't you? I've always kept my promises, haven't I?"

"Yes," Kelly murmured as her mouth explored Rachel's jaw and ear lobe. "She is coming back to me, as you said she would."

"You'll have no more need of me, then." Rachel pulled Kelly's head down with a throaty moan, offering her breasts.

"No, yes. I —" Kelly stiffened. Ursula was coming, but Autumn was with her. "I don't know if she'll be mine again."

"I made you a promise that she would be yours. She can be with you just as I am with you. When you like, how you like."

Kelly shivered. All her dreams spiraled to this moment. She knew what it would take — was she strong enough? If she could seize her dreams regardless what others may want, could she keep them?

:*Yes, you have the means, now. You know who you are.*:

She must do this, and make no apologies. She had the power and she had to use it. To do less was to deny who she was.

"I'm ready," she whispered into Rachel's throat.

"Make me yours," Rachel whispered. "Make me a part of you."

There was no resistance left in her, no dim recollection of understanding that a strength that could not restrain itself

216

was weakness. Strength was its own excuse. Someone like Taylor, who'd slaved for two masters to the appreciation of neither, could not master it. Autumn would soon know it. Ursula — Rachel moaned against her, her skirts around her waist, her legs open. Ursula would understand because Kelly now knew that she could make her.

Taylor coasted to a stop in the passenger loading area and peered through the darkness at the station doors. It was bucketing rain. She decided she would park there, in spite of the dire posted warnings. The place was nearly deserted. It would be a devoted parking officer who stepped out into the downpour to issue a single ticket.

She bolted through the gurgling puddles, wishing she had more than sneakers on, and shoved the doors hard inward. She realized too late that someone was just beginning to push them outward. There was a surprised "oomph." A dog barked, once, sharply. She had an impression of spinning red hair, then a flash of white before she found herself on her back with a woman's knee in her chest.

"I'm sorry," she stammered, smearing rain out of her eyes. She looked into her captor's face and knew the fierce expression, the unflinching, ocean-green eyes.

She was recognized as well, evidently. Autumn's face eased into more gentle lines and she took the weight off her knee.

Taylor picked herself up as Autumn turned away. She saw that she had knocked Ursula sprawling and joined Autumn in lifting her to her feet. Then Ursula was in her arms, laughing, and saying how happy she was to see her again.

Taylor felt the forgiveness. It was genuine and eased a portion of the ache inside her. Yet there was something more, something that had not been there before. Ursula had more presence, somehow, and the forgiveness was not just from a woman who had been mercilessly battered by Taylor's misguided attempt to help. It went deeper. She felt, for as long as it took her to realize it, that if she asked Ursula exactly the right questions, Ursula could explain *everything*, even the Norns.

Ursula looked into her eyes, and Taylor reined in her fanciful thoughts. She didn't see more there than she had before. It was a woman, after all. On a night like tonight, after such agonies endured, a mere woman, this woman, was certainly enough.

Ursula was about to say something more, then she just stared at Taylor's bare neck.

"Things have changed." Taylor absentmindedly rubbed the back of her neck. At this moment she couldn't find a single regret.

"How was this done?"

"I went to Aldtyme. I met your aunts, I think. Beyond the gate."

Ursula's slight nod held understanding.

She glanced at Autumn, who was still tense, and let go of Ursula's arms. "We haven't been properly introduced. I'm Taylor St. Claire."

"Autumn Bradley." The firm handshake told Taylor she was on probation.

"How is Kelly?"

Ursula's voice was free of anything but curiosity, but Taylor felt Autumn's grip tighten in reaction to the question. "Kelly is making something hot to eat."

The dog whined and leaned hard on Autumn's legs. Taylor had forgotten about the dog. Her brief recollections of their meeting in the abbey had only a hint of a large creature, more wolf than dog, standing guard near the horses. This dog was nothing like that size, but its eyes shone with intelligence.

"Is there a twenty-four hour market anywhere along the way?" Autumn scratched the dog between the ears. "Scylla is starving. Sandwiches just don't do the job."

"We'll look," Taylor said. "I don't know the area well myself, but there must be something."

Ursula took a deep, bracing breath. "Shall we brave the storm, then?"

As Taylor led them to the car she knew that Ursula had not been speaking of the rain.

Autumn gave Hilea a guilty shrug as she eased open the locked door to the prioress's office. Compared to other things she had done, it was a minor infraction. She was too quiet, it seemed, and the couple inside sprang apart. Autumn was heartened by the clothing askew and Elspeth's brilliant, unrestrained smile, the likes of which she had never had a chance to see.

"Abbess, I'm sorry, I —" Claire looked as if she would faint.

"Peace, sister," Hilea murmured. "Elspeth,'tis good!"

Autumn went to Claire. "Everything is fine. They know each other, as you see."

She stared at Autumn. "What does this mean?"

"Trust your heart, prioress. I don't know, truly. But you have known her before." She would not say they had died together in the same minute. She didn't think that Claire needed to know. Not yet.

Claire shook her head. "I am touched by something — by things I have put aside." Her hand went nervously to her headdress.

Hilea turned at Claire's words. "I have set aside many

things in my years. And taken them up again. I do not know what thread weaves you together but it is not something to ignore. Not this kind of gift — it comes from too high a place."

Elspeth went shyly to Claire's side and took her hand. "When we arrived I felt how quiet it was. I should have known that the quiet was not of Hilea's making."

Hilea snorted in a manner not usually associated with abbesses.

Claire looked dumbfounded. "I am bemused. This is outside all my expectations."

"You are the quiet," Elspeth went on. "All the quiet I shall ever need." She glanced at Hilea. "My cousin will be vexed if she misses much more."

"By all means," Hilea pronounced. "Send for Lord Aldtyme, Sister Claire." Her color was high.

Claire walked unsteadily to the office door, but there was nothing uncertain in her instructions to whomever it was she saw outside. She closed the door again. "I'm told the lord is still at table and will join us momentarily."

"We have some adjustments for our private equinox celebration." Hilea picked at the sleeve of her robe while she spoke. "We will need to discuss it at length."

"As you wish, mother," Claire murmured. Autumn thought that if Hilea had just pronounced a plan to move the cloister house, stone by stone, that evening, Claire would have responded in exactly the same way. She started back to where Elspeth stood smiling, then hesitated with a glance at the door.

"I'll let the lord in," Autumn said. "It will be better."

In spite of her gruff expression, Killera looked both fearful and hostile at the sight of Autumn responding to her knock.

Autumn stepped back to let her in, announcing, "Lord Aldtyme, prioress." She shut the door as soon as Killera was clear of it.

The silence was broken only by the hiss of Killera's indrawn breath. Autumn searched Killera's face for any expression of pleasure at these events, any flicker of emotion that might mean some day Killera would forgive Autumn for what she had done to bring this meeting about.

Between one thudding heartbeat and the next she had her small measure of reward. Killera took in the sight of her changed cousin, looked twice at the prioress's face and only then did a glimmer of relief grace her face. "It was the only bright moment in that old nightmare of mine," she said lowly.

Killera moved then, turning slowly from her cousin and Claire to the other occupant of the room. Hilea stood with her hands tucked in her sleeves, looking more like a statue than a woman. "I did not believe," Killera said. Her shoulders relaxed. "I did not believe."

"Now you do," Hilea said, clear but cool. "Providence is kind." The calm façade broke, and she took an eager step forward, only to halt at Killera's next words.

"Do you know where She is?"

Autumn watched Hilea control her disappointment. She had a new thought, one that had not occurred to her in all her many lives. "Abbess Hildegard has agreed to help us as much as she is able."

"It may not be of use. It may be everything. We shall try," Hilea said.

"How may I be of assistance, then?" Killera nodded respectfully, a lord offering aide to a holy woman.

"You shall come to Vigil. A nun's robe will be made available. Autumn will bring you to the cloister chapel." Hilea glanced around as if everything was settled. "I'll go back to my study and concentrate on what must be done, then. Claire, I'm sorry, but I will need you." She took her leave abruptly, the door left open for Claire.

Claire was obviously still full of misgivings, but she clasped hands with Elspeth. "I will try to believe," she murmured, then she followed Hilea into the cloister confines.

Autumn was amazed to see a glimmer of hope in Killera's eyes. If more good was forthcoming from their night's work, she might be forgiven after all. She allowed herself a small hope.

"I think that sleep would do us all good." Killera nodded to both of them.

"As you say, my lord," Autumn said humbly.

"I know all this," Ursula said, her voice full of wonder. "The road, the gate. It did all come back."

Autumn studied Ursula's profile as she gazed at the darkened countryside. Ursula was reflected in the window and Autumn combined the two images to form a soft, eager smile. The closer they came to Kelly's farm the more relaxed and happy Ursula seemed, while her own anxiety seemed to grow in direct contrast.

They rumbled over a grate toward a small house where lights were burning. Scylla raised her head from the bone she was enjoying in the large cargo area of Kelly's Explorer and whined.

They stopped near the front porch and Ursula was out the door.

"Kelly! Kelly, where are you?"

Autumn busied herself letting Scylla out of the back. "Have a nice, long explore, girl. You've earned it." Scylla loped into the night.

She turned in time to see Ursula swept up into Killera's strong arms. They spun in a circle and Ursula's laugh of joy carried across the fields. Not Killera, Autumn told herself. Kelly. Perhaps Kelly doesn't know what happened in the past.

She took a deep breath and made her way up the porch steps.

Ursula was still laughing. Autumn took in Kelly's rapturous expression just long enough to feel as if she should look away. It didn't seem as if Kelly would ever release Ursula.

Autumn could not imagine anything that could make Kelly let go. Only Ursula could do that.

"You've not met in this life," Ursula said as she eased from Kelly's grip. Her face was shadowed for a moment. "I know it isn't easy for either of you." She stepped back and left the path between them clear.

Autumn stared at Kelly and oddly enough saw her own emotions echoed there. They both wondered what they should do now, and how to make Ursula feel less awkward. And she saw more, the fortress she had helped build around Kelly's soul. She was stunned for a moment by a vision of watch-towers burning, by the sound of steel on steel and the cry of men dying.

Kelly finally spoke. "There was a time, long ago, when you saved us all. I haven't forgotten."

Autumn could have taken the statement as an olive branch but her instincts told her that would be a mistake. She was not forgiven for anything. Better to turn their attention to immediate concerns. "I have tried to keep her safe, but I believe that we are still pursued. When we forgot our gates for a moment, the darkness was over us both. That's why we ran."

"It's the equinox, isn't it?" Ursula looked to Taylor for confirmation. At her nod, she went on, "I didn't know if we could make use of it, somehow. To bond us, to test a circle. We don't have to do anything, I suppose. It just seems a waste of the auspices of the day."

"I think it would be ill-advised to try anything," Taylor said. "I'm not what I was. Besides, we think we have a lead on our missing member."

"Yes, where is Liz?" Autumn thought that Liz would have returned here by now.

Taylor bit her lip. "She had to . . . she stayed in Aldtyme. I haven't heard from her except for her call to say you were on your way. But I wasn't referring to Liz."

223

"Hilea?" Ursula grinned at Taylor as she grasped Kelly's hand. "You have found her?"

"Not exactly," Taylor admitted. "She is here, in this time. We know her name."

"To see her again — it would be wonderful. With her to lift us up I don't think there's anything we could not do." Ursula was shining with hope.

"We were defeated in the past." Autumn could not help her cold tone. "We are all less than we were."

"We were unprepared before. Ambushed. This time we can make the most of our strengths." Autumn hated the whole idea, and if asked her honesty would force her to say so. She didn't want to start this reunion off with a fight if she could help it, but they were not ready.

"That may be, Ursula." Taylor gestured at the table. "The eggs and bacon smell great, Kelly. Why don't we eat and talk?"

"It'll keep," Kelly said. "For a few minutes. I want to show Ursula something in the barn — from where I lost her. To put it to rest for me. Closure, I guess."

"I understand," Ursula said kindly. "I'd like to show Autumn."

Autumn saw Kelly's jaw tighten.

"I suppose it wouldn't hurt me to confront it, as well." Taylor reached for her still streaming coat.

Autumn thought it could have waited until morning, but she wasn't going to leave Ursula alone with Kelly. She turned up the collar of her long leather jacket and followed everyone else into the night.

Killera was roused in time for Vigil and made her way with a few other penitents toward the monks' chapel. It wasn't a major feast day and the smaller buildings were in use for the first of the day's offices.

Halfway down the path a flash of white caught her eye.

Autumn waved her into the bushes. She held a gray robe and headdress, twins to what she already wore. She held them out in silence.

With great reluctance, Killera removed her cloak and boots, realized her hose would show in the plain sandals Autumn held and removed those as well. The robe was tight, but still hid her tunic. The headdress covered her hair completely.

Autumn led her toward the rear of the nuns' house, into a garden, then along a path that ended at a heavy, locked door. Her hand rested briefly on the lock, then she swung it noiselessly open.

Killera heard the lock click again after the door was closed, but she did not look. Witch, she thought. Nothing has changed.

Autumn led her through a narrow passage into a darkened hall. An orderly procession of nuns was filing through doors at the end, beyond which candlelight glowed. They were the last two to enter the chapel and she followed Autumn's example and kept to the rear.

Truthfully, being a lord had its advantages. One of them was not attending Vigil. It was the dead of night, when it seemed to her that all decent people were tucked safe in their bed. She had to struggle to stay awake. She kept reminding herself of what would happen next, that they might actually find a way to talk to Ursula, to reclaim the saint from where she had been taken. And then . . . and then, she thought, she might know the saint again, as a woman, a friend, and the center of her existence.

It seemed the dead of night did not call for brevity. The music was not Hilea's. She didn't imagine anything by Hilea would put her to sleep unless that was Hilea's intention. The invitatory seemed endless. It gave way to an equally tedious hymn. The subsequent responsory and versicle were better compositions, but no less somnolent, and Killera wondered if her brief exposure to Hilea's music had spoiled her. It had been good to see her, but something had kept her from saying so. Pride, perhaps. She'd been brought here by force, after all, and to allow that any good feeling came of it was to excuse Autumn.

There was no excuse for what Autumn had done, and she would pay for it.

When the final responsory began her entire being focused on the first note, and carried through to the very last. Hilea's composition, as charged with magic and mystery as her devotions to Ursula.

The golden season turns
Toward the white winter of the serpent,
In a garden of queens,
Queens of pure virgin heart.
Winter's breath could damage no flower,
In a garden of queens,
And a splendor of colors.

To hear it sung in the upward leaping unison of women's voices was captivating. She could not discern Hilea's voice, and wondered what magic she might feel if Hilea did sing.

And then, only then, did she believe that there was true hope. The saint might be found.

The sisters were filing out before she recollected herself. She rose when Autumn did, making out Claire and Elspeth still kneeling at the rail. Finally, they rose and walked side-by-side up the center aisle, and she and Autumn fell into step when they had passed. Their feet echoed on the newly cut stone steps.

They didn't stop when they reached what had to be the abbess's own quarters. Instead, Claire led them, with careful, modulated steps, to a door hidden by tapestries. It opened to a second passage, tightly winding and narrow.

Killera was the last to enter. For a moment she thought she would run. The passage was dark at the top and she did not understand the mysteries that would greet them. The sight of Autumn's white hair in the dim light stiffened her resolve. If anything good came of this she was determined that Autumn should have none of it.

Hilea was alone, but something about her shimmered in the light of four thick, white candles on heavy, shoulder-high candlesticks quartered around the circle. Claire stayed them with a gesture, then she bent to pick up a tied bundle of white broom. With a sweeping gesture she traced a door in the air and the glimmer disappeared.

It was like nothing she had ever seen done before, but memory stirred — not memories of dreams or nightmares, but of pasts. She knew this and part of her welcomed it.

Part of her hated it, for surely this kind of magic had made it possible for Autumn to sneak inside her mind.

She stepped across the threshold with some trepidation, but her first reaction was to the silence. The flicker of the life all around them, a noise she had not noticed was even there, dulled to nothing. The sound of her own breath was abruptly loud in her ears.

Claire used the broom again and the silence deepened.

Hilea bowed to them all, then picked up a lute not as tall as the one she had used in all of Killera's memories. Her fingers moved as lightly as a breeze at sunset. One note, another one step higher, the next one lower than the first, each spilling like gold into the circle Killera now sensed enclosed them.

Her senses were sharpening, and she was aware of Elspeth's trembling. Elspeth felt things so strongly, as if she had no defenses. Autumn stood like stone while Claire's deep, rhythmic breathing was obvious.

The golden notes seemed to be interweaving them, drawing them closer though none of them moved. When Hilea, not stopping the motion of her fingers on the strings, slowly lowered herself to her knees they all followed suit.

Hilea's fingers moved more quickly now, repeating the

same three notes that took on opaque form. Golden circlets seem to line the inside of their circle, with pink light, like roses, washing down on them.

The music was a circle, a whirlpool, and Killera fell through the centuries, following the thread of gold.

The barn was as Taylor remembered it. With little effort she might have been able to outline the exact circle in the dust that had confined their ruined work.

It must have been obvious to Kelly as well, because a candle sheltered by a slender hurricane glass burned at what had been the circle's center. Next to it was a bundle of white broom, tied with a white ribbon.

She stayed Autumn with a gesture. Her dog, which had startled Taylor by loping toward them out of the dark, also stopped before crossing the broken circle's perimeter.

"Nothing can happen until this is behind them," she said lowly to Autumn.

Autumn made no reply, and they watched as Ursula stopped at the candle. Taylor could see the tears on Ursula's cheeks.

"You told me I had to prove that I loved you. I did. I let you go." It was painful to hear Kelly's forthright voice full of uncertainty, low in her chest.

"I am sorry that I pushed you to it that way," Ursula replied. "I knew you loved me. I should have trusted that you would know what had to be done."

Kelly's nod was imperceptible. "I've never seen you with your hair loose. I like it."

"Sooner or later I think it will be braided again."

"Will it? Will you go back to this?" Kelly indicated the white broom on the floor between them.

"I must. I am lost without it."

"They didn't even look for you. They weren't even worried."

"It's who I am, even though I understand so little."

"I proved that I loved you." Kelly's tone grew more taut as they spoke, and Taylor sensed frustration rising.

"I know that you did. And I love you for it."

"But you don't love me. Not like her."

Ursula hesitated. "Once I might have tried to speak softly to you, but you are stronger than I have ever trusted. This will not break you." Her expression was all compassion. "No, I do not love you the way I love her."

Taylor sensed an uncoiling in Autumn and realized that Autumn had not been certain, not until that moment.

Kelly's breath had shortened as she struggled with tears. Liz had said the Kelly never cried. "It's because of what I did, isn't it?"

"No — I loved her before that."

"I proved my love. Ask me to do anything and I will prove it again."

"This is pointless," Autumn muttered, but she didn't move.

Taylor stepped forward, thinking she could help. Then everything changed.

Twelve

The spiraling music was a river and Autumn didn't fight its current. She rushed backward through centuries, buoyed by Hilea's magic through lives of endless journeys, of endings too many to count, but no new beginnings. Starting over in a new place, a new time, but not a true beginning because she remembered everything that had been, all she had lost and learned, and especially the emptiness that had once been filled.

The caw of a seabird caught her ear. The *Verdant Bough* lurched with an errant wave, and a blackbird plummeted past her shoulder. Tain lay dying on the deck from the fall and Autumn wondered why the music brought her back to this place. Tain, her father in truth, had given her his white hair and the magic in his fingertips. She could not say goodbye because she held the tiller. He died and she did not know then that his blood was in her veins.

Why was she here? Ursula had not happened to her yet. What could be learned? The sea swelled below her, deep of life and full of truth.

"What is truth?" Ursula was next to her, then, watching the waves as they frothed white in their wake.

"You know the answer to that." Autumn looked across the unbroken horizon.

"I don't. I sometimes think I know. I feel it. The old ways are true and yet some of the new ways are true, too. Because they mean something to us. But what is truth to you?"

"The sea is truth. It is always there, always the same, the rules never change. Even the sun sets, but the sea is forever. It is the only thing I know of that is permanent. The only thing that can't ever be taken away from us."

"What about love?" Ursula's words were quietly said, but they brought a hot flush to Autumn's cheeks. She did not yet know the feel of Ursula in her arms and had therefore not yet forgotten the pleasure of it.

"Can love be that permanent? Here today, here in a hundred years, a thousand, here when empires fall and new gods are born, here like the sea?"

"I think so."

She thought she remembered it all, but she had forgotten what love was, stronger than empires, longer lived than gods. Like the sea, love was the mother of all.

Autumn turned to gaze in to the black eyes that she had hungered after for so long, but Ursula was a golden note, rising toward the sun.

Taylor fell to her hands and knees with a startled, muted cry. Ursula turned, surprised, and Autumn saw Kelly's hands move.

Taylor raised a hand and managed to choke out, "I'm okay — there's something here. The equinox, I think. There's so much power. I thought the circle done. No, Autumn, don't come in!"

Autumn caught herself before she stepped forward. In where? She glanced at Kelly, nervous at how close she had moved to Ursula, and not reassured by Scylla's sudden whine.

"Why shouldn't Autumn come in?" Kelly held out a hand. "She is Ursula's chosen and I hope that Ursula can share more with her than she ever shared with me."

Ursula turned back at that. "Please, forgive me for that. I made so many mistakes."

Taylor drew in a sharp, deep breath, but said nothing.

Kelly suddenly took Ursula's face in her hands. "This is not a mistake." She kissed Ursula, then, and Autumn ignored Taylor's warning.

She hurried forward, and everything changed.

Taylor could not name what held her, but she wasn't frightened at first. Still, after all she had lost, she was overconfident. More mistakes, more pride. She couldn't fight this. She should have cried out for help, warned Autumn something was here she couldn't handle.

She fell through centuries of memory, of lives she'd never known she'd led, moving so quickly that when she saw herself in a golden circle with Elspeth at her side, with Hilea and Killera and Autumn, it was only a flicker.

The abbey where she had died with Elspeth was another flicker, gone before the horror of it had any impact on her senses. Earlier still, to lives that walked in old, old paths. She would shatter against the rock of time, she thought, because still she did not slow.

Her headlong flight into the past finally stopped with a bone-crunching thud. She spun into the bushes, on her feet again in an instant. The stag, its neck streaming from her dagger blow, lurched into the underbrush. The priestesses swarmed it, catching the sacred blood and releasing the animal within to the spirit of the forest.

The night danced over her, the axe was in her hand. Taylor felt a wrenching chill. She'd been in this vision before, but this time couldn't push it away. It could not be a true past. It was a nightmare from Uda.

The bonfire cast orange light on the sacrifice. She knew him immediately, though it mattered nothing to her purpose this night. Small and white-haired, from the far north, they would miss his laughing way. He had been chosen and she let herself feel his joy at the journey he began. A flash of light — was she in the clearing or the abbey, with Uda laughing over them as her minion cut them in two?

The axe fell, yes, her axe and the blood was mingled with the stag's. The acolytes took his body so it would ripen their harvest, ease the coming cold and continue the turning of the seasons. Now waited the last sacrifice, her gown white and tread steady.

The virgin was stretched out on the altar, willing, honored. She raised the axe and the hood was removed.

This time, recognition took her breath away. Those eyes, that mouth, what evil brought this about? If she did not strike the acolytes would tear them both apart and they would be forever lost to each other. She would profane the love the goddess gave them if she struck, and profane her vows, blight her people if she did not.

"I will find you again," the virgin whispered.

She could not strike. She did not strike. It had not happened. This past was a lie; she had never been the goddess's axe. It was not part of what she was and meant nothing to what she would become.

The axe was torn from her hand. The acolytes took up a ululating cry as sharp as the knives of bone they carried.

Their blood mingled for the first time.

There was a long, long dark, so deep that Killera thought it might not end. Then flashes of light showed herself in earlier days, fighting, crusading, surviving, struggling, never lifted by a sense of purpose, frozen of love and desire. She wanted to cry out when the crow's nest flashed past her eyes as she swooned at the sight of her bloodied hand. Earlier than their leave-taking, a few years only, to a glade encircled by a hundred joined hands, all witnesses to the coming of a goddess for the first time in so long. With the darkness of men's wars at the doorsteps, the names of the true land lost to the young, they called for her to walk among them and let them know her grace.

She worried for Ursula, for she loved her and always had. She was young for such a burden, a woman but by a few years. The crones gathered around her, braiding as they sang and Ursula seemed transported as the energy in the glade grew.

Hilea sang for them, her carefully studied words and music heightening the magic that was coursing through Ursula even now.

In a garden of queens,
A queen of pure virgin heart,
Winter's breath could damage no flower,
In a garden of queens
And a splendor of colors.

Ursula rose, red light streaming from her fingertips. She turned in Killera's direction, smiled, held out her hands.

Killera knelt and lifted her hands, palms together. Ursula, goddess and woman, took them between her own and they pledged perfect trust, perfect love and sealed their pledge with the kiss of peace.

A pledge for all time, Killera thought. She heard Hilea's music again, this time drawing her forward to a moment when Ursula had spoken of a different kind of love, for the captain's daughter, the thief. It was the moment when perfect love had been betrayed by perfect trust. Killera had paid then. She still paid. The world steadied and she saw Autumn had bent forward to touch her forehead to the ground. It was a great show of piety, but she was not moved. Autumn, so far, had paid nothing for what she had done.

What evil was this, buried so deep in the earth below her that she did not sense it and yet so powerful that it created a dark vision that had to be a lie? Taylor was aware of the dust of the barn floor and she looked at her hands. All her fingers were there, her skin unmarred by knives of sharpened bone. Of all the places in all her lives, why had she been pushed there? What had she been?

Her mind was unchained in time sweeping backward and forward, seeing all the pasts that had been taken with her braid. Why should she know them now when she could do nothing about them? She stood with Elspeth in a circle of music. The Voice was guiding them in their search.

Someone groaned next to her and she managed to turn her head to see Autumn on her knees, one hand on the floor while the other seemed raised to fight off some private vision.

Scylla paced outside the circle, growling, but not breaking the line.

Ursula, Taylor suddenly thought. No, she was safe in Kelly's arms.

Except Ursula was saying, "No, please, don't."
Kelly was not listening.

Autumn tried to stay in her time, not to lose sight of Kelly pulling Ursula so hard against her. Her hand grappled with the air as her mind began to turn cards: queen of hearts, queen of spades, queen of diamonds, queen of clubs . . . queen of cups, queen of wands, queen of pentacles, queen of swords . . . queen of love, queen of energy, queen of mind, queen of earth. Queen of oblivion, no, she cast the card aside and had to begin again.

Queens . . .

Queens . . .

Red and black, with her oceans-deep eyes. The eyes went blue-now-green and the queen of the axe laughed as she scythed through all the cards Autumn had turned.

She began again, desperate, only then realizing that she had no air. She needed more power than she had. Only now did she realize she had a weapon that could have use here, but the lid of Tain's box was in her satchel, still in the car.

She faltered and fell into the past.

Autumn followed the golden note into the sun. Hilea's music caught her safely. She felt as she had when Ursula had guided them that incredible night they had spent together, floating among the stars. Her body felt suffused with bliss and she bent slowly, arms around her waist, and let her head rest on the floor.

"Come back, all of you," Hilea said softly. "Tell me what I have wrought."

Killera was the first to speak. "I was remembering when

236

Ursula was made the goddess walking. You were there," she added, nodding to Elspeth and Hilea.

"I remember it well," Hilea answered. "And you, Elspeth, did you go there?"

When Elspeth didn't answer, Autumn pushed herself up to her knees.

Elspeth and Claire were ashen. "I cannot speak of it."

Claire reached for her and Elspeth flinched. "I did not do that thing. It was not me."

Elspeth shivered. "I remember only the axe. I told you I would find you again."

"I did not strike. I could not."

"I have searched for you," Elspeth whispered.

"You have found me," Claire was still holding out her hand. "My love, let it be enough to remember in the lives to come."

Autumn didn't know what fear Elspeth faced nor what axe Claire spoke of, but she saw the effort it took for Elspeth to take Claire's outstretched hand. Claire began to sob and Elspeth gathered her up, her face shining with the courage it had taken to conquer the dragon of the past.

"This was not my intent," Hilea murmured. "I meant us to remember our best moments, when we were strongest."

"I remembered when my father died, the day before we sailed into Aldtyme to take Ursula and her party to her wedding. I don't know why I would remember that, instead of when I first saw her. When I knew I was hers."

Killera rose to her feet. "The experience was memorable," she said shortly, "But I don't know what we've accomplished."

"We've only begun," Hilea said.

"Begun what? I hear only music and dreams."

"You need not help if you do not wish it," Autumn snapped.

"When have my wishes mattered to you?"

Autumn fell silent because she deserved the remark.

"Peace," Hilea murmured. "Let us try something else."

"No, I am done," Killera said. "I do not believe we can find her. She no longer exists except in our memories."

"Killera," Hilea chided. "Have you lost your sense of adventure?"

Killera reddened with fury. "When you have lived my life, when you have had control of yourself taken, you can judge me." She sent Autumn a look of pure rage. "This witch brought me here by force. You will have to pardon me if I am not grateful."

Claire was watching in a daze while Elspeth followed the exchange with close interest. Looking at Autumn, she said, "What does she mean, by force?"

Autumn was trying to think of a way to answer Elspeth truthfully without giving any damning facts, but her wits failed her.

"What did she mean, by force?" It was Hilea now who asked.

She tried to explain. "I heard your music. I knew that Lord Aldtyme had commissioned it. When I saw the lord —" she waved a hand helplessly in Killera's direction. "After so many lives, so much searching, I had found someone. But she didn't remember anything. I had to get here, to find you, and I wanted her to come, as well. So we could work together, don't you see? But she never would have agreed."

"You did not even ask. You gave me no choice."

"You deserved it for what you did to Ursula." It was a coward's statement, but she could not bear to have them all looking at her with such doubt in their eyes. Was she a coward, now? Had she no honor left? "No, do not listen to me. That was not fair."

"She cannot speak the truth to save her soul," Killera said. "She has no soul."

"I don't believe that." Hilea searched Autumn's face for reassurance, but Autumn could give her none.

"I told you," Autumn reminded her. "I told you I was not proud of what I had done."

"I didn't know it was Killera you harmed."

"Does it make a difference?"

"Of course — the wound is greater. You betrayed friendship."

"I didn't set out to do so," Autumn answered. She lifted her chin, for that was the truth. "I needed to get here and bring her as well. Elspeth knew it was necessary."

"Yes, but I did not know the means you used." Elspeth and Claire were twined in one another's arms, but Elspeth's regard was clear and piercing.

"What was it," Hilea demanded. "What did you do?"

Autumn could not find the words and was grateful, even though Killera painted it so black, that Killera finally spoke.

"She played the whore for me, inside my head. Whenever I began to think for myself she would lure me to bed again so I forgot to question what she did. She panted and whored and doubtless liked it, bringing me to heel with memories of the one I truly loved."

Hilea turned to Autumn, disbelief tinged with anger.

"It was happening before I knew I was doing it," Autumn protested as she got to her feet. "It pleased her, at first, I truly thought there was no harm, like festival. I felt close to Her. I know Killera did, too, though she hardly knew why." She blinked back tears. "And I am so sorry for it. It weighs on me, it does." Killera clearly did not believe her.

"Nothing but lies," Killera said.

"Enough." Hilea's voice was edged with command. The gaze she turned to Autumn was critical. "I cannot say that I have not labored in beds to survive this long, long life. But this was not for survival."

"I know." Autumn struggled to keep her lips steady though tears trickled down her cheeks. "It felt like I had reached an ending and a beginning. That if I did not act I would not get another chance for hundreds of years."

"What are you saying?" Claire pushed Elspeth away. "What black magic is this? These nightmares, that axe, these horrors — where are you taking us all? What was I? What will I become?"

"Peace, Claire," Hilea said.

"No, mother. This is not natural. What I saw in that vision I cannot bear to think I once did. I do not understand!"

"This magic is summer white, and once you knew it, too," Elspeth began.

Claire rounded on her, spurred by obvious fear. "What kind of witch are you? I've never forgotten my vows before, regardless of temptation. You were quick to my arms, and would be to my bed as well. Would you play the whore for me as she did for your cousin?"

No, Autumn, thought, no, it was not supposed to be like this. She had brought them all to ruin.

Pure silver cut through the room.

"*Nos sumus in mundo, et tu in mente nostra.*" Hilea fell silent for a moment, then another lance of silver sent Autumn to her knees. "*Et amplectimur te in corde, quasi habeamus te presentem.*"

They were all kneeling now, even Killera.

"You have all forgotten so much," Hilea whispered. "But not this truth. 'We embrace you in our heart as if we had you present.' This truth drew you to me, Claire. Drew Autumn to Killera, Elspeth to Autumn. And now we are all here."

Autumn felt a rising wind around her ears and wondered what magic Hilea was calling.

"Abbess, I did not mean —"

"Peace, Claire. We are at a crossroads, all of us. We run to her on a different path, now. None of you, it seems, remembers the evil. I remember. I forget nothing. The darkness will use our bitter hearts, our angry souls, our pride and arrogance against us. We do not struggle to find Her because we must

240

have Her back, for ourselves, *but because She does not belong where She is.*"

Autumn felt like the dust itself. She spoke the truth she had to confront. "She would stay where she was, endure anything, if she knew what I had done to bring her back." She pulled off the flimsy headrail and clasped her hands in her hair. "I thought to restore her to my life and instead brought fire between all of us, where she would never have wished it."

She was no longer worthy of what she had sought for so long. How could she ever take up this quest in the next life when Ursula would reject her for what she had done?

"You are angry, with cause," Hilea said to Killera. "Let us find atonement and forgiveness."

Killera shook her head. "No. This has all been madness. I cannot have her back. She is a saint and you would pull her down to earth, dirty her with our affairs and lusts. You would make me defile her. There is no atonement for what the thief did."

"Then there is no atonement for what you did to her, out of jealousy and anger," Autumn shouted. "You are as guilty as I am!"

Killera stared at Autumn for two beats of Autumn's pounding heart, then said, "I know my guilt. I know my punishment. I have lost her forever." She spun on her heel and moved quickly to the door.

The circle was still intact and Killera rebounded from what she could not see.

"Let me out," she said. Autumn heard the dangerous edge to her voice.

"Let her go," she advised Hilea. "We can accomplish nothing tonight."

"You'll never have my help," Killera raged. She swung round to face Hilea. Her robe caught on the candlestick nearest her, toppling it to the floor. The candle split from the long, narrow spindle that had held it in place, and went out, but not before its flame touched the hem of Killera's robe.

"I don't believe you'll do this," Ursula said. She did not struggle. She knew she was not strong enough to get out of Kelly's grasp. She felt the gate opening behind the candle. If she let herself she would be terrified and senseless. She knew the gate. She knew where it led. But Kelly would not do this.

She had thought she had lost her belief in perfect trust, but she had not. Faith was demanded of her, now.

Kelly kissed her again, holding her so tightly that Ursula could not turn her head. "No can become yes so easily, if you want it to. She lied to you, she bewitched you, I'm not jealous that she went to bed with you. I understand that it was all her."

"She didn't sleep with me. She's taken nothing of me that I didn't give her freely."

"You don't know her the way I do."

"I know her soul and I know yours. I know you won't do this." Ursula felt a swell of compassion and understanding.

"You don't think I'm strong enough to do it."

"Dearest, I think you're strong enough not to."

Kelly swallowed convulsively. "Know me for what I am, Ursula. You never wanted to see it."

"I love what you are —"

"How can you when you don't have any idea who I truly am?"

"You're stronger than I ever was willing to trust, I see that now."

"I am this strong," Kelly said and for the first time, Ursula felt Kelly's mind pressing skillfully, powerfully against hers. She could have stopped it, but the gate was pulsing open behind her and she was far too close to it. Energy she might draw on would have uncertain consequences if used near a

242

gate of that magnitude. The only way to stop Kelly was to know her heart and show it to her. She had wondered what she was good for without her braid or her beliefs. Let it be this.

She saw Autumn, then, through Kelly's eyes in a past when Autumn had whispered love and desire, all the while planting answering echoes in Killera. She heard Autumn moaning with pleasure, spreading herself out for Killera's taking. Killera had had more of Autumn's body than she had ever enjoyed. Was that twinge jealousy or regret? Neither had any use here, not now. She wished Autumn had told her, but understood why she had not. She had not told Autumn about the crow's nest. Autumn had found out about that on her own. Secrets would be their downfall.

:I am strong enough to make you love me again. You see what she did. I learned from it. I thank her for it, now.:

Ursula didn't think, until Kelly lifted her off her feet, that Kelly would do it. She wanted to have faith again in perfect love and perfect trust, to give Kelly the chance to choose differently this time.

She was in the crow's nest for a moment, not believing that evil would come to her through someone who loved her so dearly, whom she loved as a true sister in return. She felt the energy of the dark gate against her back and Kelly's arms like unbreakable chains.

She did what she did not do before.

This time she fought.

Thirteen

Queens . . . queens.

Autumn had a disconcerting flash of cards before her eyes, swept aside and being dealt again. She thought, feeling disconnected in time, that someone should put out the fire.

The smell of burning cloth brought her back to where she was. She was on her feet, pulling off her own robe as she went, then smothering the flame that licked up Killera's leg.

Hilea leapt up as well. She gasped as she looked at the floor. "What is this?"

Killera seemed frozen, staring into the spilled wax from the fallen candle.

The wax had turned black and fathomless, like a gap in the world tapestry. Claire and Elspeth joined them around the circle in the floor gazing downward. Stars flitted in the depths. There were strands of light, twisting endlessly on each other, but the light made no difference to the black. The vortex drew them deeper still, until they were all in the lights. Music and cacophony lanced pain through Autumn's mind.

"Look away," Hilea cried. "This is not for us to see!"

Ghosts seemed to dance, spirits wailed. Autumn smelled roses and manure, saw grace and suffering.

Hilea pulled Autumn back from the wax circle's edge and its spell was broken.

Claire held Elspeth again. "We cannot survive that place. It is from the old ways! They are done."

Hilea seized Killera, but Killera pushed her aside.

"Help me," Hilea said to Autumn. "She must not look."

Killera was immovable. She pushed them away as if they were gnats, her eyes never flinching from what she saw. Finally, though, it seemed that even she had her limits because she cried out.

It wasn't in pain, but triumph.

Pointing into the maelstrom, "She is there! There!"

Autumn made herself look again. Her eyes burned, her mind was on fire. There was a flash of red, then she saw what Kelly saw. "Gods!"

Hilea saw her as well. *Ecclesia gratias!* I see her."

Autumn reached down through the roiling light to try to touch her, but Killera knocked her hand away and reached herself.

"No," Autumn shouted. "I'll get hold of her and you pull us both up. It's the only way."

Killera gave her a look of distaste and mistrust, then nodded curtly. "You'd never hold me, that is true."

Autumn leaned over the black tear that seemed to have no sides or bottom, no time or stopping. The pain behind her eyes bathed everything in white-yellow. She felt strong arms wrap around her knees and knew then, that she had to trust that Killera could hold her.

Hilea's voice soared to a vibrant pitch and the chaotic noise and visions seemed to falter, making way for the red that rose toward Autumn's outstretched hand.

Objects brushed against her fingers, shapes in mist. A bell, a cup, a ring. The deeper she reached the more substantial these things became and the more real Ursula seemed.

Her body slowly tumbled without direction or intent, surrounded by a red glow. Another roll and the face turned toward them.

Ursula's face, Ursula's eyes. They were empty of all but pain. :*Who am I? What have I done?*:

Only that, an endless cycling question, seeking an answer for what she suffered.

Autumn called out. "Ursula! You are Ursula!" She felt as if her voice was smothered by sand. Ursula did not look her way. She trusted Killera's strength as she stretched deeper into the chasm, pushing away a feather that tickled, then a long, sharp blade that stung.

"Beloved!"

Ursula turned her head. :*Beloved. Beloved.*:

"Lower, let me go lower. She knows me." Killera must have heard her because her grip carefully shifted from Autumn's knees to her ankles so that Autumn was hanging upside down, suspended from Killera's iron grasp. She strained toward the floating red hair. It was almost at her fingertips.

Hilea's voice did not falter. Autumn could hear another voice and their phrases overlapped.

Ecclesia gratias, we feed among the lilies . . .
Kyrie eleison, Lord have mercy . . .
Ecclesia eleison, gloria spiritui sancto, Columba bless us . . .

Autumn wished she had some meager magic to add, but there was only her love. :*Give me your hand, beloved.*:

Killera lowered her farther and Autumn realized that Killera was now half into the depths of this place as well. "I can almost reach her," she shouted.

The pain in Ursula's eyes was tinged with something new. :*Beloved? Autumn? I have longed for you, but never would I want you in this place!*:

"Gods," Killera exclaimed. "It is her. I hear her!"

:*I am the path to the world again. Take my hand. We are all here for you.*:

Ursula reached up. Their fingertips brushed.

Queens... queens ... queens for dancing, queens for tears. Autumn turned cards and turned them, denied the scything axe that shattered what she tried to build, and started again.

Taylor stumbled toward Kelly but didn't make it, clasping her hands to her eyes as if she saw visions she could not bear. Kelly had lifted Ursula in her arms. To her horror, Autumn saw that a gate, livid with blue-now-green energy, had opened behind where the candle burned.

Red and black queens. Ursula was red. Her eyes were black. She was the queen and Autumn let all the cards become her. Red and black, red and black, split the bet, watch the marble tumble. The wheel turned, the circle spun and she lifted it over her head.

Autumn got to her feet. She felt pierced by the light she wielded. "Scylla."

With a howl of fury, Scylla crossed into the circle. Her teeth found Kelly's calf and she stumbled backward, carrying Ursula away from the maw of the open gate.

She had wanted time. Time to run, time to stand. Time to stand still.

"Yes," Autumn said. She felt stretched between two expanses. Up and down were competing for her sense of balance.

Hesitation would be fatal and she had no choice now. She addressed herself to the gate. "I am ready."

"I almost have her," Autumn cried. Their fingertips brushed again and Autumn felt something stir in her. Her hands almost looked as if they glowed.

Ursula's hair was streaming upward and Autumn realized she had never seen it unbraided. It was lank and dirty, like a red death. A lock of it whispered past her fingertips, then she could gather a coil in her hand. Gently she pulled upward and Ursula began to rise toward her.

A bolt of lightning, sickly green, struck her hand.

She screamed, not because her hand spasmed with pain, but because Ursula was falling, her body sinking back into the abyss of unbearable light and darkness.

Another lance of green flew toward her. She flinched from it and it stung her shoulder as it passed upward, burying itself in the circle that Hilea had raised. The golden circlets of the protections cracked.

"Let me go," Autumn pleaded. She kicked at the hands on her ankles. "Let me at least be with her."

:No, leave me. If you cannot end this, you must endure. You are all I have.: Ursula was sinking into the depths. *:Have you your bow? Please, I beg of you.:*

Another bolt of green exploded on the circle wall.

She had no weapon, but as soon as her mind conceived the bow she had once carried it shaped itself out of the mist. She seized it. *:A deadly arrow, sharp and fine.:* That too appeared as she envisioned it.

She had failed at the abbey, had not been able to release the arrow. This time, she thought, she would do it. She would consign Ursula to oblivion rather than have her exist in such agony. She nocked the arrow to the ethereal string and aimed for the beautiful neck slowly drifting from her sight.

She stood abruptly on the *Verdant Bough*'s surging deck, making every arrow count. Smoke and fear did not stop her and she swayed with the rocking netting and the rising of the sea. She never missed.

:Forgive me, beloved.:

:Do as I ask. I forgive you, forever.:

"What are you doing?" Killera was shouting to be heard and straining better to see. She seemed completely oblivious to the pain of this place as well as the next bolt of green fire that Autumn felt fly past her ear.

Her aim was careful. The arrow would fly true.

Taylor struggled to her feet again, pushing as hard as she could against the memories that were cascading through her mind. Killera so bitter and angry, the vortex that Hilea opened — she did not have time to comprehend the past.

The dog deflected Kelly from her path. With a curse of pain, Kelly kicked out. The dog snarled and began to circle.

Ursula's eyes were closed and her brow furrowed as Taylor tried to wrench her from Kelly's grasp. She knew where that gate would take Ursula now. She would not let her go there, not again. Kelly upended her with a kick and pulled Ursula toward the gate.

Ursula seared with a red light so bright Taylor thought for a moment she was blinded. The light eased and Taylor saw that Ursula was forcing the gate closed, standing between it and Kelly, who had frozen in place with Scylla sunk down on her haunches behind them both.

The red light was tinted with white now as Autumn walked purposefully toward the narrowing gate.

"Keep her safe." Autumn spoke to Ursula. "The darkness cannot have her either."

"Let me close the gate. I can do this."

"We must end it now, for all our sakes. So we can learn to trust each other again."

Ursula faltered, then the gate spiraled wider. A woman stepped through, the figure of Taylor's greatest nightmare.

She tried to get up, to stand with Autumn. She could bear this moment, she had done it before. She had never been a fighter, but she was not what she had been. Her hand went to the back of her neck as she stood.

She reached for what spells she remembered, what power she had reclaimed and the nape of her neck seemed to burst into flames. She screamed and fell into nothing.

Taylor's agonized scream shook Ursula, but she could not help. She knew the pain, had experienced it herself when her braid was undone. Why Taylor's had been delayed she did not know. But she would end this and the pain would stop.

Distraction, she warned herself. You are in danger.

"Would you shield a traitor?" Uda moved sinuously toward Ursula with a knowing glance at Kelly. "Would you save someone so weak that she was mine in an instant?" A lazy hand gestured at Autumn, who stood poised as if choosing her moment to strike. "This one at least resisted me for a minute. I had my pleasure of her anyway."

"This is all distraction." Ursula replied as calmly as she could. "I deny you. What you desire you shall not have." She let her shields flare again to show Uda she had energy to spare. Her shield was spread wide enough to hold Kelly safe inside. She felt familiar coldness steal over her.

Uda stood her ground. "You took my servant from me, though you had no right to do so."

"I freed him from you."

"Will you free this one in the same way?" Her eyes dismissed Kelly. "Show her her own guilty soul, the women she has hurt for anger's sake."

"This is all distraction," Ursula said again. She would not let Uda penetrate her defenses with the temptation of judgement.

"Let me show you what she is." An image flared between them, of Kelly with Uda on the bench not far from where they stood, tearing clothes in haste. A barrage of women, all crying, accepting pain for a moment of pleasure. Then it was Kelly on a bed, heedless of hands pummeling her shoulders.

Kelly moaned and Ursula groped for Kelly's hand. Kelly would have never found this darkness inside her without Uda's help. She would not judge Kelly. "This is all distraction."

The image changed, it was Autumn with Uda now. Autumn trembling with satisfaction, her body still coiled in anticipation of more. Ursula tried to hide that she had not known about this, but she could not help a glance at Autumn. Autumn looked stricken as she pressed one hand to her chest where the scar had been. She would not meet Ursula's gaze. Gods. Uda had been the one who had stabbed Autumn, after . . . She closed her ears to the sound of Autumn's moan.

There was a dagger in Uda's hand and Ursula did not know how it got there. Her shields faltered, then she found her center again. "This is all distraction."

"You must protect Kelly," Autumn said. "For my sake, now. I owe her this battle." She raised her arms and white light danced in her hands. "I am ready," she said to Uda.

From behind her Ursula heard Kelly's low plea. "Let me go to Taylor. I'm free now. Let me try to help."

Autumn wanted her to keep Kelly safe. Kelly needed to know she had Ursula's love and trust.

There was only one thing she could do when Kelly had been so deeply wounded, by her, by Autumn, by all of them in their lack of faith in her strength. She trusted.

Lifetimes of searching, of learning and remembering had brought Autumn to this place of terror and pain. She had lost her sense of direction and only knew which way was up by the pain where Killera gripped her ankles. The sharp tip of the arrow glinted in the shrieking light. Destiny had put a heavy price on her mistakes, but if this was what she must do, she would do it though it cost her her soul. She could finally die, forever. In death she might find Ursula.

Autumn loosed the string and let fate claim her.

"Nooo!" Killera's cry echoed through the light, rending Hilea's magic. Autumn saw the arrow pass cleanly through its target, piercing the graceful neck with silent death. Ursula was smiling as her red light began to fade.

The madness joined Killera's scream of disbelief and the air filled with the beat of a thousand wings, pressing against her.

Killera was pulling her out of the maelstrom, but too slowly. A figure was forming out of the mist, regal, with her chestnut hair bound round her head like a crown.

If Uda had taken vengeance first Autumn knew she would have met oblivion. Instead, Uda pulled the lifeless Ursula to her, hands around the bleeding, mutilated throat.

Autumn knew she should feel something at the sight of Ursula so limp, but she did not. Numbness had taken her.

Killera's grip was relentless and Autumn was finally clear of the vortex. She spared herself what she could when Killera tossed her headfirst to the ground.

"She is there," Autumn gasped as she struggled to her feet. "Uda. She will come for us all next."

252

"Murderous witch!" Killera's backhand sent Autumn reeling across the circle. Her head was spinning with what that place had done to her senses. She only knew Down because it was the direction she fell. She could not win against this kind of strength. She'd spent too much time on her dice and not enough preparing for a fight such as this.

Hilea gave a great cry and cast her lute at the opening. Killera fell hard on what was now only a wax-covered floor.

Autumn coughed and spit out blood. Where was her robe? She needed a weapon.

"You had no right," Killera shouted at Hilea. "I could have gone to her. I could have helped her bear it. None of you had any right. We won't even have our dreams now!" Her enraged gaze fell on Autumn. Autumn scrambled backward, felt her robe under her hand. Her knife and Tain's box were her only weapons and she rolled, gathering both to her.

Killera's kick knocked them both from her hands. The box flew across the circle to shatter against the golden protections. The splintered pieces turned to ash. Only the lid remained intact. Black and red stones, with green dots for counting, fizzled like the deaths of shooting stars.

Stunned by the loss of something so precious and ancient, Autumn forgot Killera was going to kill her until Killera lifted her off her feet by her undershirt.

"She's lost forever because of you." Heedless of Autumn's kicking, she shook her like a rag. Elspeth clutched Killera's shoulders, looking as if she would be ill at any moment, but Killera pushed her away.

"Killera, you must not do this." Her voice was calm and even and Autumn sensed a spell behind the words, but Killera's anger did not abate.. "I have never lied to you, I was always your friend, and more."

Killera tossed Autumn to the ground and Autumn felt a

rib splinter. There was a sharp pain in her lungs. She realized, far too late, that she should not have left Scylla behind.

"If you defend this evil creature, then you are evil as well." Her boot found Autumn's hip and Autumn rolled with the blow because it took her in the direction of her knife.

"Killera, no!"

Autumn turned in time to see Hilea frantically clinging to Killera's back even as Killera shoved Claire to one side.

She came up with the knife just as Killera kicked her a last time. She went down hard on her chest.

Elspeth screamed.

It was such a small pain at first. The weight on her back hurt more, at least at the beginning.

She could not rise. She was momentarily puzzled, then she realized she was pinned to the floor by something thin and sharp.

"No matter what happens," Killera said bitterly, "I shall not regret this."

The pain multiplied as Killera slowly pulled the candlestick spindle out of the floor. Autumn heard it grate on bone on its second journey through her breast. Her breath sounded wet to her ears.

She had lied, she realized, yet again. She had said she would not die at Killera's hands. It was a violent death, one she had courted with her own choices. Tain's box was lost. What would this cost her in her next life, she wondered.

Fool, she thought. You gave Ursula oblivion. There will be no next life.

She was cold and could not move. She heard Elspeth crying and Claire's attempts to comfort her. Hilea gently turned her over but it was still an agony. Autumn would have screamed if she could have drawn in breath.

:O rubor sanguinis, O redness of the blood. In a garden of

colors, in a splendor of dreams.: Even the beauty of Hilea's voice could not save her.

Her name was Autumn, she would remember that, and her love was Ursula, she would remember that as well. They had met in Aldtyme, their bard was . . . they sailed together on the . . . on the . . .

On the . . .

Autumn staggered, pinned between the echo of Uda's dagger blow in her chest and Killera's spindle through her back. She remembered, then, the foreboding she had had that when she next died it would be forever.

She reached down for her essence, a warrior, a magician, a woman in love. She let her shields flare with the heat of her convictions and raised her glowing hands. She formed a weapon that had never failed her, not on a moving deck, not in the depths of the chaos. She would finish this before death could make any claim on her.

Kelly bolted from behind Ursula, somehow beyond Ursula's shields. Ursula did nothing, Uda did nothing. Autumn was stunned by the trust they both displayed in a woman so torn by past and present. For a moment it seemed as if Kelly would cannon into Uda, then she spun on her heel to seize Ursula through shields that had not been designed to keep her out.

Ursula gave a noiseless cry as Kelly threw her at the gate. She grappled at the rim with a scream of utter disbelief and grief.

There was a high-pitched wail of what might have been a guitar. Ursula managed to get one arm over the edge of the gate, but Uda raised her hand. The gate sucked harder at

Ursula, lifting her off her feet. She clung though forces were pulling her inward, shrieking Autumn's name in terror. *:I won't go there again!:*

Autumn faced the moment. The bow she held was of her own making, with magic and deadly intent. Uda had reached Ursula in time to heal her before, but this time she would not be quick enough. Her heart breaking, she told herself she had no time for grief. She was here to give all that she had to Ursula's service. She remembered, only then, that she had wondered what she would do — or fail to do — if it meant losing Ursula for herself. The thought was not worthy, and for so many lives she had tried to redeem her mistakes so she would be pure enough to serve.

:Oblivion before a return to that place! Please!:

Uda was turning toward Ursula, smiling with victory.

Autumn chose her target and sent the arrow of light into the pleading pain of Ursula's black eyes. She went to her knees before the arrow found its mark. *:Forgive me!:*

Ursula shrieked, but not because Autumn's arrow had broken her skull, but because it missed.

Stunned, Autumn fashioned another arrow but by the time she drew Ursula was gone in a flash of blue-now-green light.

With a cry of anguish, she loosed it at Uda instead, but Uda dissolved into mist. Autumn realized she had never been there. Only the gate had been real, that and Kelly's betrayal.

"No, wait!" Kelly spread her arms where the gate had been. "She is mine!"

One last arrow then. The magic in her hands was fading and the arrow was small. It found Kelly's shoulder, slamming her to the floor.

There was only retribution left. She flung herself on Kelly and met no resistance to her attack. She pounded her anger into Kelly's face and chest and did not stop until her river of loss and rage had crested. She let Scylla pull her to the ground.

The barn roof was hammering with the sound of rain and water rushing through the night.

"Can you trust what you do not understand?" Black eyes gazed at the distant shore.

"I do not understand the wind, but I trust that it will blow," Autumn answered.

"Is that trust or faith?"

"Is there a difference?" Autumn concentrated on the tiller, afraid that her feelings might show. She did not yet know the feel of Ursula in her arms and had therefore not yet forgotten the pleasure of it, nor relearned it only to lose it once again.

"I think so. Faith is trust hoped for. Trust may falter, but faith will shore it up."

"But if you do not understand what you have faith in, faith may not be enough." Autumn might have added that she did not understand Ursula, but she trusted her with more than her life.

Taylor stirred in the dust, her head pounding so painfully that her sight came in pulses. It was dark. The candle had gone out.

The gate was gone.

She heard the dog whimpering.

She found the candle by accident as she crawled in the dark, and used her meager powers to light it once she had set it upright.

The light only added to the pain in her head and she had to shade her eyes.

First she saw Autumn, face down in the dirt, her hands stretched ahead of her. One sleeve looked as if the dog had shredded it, and her hands were spotted with blood. She was frighteningly still, but breathed.

Then she saw Kelly, twisted on her side, one leg bleeding, her face bruised and clothing torn. Her fingers were bloody and caked with dirt. A closer look revealed a wound in her shoulder, leaving a pool of blood. She, too, breathed, but would not for long without help. The dog whimpered again, her mouth smeared with red and ears flattened against her head.

There was no sign of Ursula.

Taylor cast out with all her senses, looking for a trace. She found all that she could, a dim pulse of disbelief and grief surrounded by an echo of triumphant laughter.

They had lost, as they had in all the pasts. Ursula was taken again, but this time not by the one she loved. Taylor crawled to where the gate had ended Ursula's presence in this place, in the same place where Uda's gate had appeared before. She must close this doorway, but remembered she had no skill for that. Not any longer.

She had not thought there was more to lose, but each time she had hope she lost even more of what she had been. She'd had no time to find a new path. She'd had Ursula in her grasp and lost her in the same dark night. She had lost Liz, and the visions she had seen spoke of a betrayal so powerful and ancient that she might never find her again.

She stretched out her hand to learn the essence of this gate's energy and only then did she sense that it was familiar to her. She had felt its like before. She tried to remember, but it triggered flames in her mind.

Memory was singed to nothing.

Inferno

The night danced over her, the axe was in her hand.

No longer priestess, no longer cleric. When she closed her eyes she saw the axe gleam in the fire's leaping light. It fell, rose again. Did she strike that second time? Had she sacrificed love and humanity?

Became. Becoming. Shall be. Was that why she had wandered so long without finding a true path?

The mirror told her no truths, but two mirrors told her a secret. Her neck had burned with pain when she had tried to help Ursula, fire leaping from what she could now see was a mark on the back of her neck. In the second mirror's reflection she could tell what it was: a white columbine, *Columba* in heaven. *O, Ecclesia*, she thought, but the music no longer had magic. She had no need of a bard. She was branded with a reminder of one who had once been a goddess, but it had hindered, not helped, when it mattered.

* * * * *

Strength is. It was a simple truth, and all roads had led her to use her hands, her arms, her back, and finally her mind. She was strong in all of it, but it brought no one anything but pain.

"Dearest, I believe you are strong enough not to," her goddess had said, only proving again that even a goddess could misunderstand someone she had once loved.

She had thought if she gave in to her strength in this life she would have Ursula again. But there was nothing of Ursula in her bruised face, cracked ribs, her torn calf, the hole in her shoulder. She might never be able to fully raise that arm again, but that was meaningless.

The rain didn't seem to stop. She was ever falling into grief and the frozen relief of winter still would not come.

She was strong enough to bear her wounds, but did not believe she would ever be strong enough to hope. Hope had made her a tool, time and again, always someone else's hammer.

* * * * *

It was a child's toy, though the package had touted it "professional." It had a mere thirty pounds of draw weight, and the arrows wouldn't pierce sand.

The warrior drew again, her fingertips raw in spite of the protective tabs. The arrow thumped into the fence next to its twin. She fired until all ten arrows were neatly in line, never missing.

Her rage was still white-hot. She was a magician, a warrior, a woman in love and none of it mattered. She'd had one chance to end it and her skill had failed her. If there could be another chance she had to be ready to seize it. This toy was not enough but it occupied her furious mind. She was alive, still, and there was no other way to give her life purpose.

There had to be a new path. She would start again, because now she remembered so much. She drew and fired until her fingertips bled and her arm shivered with exhaustion.

* * * * *

Deep within the mother of all circles, in the circle within the circle, the prophetess stood with her back against the rock of time. Became, becoming, shall be. She had lived and died there. These choices — life, death — were before her again, and although she knew the faces that demanded her seer's knowledge, she would not speak of future or past.

* * * * *

I remember it all. I never sleep. Nightmare is anger and has become my life. I am the bard, the singer, the harper, the headbanger. I am Hilea, the one who never died.

The Tunnel of Light trilogy will conclude with book three, The Forge of Virgins.

About the Author

Laura Adams is the alterego of Karin Kallmaker. She is let loose on a regular basis to pen romantic fantasy, supernatural and science fiction novels. Karin Kallmaker was born in 1960 and raised by her loving, middle-class parents in California's Central Valley.

The physician's Statement of Live Birth plainly declares, "Sex: Female" and "Cry: Lusty." Both are still true. Her genealogically-minded father recently informed her that she is descended from Lady Godiva. This information delights her to no end.

Karin lives in the San Francisco Bay Area with her long-suffering partner. The happily-ever-after couple became Mom and Moogie to Kelson James in 1995 and Eleanor Delenn in 1997. They celebrated their twenty-fifth anniversary in 2002. Readers are invited to explore her web site, which can be accessed from her author's page at www.bellabooks.com.

Publications from
BELLA BOOKS, INC.
The best in contemporary lesbian fiction

P.O. Box 201007   Ferndale, MI 48220
Phone: 800-729-4992
www.bellabooks.com

ACCIDENTAL MURDER: 14th Detective Inspector Carol
Ashton Mystery by Claire McNab. 208 pp.Carol Ashton
tracks an elusive killer.   ISBN 1-931513-16-3 $12.95

SEEDS OF FIRE:Tunnel of Light Trilogy, Book II by Karin
Kallmaker writing as Laura Adams. 274 pp. Intriguing
sequel to *Slight of Hand.*   ISBN 1-931513-19-8 $12.95

DRIFTING AT THE BOTTOM OF THE WORLD by
Auden Bailey. 288 pp. Beautifully written first novel set
in Antarctica.   ISBN 1-931513-17-1 $12.95

STREET RULES: A DETECTIVE FRANCO MYSTERY
by Baxter Clare. 304 pp. Gritty, fast-paced mystery with
compelling Detective L.A. Franco   ISBN 1-931513-14-7 $12.95

CLOUDS OF WAR by Diana Rivers. 288 pp. Women
unite to defend Zelindar!   ISBN 1-931513-12-0 $12.95

OUTSIDE THE FLOCK by Jackie Calhoun. 220 pp.
Searching for love, Jo finds temptation.   ISBN 1-931513-13-9 $12.95

WHEN GOOD GIRLS GO BAD: A Motor City Thriller by
Therese Szymanski. 230 pp. Brett, Andi, and Allie join
forces to stop a serial killer.   ISBN 1-931513-11-2 $12.95

DEATHS OF JOCASTA: The Second Micky Night Mystery
by J.M. Redmann. 408 pp. Sexy and intriguing Lambda
Literary Award nominated mystery   ISBN 1-931513-10-4 $12.95

LOVE IN THE BALANCE by Marianne K. Martin. 256 pp.
The classic lesbian love story, back in print!
                                        ISBN 1-931513-08-2 $12.95

THE COMFORT OF STRANGERS by Peggy J. Herring.
272 pp. Lela's work was her passion . . . until now.
                                        ISBN 1-931513-09-0 $12.95

CHICKEN by Paula Martinac. 208 pp. Lynn finds that the
only thing harder than being in a lesbian relationship is
ending one.   ISBN 1-931513-07-4 $11.95

TAMARACK CREEK by Jackie Calhoun. 208 pp. An intriguing story of love and danger.   ISBN 1-931513-06-6 $11.95

**Visit
Bella Books
at
www.bellabooks.com**